"A truly captivating, mind-stretching read. Highly recommended."

Dr. Phil Parker, Author of The Lightning Process

"A dark psychological thriller following three damaged children as they seek answers – and restitution. Clear-eyed, suspenseful, and unflinching, the narrative cleverly treads the line between visions and reality. A very promising debut."

Una McCormack, USA Today Bestselling Author

The Dark Chorus

Ashley Meggitt

www.darkstroke.com

First Dark Edition, darkstroke, Crooked Cat Books 2020

In memory of Iain Banks

About the Author

Ashley Meggitt lives near Cambridge, UK, with his wife Jane. He left school to join a psychedelic rock band when he realised that sex, drugs, and rock and roll was a thing. Subsequently he went back to education and became head of IT for a Cambridge University College. In recent years Ashley has retrained in psychology and is now an associate lecturer in sports psychology. He is studying for his PhD.

Ashley writes when not studying, playing his guitar, or coaching triathletes.

He quite likes his children and goats.

Acknowledgements

It has been a long journey for the Dark Chorus and many people have helped to push the story over the publishing line. I must start by thanking Laurence and Stephanie at Darkstroke Books for believing in the story and allowing it to see the light of day. Without people like you, people like me would remain unheard. I am eternally grateful.

Also, to my early writing buddies Dave Scott, Tim Ritchey, Alex Grey, Dominic Aboi, and Julian Prokaza – those were exciting days, much missed. I also owe a debt of thanks to Una McCormack, Laura Dietz, and Lucy Dawes, whose teaching, support, and encouragement throughout my MA in Creative Writing helped me to develop the groundwork for this novel.

To my friends Michelle and Richard Porch, Nick and Chris Clare, Annette Lanjouw, Louisa Bromilow, Teressa Issacs, and to all those at Wimpole Runners for their encouragement and much needed social distractions.

To my beta readers Adrian Asher and Helen Burchmore for sharing and revelling in my darker ideas, and to Dr Ahoora

Baranian for forcing me to get on with the edits so he could read the story. And to Maty Matyszak for publishing advice and checking my Latin.

To Rachael Cubberley and Sam Buchanan for their enthusiasm, time, and skills with the creation of the novel trailers. Big love to you both. To Mark Sheppard, who despite being imaginary, has been a real friend and support over the years – thanks Dr M. – have a goat.

Special thanks go to Katie Martin – my writing sparring partner and friend, without you the book would not have happened. It is a debt not easily repaid.

To my wife, Jane for putting up with the ebbs and flows of my writing journey – more to come I'm afraid. *Ti amo*. To my children Ben and Lucie and their partners, Sally and Pascal, for their constant enthusiasm and belief that the *old man* could write a story. To my brother Justin, for his advice, encouragement, and taste in T-shirts, and to my parents for always believing in their children.

To coffee houses and cafes in general – because I love coffee, I'm nosy, and love writing in the busy, warm, and chatty spaces they provide – but to Abantu and Hot Numbers in Cambridge in particular, where a great deal of the novel was written and edited.

The Dark Chorus

Chapter One

I was born right here in this asylum – literally into bedlam; delivered into a stark white-tiled cell, in what I've come to think of as The Screaming Room. As quickly as I arrived, I left. Prised from my mother's arms, I swapped one institution for another. But even as the car took me away, the darkness of my mother's despair curled itself around my soul, anchoring me to her and my birthplace. I know this because I remember.

***

The early morning sun meanders around the grime on the windowpanes, lighting up the almost empty room I sleep in. I have a bed; I found it in one of the other rooms. It has a metal frame that was once white but is now yellowed with age and worn from use. I lie for a moment, listening to the dawn chorus. It's a gift of nature that I'm always grateful to accept. It makes me happy, more so now that I am home.

I rise, extracting myself from the sleeping bag, feeling the cold air tug at my warmth, pulling it from my body to assimilate it into its cold collective. I watch the process for a moment, but I'm thirsty, so I pull on an old jumper and head to the kitchen to make some tea. It's not far, just down the corridor and, as I walk its path, I pass other rooms, all empty, all grey with dirt, all neglected. My home is now abandoned, closed to its disturbed guests, but open to decay and boredom – its destiny uncertain.

The kitchen reminds me of the one at Shelly Fields, the children's home where I spent most of my life. The layout is arranged in a similar fashion, but it's the smell that triggers the strongest memory; ingrained boiled vegetable and disinfectant soaked aroma. Shelly Fields was not a bad place in which to be brought up. It provided shelter, food and books. I needed little else. Other children kept their distance, wary of my difference, sensing a strangeness that sets me apart. They mostly came and went, either moved on or adopted. I was neither moved on nor adopted because I didn't want to be. Occasionally, the home would make an attempt to place me, send a couple for a viewing hoping that they might be able to remove this quiet yet stubborn blot on their performance landscape. The couples always left without me.

There is no electricity in my new home, but there is running water and, miraculously, gas. I light the hob and boil some water for the tea. Steam pours from the fresh-brewed cup and I let the hot vapour envelop the cold skin of my face. Some of it condenses on my forehead and cheeks and they become warm and wet as tears of tea drip from my eyelashes. I think of it as my morning sauna – I read somewhere that steam keeps the skin young. It's important that I stay young, so I do this most mornings.

A bee bumbles against the glass of the window, its comically small wings buzz in annoyance - it wants out. I hum quietly to it to calm it down. I have always had an affinity with bees, in fact with all sorts of creatures, but bees in particular. It quietens and as I put my hand out it lands gently in my palm and turns its engine off. I take a moment to admire its beauty and then carefully place it by a broken windowpane. It senses freedom, fires up its engine again and launches itself into the fresh autumn morning.

I'm waiting, so I spend the rest of the day walking the buildings letting serendipity guide me, amusing myself by checking through the scattered remnants of the inmates' belongings. I find a few photographs, some medical notes, and sad, unintelligible letters never sent; snippets of lives never knowingly lived.

Dusk comes, and I sit and watch from the comfort of a peeling wooden bench. It washes over the late afternoon sky and with each moment the granularity of the darkness becomes finer until night finally falls. I listen to what I call the Dark

Chorus; the chatter of the lost souls, those that have died here but, for whatever reason, cannot pass on. The chatter is not beautiful like the dawn chorus, it's chaotic, jumbled, laced with anxiety and fear. It doesn't frighten me. I've heard it from birth. It's sad, and I wish I could help them.

It's time.

Almost every day for the past six months I have gone about the business of collecting these souls. I do this because I am looking for one in particular. I know she is here, but I cannot pick her out from amongst the cacophony of incessant monologues. So, I collect these immortal remains one at a time in order to lessen the noise, to hear more clearly.

I know my mother is dead because I felt her die. Her death pulled at my own soul, nearly tearing it from my body. Our connection stretched and pulled and threatened to slip from my grip. I held on with grim determination to save her from passing on, but in my ignorance, I condemned her to a half-life in the Dark Chorus. From that moment on guilt has clouded my every thought, so I decided to leave Shelly Fields and return to my birthplace, to put things right.

But how to catch souls? I could see them and hear them, but could not hold them. Dreams provided the answer, although I am not certain they were dreams, so sharp and clear were their instruction. They provided me with both the physical actions of a ritual, and the mental imagery of soul manipulation. It took time for me to put the dream instructions together, but eventually I found a perfect balance of mind and ritual, and so my trap was created. I left the children's home soon after; slid silently into the night, a thirteen-year-old boy with an unbreakable certainty of purpose.

I expect the carers are relieved that I've gone; my attempts at soul catching frightened everyone. I think in those moments even the mundane minds could feel the spirits.

There is a room in the asylum where the lost souls tend to congregate once the light has left the day – it's The Screaming Room, the room I remember from my birth. This is where I've been concentrating my efforts. My theory is that the door to the other side is in this room somewhere, and they know it, but cannot find it.

I leave the bench and go to my room to collect the paraphernalia I need for the ritual. The full moon lights the way, throwing shadows across my path. I'm excited. Yesterday I heard my mother for the first time, just for a moment in amongst the thinning crowd, and although I didn't catch her that evening, I did remove another voice. Things will be clearer tonight and my own spirits are high in anticipation.

The Screaming Room is dark as I enter and my footsteps echo, bouncing around the tiled surfaces looking for an escape; the windowless room offers no such option. I light a candle so I can see what I'm doing and place it on a stainless-steel work surface. I've removed the restraining table and other such medical detritus – I don't want reminders of my birth.

I've painted a dozen floor tiles black so that I can draw on them. I kneel down and, with a piece of chalk, carefully sketch out a large circle, big enough for me to lie in. I then draw a square that fits exactly inside the circle with each of its corners just touching the circumference. At these intersections, I place lit night-lights. In the dead centre of the square I place a large jar that contains another night-light, its flame flickering and smoking as it struggles to breathe. I blow out the candle on the work surface and with exaggerated care sit down inside my trap and wait.

It isn't long before I hear the chorus of the dark coming, their chatter faint at first, but growing stronger as the minutes pass. The souls enter the room for their nightly search, small glows of translucent light, seeking the elusive portal to death. My trap holds them at bay; they are attracted by the flames, but are unable to pass over the chalk boundary. I listen, trying to pick out the voice of my mother, but others dominate, brittle and discordant. And then I hear her, her voice rising above the confusion. She's screaming, cursing the doctors that took me away, cursing her parents, calling out for me, over and over again. A soul bumps up against the invisible chalk barrier. I crouch down to look. Yes, it's her.

I hurriedly dust away a small section of the circle allowing her soul to slip through the gap. I then quickly close the breach with fresh chalk so no others can follow. I do the same with the square allowing her to progress to the heart of my gentle trap. The flame senses the soul's presence as she hovers near the jar, burning with more intensity as if concentrating on its prey. Then, like the sticky tongue of a fiery lizard, it extends itself snatching the shimmering spirit from the air, pulling it down into its transparent lair. The lid goes on. I have her.

***

I make my preparations and then leave the asylum and walk with a divine sense of purpose towards the nearby village. The institution sits hunched on its outskirts, an outcast, like the unspoken family secret. The silver light of the moon soon gives way to the anaemic yellow of the streetlamps giving the medieval buildings a surreal and lifeless appearance. I find a gap between two houses where the light does not reach and stand quietly, watching. A few moments later I hear the tinkle of the shop's doorbell sounding the last act of its commercial day. Footsteps approach, sharp drops of sound splashing in the still night. I can tell it's her. She is my hope, my vessel, my saviour. As she comes level with me, I step out of the shadows.

"Good evening, Mrs Johnson," I say. She takes a step back in surprise, but on seeing only me, quickly recovers. Before she can say anything, I catch her gaze, holding her eyes steady and open. I then focus, my gaze becoming a hypodermic stare spearing her pupils and piercing the flesh of her brain. She has beautiful eyes hiding a great sadness that makes her feel empty inside. I sense this; it sits at the front of her mind and spills out as I make the connection. Now I inject my will, like a single drop of dye into the turbulent waters of her mind, colouring her thoughts – *trust me.* I carefully remove the connection.

"I'd like you to come with me. I have something to show you." There's no resistance, just a quizzical look.

"That'll be nice," she says. "Where are we going?" I don't answer, I just smile and lead her towards my home.

As we pass through the asylum gates, Mrs Johnson

becomes a little anxious. I think she can feel the spirits passing around us even if she can't see or hear them.

"Please don't worry, Mrs Johnson, there's nothing to fear. Trust me – everything is fine." The words calm her down.

"Trust you? Yes, I trust you," she says and gives me a little absent smile. We head inside and move through the darkness to the kitchen. The flickering golden light of several candles throws itself effortlessly around the room, creating chaotic shadows to anything it touches. I open an adjoining door to a large storeroom.

"Come," I say, beckoning. She walks into the store with me. "What do you see?"

"My goodness, there's hundreds of jars with little night-lights in them. This is an odd collection." She picks up one of the jars. "What are they for?"

"I'll show you," I say. I put my hands up to her face, and steady her head. She looks at me and I once again catch her gaze. This time I simply remove the filter from her eyes, the one I was born without, the one that stops everyone from seeing what is actually there.

"Look again," I say. "And now tell me what you see." She stares at the jar and her eyes widen in amazement. She can see what I see, a soul hovering over the lit night-light, brighter and more visible, nourished by the flame.

"It's beautiful," she says. "Like a paua shell, shimmering, all wonderfully translucent blues and greens running together. What is it?"

"It's a lost soul, Mrs Johnson." I wave my hand towards the rest. "They are all lost souls."

Mrs Johnson struggles with my answer, but seeing is believing, or at least seeing puts doubt to her disbelief. "Really? But why have you collected them? Are they valuable?"

I take the jar she is holding and stare for a moment at the shimmering object it contains.

"This one is priceless," I say quietly. I pull my gaze away. "I think it's time to take a closer look, don't you?"

We leave the bright light of my soul collection and I lead

her through the kitchen to The Screaming Room. A number of souls flit past us as we enter, their faint blue glow barely visible in the dark.

In anticipation, I have already drawn the circle and its inner square and have placed night-lights where the shapes collide. I light the candles and place the jar I've brought with me at the centre of my creation. I beckon Mrs Johnson to come and join me in the circle. She hesitates, uncertain.

"Everything will be all right. Trust me," I say. "Come and lie down." I pat the blanket I have laid out for her. Again, my words soothe her, and she enters the circle, uncertainty gone. She lies on her side with her legs curled up beside her and her head resting on an arm. Lying next to her I mirror her position and we look at each other for a moment. The jar sits between us.

"I can help you, Mrs Johnson. I can stop the sadness."

"Can you?" But the dye of my trusting thought allows her to answer the question herself. "Yes, I expect you can."

"Shall I?" I wait for her reply.

"Yes," she says.

"I will then, and thank you." She frowns, unsure of my meaning, but in that moment I catch her stare and she is still. Once again I enter her mind, pushing deep into the centre of her brain. There is no single drop of actual thought this time, no attempt to control, I simply pour the one burning desire I have had since I was born, my most cherished want, my most desperate need into her mind until I have coloured every part of her consciousness, until she can take no more. I don't remove my piercing stare, but instead blink, disengaging the connection with me, leaving an open path to her mind. Mrs Johnson lies still, her eyes are wide, unblinking – she is ready.

I sit up and unscrew the top from the jar. The soul flickers inside the container, mimicking the dance of the flame that has it in its fiery grip. I gently blow out the candle, releasing the soul, which slowly rises, drifting leisurely in the almost-still air. After a moment of listlessness, the soul starts to move with purpose – catching a hidden current it is pulled towards the open connection, my invisible conduit to the future. The soul spins and twists and throws colours at me as it stretches and folds, shaped by the hidden force. I watch in excitement and anticipation as in one swift movement the soul is inhaled – gone.

I lie down next to the still woman. Her eyes are now closed, but I gaze at them anyway and wait. Several minutes go by, lost souls wander past noisily, but I have no time for them now. Slowly, very slowly, the eyes open and focus on me.

"Hello," I say.

My mother smiles.

Chapter Two

There is a path that starts from a handle-less metal door at the rear of the asylum and winds itself down into the wooded garden. I have walked this path many times since I came home, following its haphazard route, treading where thousands have trodden before, joining in with the shuffling ghosts.

Now, as morning breaks, I set off to walk its route once again, the fresh dew-laden air filling my nostrils. But today, even its invigorating scent cannot lift me. My certainty is lost, replaced with biting despair at the realisation that my future will be as motherless as my past. I have failed.

***

My mother has not smiled for three days, not since I first brought her back from the Dark Chorus. For the first day she said nothing, just sat and stared straight ahead, neither acknowledging me nor her surroundings. On the second day, her dream state broke; she began to speak, rapid fractured sentences, spliced cuttings of whatever was projecting through her mind. Then, without warning, she started to scream and curse and throw herself around the room; she hurt herself, tearing at the skin on her arms and repeatedly beating the walls. I had to stop her, and after a struggle I managed to tie her to the bed with strips of torn linen.

When I'd finished, I fetched some cold tea and bathed her arms and hands with it. A carer at my orphanage had said that tea was a cure for all ills. I'm not sure I believe her but it's all I had.

This is very wrong. I'd brought my mother back to the world of the living for her to be free, to live the life she'd missed, to be with me. But instead, I've imprisoned her again, shackled to an asylum bed as if she had never left.

I had spent that night sitting in the corner of the dark room watching her and listening to her babblings and screams. By morning she was silent and appeared to be asleep. I had gone to the refuge of the kitchen and made some tea but hadn't bothered with my sauna. I had let the steam go unused and instead watched the vapour rise, bullied by the air currents, the chaos of its journey matching that of my feelings.

On returning to the bedroom I had found my mother awake, and as I entered, she had turned her head and looked at me.

"Are you my baby? Are you my son?" Tears had rolled down her cheeks. Hope leapt at me, catching me mid-stride, my step faltered. I became suddenly nervous, excited, shy.

"Yes, Mother, I am." I had approached the bed and crouched down to look at her closely – to gaze into her eyes, to see if this really was my lucid mother. For a fleeting moment it was her, tearful and beautiful, and then she was lost as a cataract of insanity formed, haunting and terrible.

She headbutted me.

"Liar," she had screamed. "Where is my baby? Give him to me you bastard, give him to me." She had then pulled violently at the restraints and continued to scream obscenities at me until she exhausted herself. I had gone back to the corner of the room and sat clutching my knees, my face as bloodied and as broken as my dreams.

***

At its farthest reach, the path rounds a beautiful old beech tree, which stands proud, guarding the edge of the asylum's territory. I sit at its base, my back resting against its smooth trunk and close my eyes. A light wind plucks at its branches creating a wonderful natural song. I'm transported to the seashore to watch the waves rush up a shingle beach in excitement, causing tiny stones on its gentle rise to tumble against each other. This unrelenting action is played out again and again and again, and with each unfurling of a wave a different tune emerges. Beech trees are surely the most musical of trees.

Tears leak from me. I've not cried before and it takes me by surprise, but I let them flow – it seems right. I've never thought of myself as a child, but now as I sit here, enveloped by ancient sounds, I know that I am one and I feel lost and very lonely. I continue to cry, but after a while I start to feel a little better. The pain of my own sadness lessens, and I dry my eyes. I wonder at my crying. Perhaps the purpose of tears is to draw the sadness out of you.

I let time take a few moments and then pull myself to my feet and thank the tree for its help. It sings back an acknowledgement and I continue on my walk. My head is clear now and two unquestionable truths push themselves forward: my mother loves me, and she needs to die.

As I follow the path back to the asylum I think when my mother first died, a gateway to death had opened up before us and beckoned her in. But I'd held on to her soul, stopping her from leaving this world, and so when she did not pass through the gateway it closed and disappeared. It seems to me that each of us carries within us our own portal to death, our own gateway. It opens when our body fails us so that we can move on, so we are not left stranded and eternally lost to the Dark Chorus. I think this might be what the priest at the orphanage referred to as Purgatory, or at least a version of it, as all I can see is the cleansing element of infinite time. So once a soul loses its body it cannot die; no soul in the Dark Chorus can ever move on.

Ever.

I stop and look up to the sky.

Ever?

No. This cannot be right, there must be a way. I will find one. Although it is the middle of the day I catch sight of a soul, translucent, swamped by the daylight, and it prompts me for my next move. I must remove my mother's soul from her failed surrogate body and catch it in a fire-jar. That way I will be able to carry her with me while I search for our redemption.

I move on, my mind filling with ideas and images; a ritual

must be conceived and to it I must tie the imagined mechanism of soul extraction. Once I imagine, properly imagine, how a thing can be done, then all I have to do is believe in it and it will work. I have often wondered why I can do this but have no answer other than a feeling that I am connected to more than just my mother.

I arrive at the old peeling wooden bench, with its suggestion of green, and sit. I like to sit with my knees together, my back straight, my arms each side of me, palms flat on the crumbling wood. I close my eyes and breathe – slowly, deeply, deliberately. The body's rhythm slows, calming my mind and letting the artist within take over, the artist that can paint a reality. My head drops to my chest.

Time passes, as unconcerned as always.

I open my eyes. This may be tougher than I thought, but I think I have what I need now. Some tea first, and then I will get on and prepare the way before I approach my mother.

***

Preparations made.

The night is back.

The Dark Chorus sings.

I return to my mother to find her quiet, lost in dreams or perhaps just lost. I remove her restraints and guide her gently back to The Screaming Room. She moves without resistance, without recognition, without the realisation of what is about to happen. The shoulder bag I carry clinks rhythmically as I move, breaking the silence in the empty corridors.

Members of the Dark Chorus have gathered in the room, as if expectant, an audience ready to applaud the freeing of a fellow soul.

I have already drawn the chalk circle and square, a prerequisite for my dealing with souls, a cornerstone for my rituals. I have thought carefully about this act; the release of the soul through the death of the body. As my mother's soul has no route to death, no path by which to leave the body, I will have to supply her with guides to show her the way.

Carefully avoiding the lit night-lights, I lay my mother down on a sheet I have prepared for her. The cloth is arranged to fit within the chalk boundary. I wrap the sheet around her like a shroud, leaving her hands bound but exposed at her side. I secure the shroud with lengths of ivy cut from the woods, binding my mother at the feet, waist and shoulders. Her unshrouded head lies on a pillow of leaves; her passing needs to be right, to be beautiful, to be as painless as I had painstakingly imagined it.

From the shoulder bag I remove a knife and the bodies of a dozen birds. I collected them during the day, trapping them easily with offers of food. Their now lifeless forms are weightless in my hands. I run a forefinger through the plumage of one, a mustard yellow and powder blue, soft and still warm. Tiny feet curled up; a sad but necessary sacrifice.

I sever their heads and place the decapitated bodies in a semicircle around my mother's head; a halo of helpers, ready to offer themselves as surrogate bodies. I sit back on my haunches – I'm almost ready and I start to feel happy again.

From my bag I pull out a jar containing a night-light – my fire-jar – and place it carefully above the halo, just inside the edge of the chalk square. I light the candle; my fiery lizard is ready to catch the soul when it appears. I take a moment to sit quietly and gather myself, shutting out the chattering souls around me. I'm not sure this next part will work. I sit forward and look into my mother's eyes. They are open and dreamy and offer no resistance. I connect and observe. I'm grateful that she is calm; entering her mind and navigating its turbulent waters would otherwise have been unduly difficult. I feel for a channel that will lead me to her soul, to the dimension where the soul is contained. I find one and follow it.

The soul, its paua-shell colouring striking in the darkness of its containment, is held in place by bonds that seem to have no end. It hangs, suspended, an immortal fragment bound to an earthly existence until it is no longer required. I try to break the bonds, to simulate death and so free the soul from its captivity, but I cannot. My attempts fail, my imagery of their breakage is not strong enough, and I start to feel tired from my efforts. I think it is best to leave. As I retract my connection, I wonder what would happen if I became too tired to retreat.

I have no alternative but to kill the body in a more traditional way. I thought it might come to this and have prepared accordingly. I pick up the knife I had used to behead the birds and slit my mother's wrists – long vertical cuts that open the veins wide. Blood jets rhythmically from the wounds as each beat of her heart pushes life from the body; the crimson fluid soaks the shroud.

Minutes pass as life ebbs away. There is one last act to the ritual, and I evoke it now. The final item in my bag is a plastic box, which I extract with some reverence. I remove the lid and carefully tip the box's contents into my mother's mouth, gently pulling her lips closed to finish. I kiss her forehead. It is all done.

I stand up and move outside of the circle, positioning myself at her feet. Now I wait and watch with focused attention, my senses acute with anticipation. In the flickering light, I see beauty in my ritual and love in my imagery; I know I have this right.

Without warning, The Screaming Room door is thrown open. There's a shout.

"In here, I've found her." A torch beam illuminates my mother. "Oh my God."

I don't turn to greet the voice. I stay focused – *nearly there*. A hand grabs my shoulder and pulls me back. A face flushed with horror forces its way into view.

"What have you done?"

I say nothing but side-step the face. I can feel the activity of my helpers, their tiny engines fire up, they are ready.

Two new voices enter, their torch beams throw out harsh stabbing light which plays over the body, its still features, the halo of headless birds, the ivy-tied shroud and the large, rich-red pools of blood. One of the new voices retches.

I'm grabbed by each arm now and forced backwards against the tiled wall.

"What have you done?" a policeman, by the looks of him, asks.

"Released her soul."

He stares at me uncomprehending. I think he wants more but the question is answered.

"Is she alive?" he says, looking at his colleagues. A policewoman steps in to the chalk circle, into my ritual, and crouches down by my mother, putting a hand on her pale face.

"I can hear something. A humming but she doesn't appear to be breathing." The policewoman bends down for a closer look but recoils with a choked scream.

At last; a bee has pushed its way out from between the now dead body's lips. It's followed by another, and another, until all twelve of them are free. They sit together for a moment, an odd living spew, and then as one they fly. And with them comes my mother's soul. The fiery lizard tongue springs from its hiding place and snatches her from the air. I push past the policeman and clamp the lid on the jar, screwing it tight.

I have her safe.

I smile.

Chapter Three

The camera looks down from the corner of the almost bare room. It takes in a boy sitting at a table, straight backed. His hands are palms down flat on the chair each side of him. His head is cocked to one side as if listening. Opposite him sit two women. One is tapping away on a laptop while the other sits back, arms crossed, waiting. The woman with the computer is a psychiatrist. The boy knows this because she's told him. The other woman is a police inspector. Everyone calls her ma'am. The boy thinks perhaps he should call her that too. She's the same policewoman that came to The Screaming Room. A man called Rigby sits beside the boy. He said he's the duty lawyer. He said he's there to make sure the interview is done correctly.

They wait until the psychiatrist stops typing. It's been twenty minutes since the interview started; the black-and-white clock on the wall says so. The boy now looks at the large jar that sits on the table. His eyes are soft and smiling.

Ma'am leans forward.

"Why Mrs Johnson?" Her question brings me back to the table. Sometimes I like to see my world as if I'm in a film; I'm a camera looking down on the scene. I can't actually do this, but I have a good imagination.

"Because I knew she wouldn't mind."

"Wouldn't mind dying? How did you know that?"

"I looked into her mind."

"You read minds too. Well, that's smart, even smarter than planting ideas into an innocent woman's head. Can you read my mind?"

"No." I know she wants more from me, but I don't like her much. And I couldn't get into her mind or anyone else's for that matter. Everyone is closed to me, too cautious, not trusting.

"What did her mind tell you?" asks the psychiatrist.

I shift my attention to her. Her eyes are clear and bright. Eyes are important. People say they are the windows to your soul. How do they know this? Perhaps there have been others before me that could climb in through these windows, the truth of their intrusions left in the consciousness of the everyday world as sayings and folk tales. The psychiatrist has honest eyes.

"She was sad and wanted to move on but didn't know how. It was a very powerful feeling."

"So, you felt this justified killing her?" says Ma'am, cutting back into the conversation.

"Can I have a cup of tea? I'm very thirsty."

"In a minute. So, you felt this justified killing her?"

"It was a trade. I helped her to move on and in return I put my mother's soul in her body."

"Now I'm confused. You put your mother's soul into the body of Mrs Johnson and then you sacrificed her. Why would you do that?"

A fly has been buzzing around the room for a while. Indiscriminate in its investigations it now settles on Ma'am's shoulder. I watch it for a moment as it cleans its thousand-lensed eyes, thousands of tiny windows, alien and soulless. Ma'am notices and attempts to swat it, but it evades her flailing hand, buzzing its contempt. Like me and the Dark Chorus, it spans two worlds: our slow clumsy one and its own, light, fast and high-definition one.

"Because my mother's soul rejected the surrogate body. I had to remove her. My attempts to do this without harming the body failed, so my only choice was to kill it. I could then collect her soul in my fire-jar."

The psychiatrist shuffles in her seat.

"In this jar?"

"Yes."

"And she's in here now?" She taps the jar's lid and looks at me intently.

"Yes," I say without breaking eye contact. "She's quiet

now."

"Quiet? Do souls talk a lot?"

"Yes."

"Is this relevant, Dr Rhodes?" asks Ma'am. "I think I've heard enough." Ma'am concludes the interview and switches off the recording device, which has sat unnoticed on the table. She pushes her chair back. "You've got your work cut out with this one."

I say, "Can I go back to the asylum now?"

Ma'am looks surprised by my question. She stands and looks down at me. "You killed an innocent woman. That's a terrible thing to do. The law says that you'll be punished for it. You do understand this, don't you?" She presses her index fingers against her temples and rubs. I can see she bites her nails. "You committed a ritualistic killing. By general consensus that's an horrific and revolting thing to do."

I don't answer. She's the one that doesn't understand.

"So, no. You'll be held in a secure home while the law runs its course." Ma'am picks up the jar and leaves the room. I watch my mother leave. The duty lawyer says something and follows Ma'am out of the room.

The psychiatrist and I sit quietly for a moment. I can almost hear her thinking.

"Let's get you that cup of tea, shall we?" She gets up. "I won't be a moment." As she leaves the room a policeman comes in and stands inside the door. Perhaps they think I'll run away.

The psychiatrist returns with two brown plastic cups of tea and sets one down in front of me. It doesn't smell like tea. She sits down opposite me again and waves the policeman out. He leaves, shutting the door quietly behind him.

"Do you mind if we carry on with our chat, just for a little while longer?"

"I don't mind, but Ma'am might. I don't like her much."

"Ma'am? Oh, the Inspector. No, she won't mind." She sips her tea. "Do you think it's wrong to kill?"

"Yes."

"But you killed Mrs Johnson."

"Yes, but it wasn't against her will. Is it wrong to help people die if they want to? Is it wrong to make people live if they don't want to?"

"How do you know she wouldn't have changed her mind, had you not killed her?"

"I don't, but how do you know she would have? I looked for someone who wanted to go, who wanted to die, and I found Mrs Johnson – that's all that mattered."

Dr Rhodes gently rotates her cup. "So, now you're back where you started."

"Yes."

"Are you angry about that?"

"No. I'll try something else."

"That may not be for a long while."

"I'll wait."

We sit in silence again, sipping our tea.

"Do you think I believe you – believe your story?" she says.

"I don't know."

"Do you care?"

"No." As I look at her, I see she's less cautious of me. Her guard is partially down. I quickly catch her gaze. I can't get deep into her mind because there is still some resistance, so I leave a thought on the edge of her consciousness: *Believe.*

"No," she says slowly. "No, I don't suppose you do." She gets up a little unsure of herself. "I have to go now, but we'll speak again in a few days' time." She leaves the room and her space is filled by the policeman.

The fly lands on the table and I let it crawl onto my hand. We look at each other, briefly coexisting in the same world. I consider killing it. Would my actions be any different to the flailing hand of Ma'am? I think so. I'd kill as a kindness so that it doesn't starve to death in this barren room; she would have killed it simply as an angry reaction. I don't think she would see it like that though. I let the fly live, but as it takes to the air and busies itself with its undivulged quest I feel I've done it an injustice.

"I need the toilet."

The policeman rolls his eyes.

***

The boy leans forward. “What are you looking at, you fuckin” little prick?” He is sitting opposite me in the back of the police van and he is angry. His face is a mask of aggression, a mask to hide his fear. Fear. I recognise it, but I don’t understand it.

“Sit back, Jenkins,” says the policeman next to him. His voice is firm and laced with aggression. The boy scowls but sits back.

“Fucker,” he says under his breath, but it’s not clear if that’s aimed at me or the policeman.

We bounce around in the back of the van as it weaves its way through London’s late afternoon traffic. Nothing more is said.

We arrive at the centre and a large sign announces it as Thorndyke House. Two sets of gates guard the precinct. We pass through the first one and have to wait for it to close behind us before the second one opens. It is as if we are being slowly swallowed. Jenkins has stopped being angry. He’s pale and quiet, and as we leave the van he starts to shake.

A red-brick building beckons. Its shiny glass doors reflect our transparent images, and as we wait to be allowed in, it occurs to me that there may be other worlds like the Dark Chorus, ones that I can’t see – ones through the mirror.

The doors open and we enter, finally swallowed.

***

“Is there anything I can get you?” says my caseworker cum carer. He is called Dave, and he is friendly. I’m being taken to my room now, to be locked in until tomorrow morning. I’ve spent the evening being inducted, as Dave refers to it. I’ve not seen any other children yet, but I’ve heard them – a mixture of hard vowels, whispered submission, and barked defiance.

“Yes. Tea, please.”

Dave raises his eyebrows. He opens the door to my room, and we enter. “There’s bottled water here,” he says opening up a cupboard. “Some squash, some biscuits, a plastic cup and a few other creature comforts. That'll keep you going until morning." He waves his hand over to the bed. "PJs and a dressing gown. Tired?"

"Yes."

"It's quiet here," he says, but pauses for a moment as we hear some muffled shouting from somewhere down the corridor. "Well, mostly. You should get a good night's sleep." He looks at me. "You don't say much, do you?"

"No."

He raises his eyebrows again. "OK, fine. I'm off now. I'll be back in the morning to fetch you for breakfast. Good night." He pulls the door to behind him. I listen to the metallic clunk as Dave locks the door, a hard, secure, permanent sound. A hatch slides back in the door and Dave's face appears.

"Forgot to say, lights out in five minutes. I control them from out here, so look lively and get changed or you'll be fumbling around in the dark." He slides the hatch closed, another metallic sound. I suspect in my time here I will get to hear the full symphony of my prison's ringing metal instruments. A far cry from my singing copper beech tree.

I sit on the bed and survey my room. Apart from the bed there is a cupboard, desk, shelves, wardrobe, and a chair. All but the chair is fastened down, screwed to the wall or floor and unmovable. There is a window, and a toothbrush in a plastic cup sitting on a shelf. It's yellow and blue, the colours of my dead birds, the colours of success and failure. Which is which, is hard to say. Perhaps time will tell. The thought forces a sigh from me, but I dismiss it as a sign of tiredness, not resignation. I know what I have to do, and I will do it. Time is on my side.

I change into my PJs and stand in front of the window. The light from my room reflects my image back at me and I reach out to touch the other me, but it abruptly disappears, dragged off to wherever light goes when it's no longer required. I'm left standing alone in the darkness.

Chapter Four

The light flicked back on as if trying to catch the darkness unawares. Dr Eve Rhodes stared at her reflection in the brittle dark of the tube carriage window. Framed by advertising posters and the Circle Line map, the translucent reflection stared back. The dark twin. It rocked slightly as the tube screamed down its blackened brick-lined tunnel, its background alive, swirling with motion and punctuated with the occasional colour of an unidentifiable object. It was performance art, unique, yet reproduced for anyone who cared to look.

When she was young she used to think that the world of dark reflections was real, that if she had wanted to, she could have stepped through, joined the others there who would understand – understand her guilt and loneliness, her life with a mother who was never really there.

Eve had just read the police report on the murder of Mrs Johnson and her mind was sparking. An involuntary shiver ran down her spine, not of fear or shock, but of anticipation and a little anxiety. She acknowledged this by allowing her dark twin the tiniest of smiles. This case was going to be a challenge, there was no doubt about it.

The boy was extremely unusual: articulate – more than many adults – self-assured, self-contained, driven. He appeared to watch everything, observing it with a keen, if somewhat detached, air. She had never come across a child like him; a child who seemed to have no doubts about the world he inhabited even though he knew no one else lived there. And his world appeared fully formed. It would seem that he'd been seeing it for years without attracting any attention; there was nothing in his social services report.

The tube shuddered to a halt at the next station. People exited and others entered. Some jostled their way in urgently, while others strolled on, seemingly unconcerned. Eve looked up at the activity, but didn't take it in. She was thinking.

The toxicology report said Mrs Johnson's blood showed very high levels of diazepam. It was no surprise then that the woman went with the boy to the abandoned asylum – perhaps seeing her own lost child in him. Did Mrs Johnson tell the boy that her own son and husband had died only six months before? Certainly. Which is why, as he said himself, he had been doing her a favour. But to kill with such detachment from the physical action and with such clarity of thought was incredibly unusual for a child. In fact, Eve couldn't think of a case that came anywhere close to this one.

Without warning the carriage lurched violently, stirred its contents in one brief shake. Eve caught herself as she pitched forward.

There was something tugging at her memory, some pattern of behaviour, but what was it? She looked at her dark twin. "What is it?" she said out loud. "Baker Street, darlin'," said an old man sat next to her, mishearing. "Baker Street," he repeated.

The lights flicked again.

***

The morning is cold and brittle. A coat of hoar frost fashions itself on the few trees and benches that sprinkle the courtyard, sparkling in the weak winter sun. Everything looks clean, untouched, sculptural. I want to enjoy its innocence, breathe in its freshness, but others come spilling out of the many staircases, and spread out like a plague, intent on corrupting the beauty.

I am pushed violently from behind, slipping over on the icy path as I try to steady myself.

"Out the way, freak," says the boy who had been on the bus with me. I stand up carefully rubbing my sore, and now cold, hands together. I don't say anything, just stare at him. His face is full of resentment, a face I've seen fear in, but one that isn't afraid anymore. I stand aside as he and his two new friends walk past.

"Freak," he says again, and the henchmen dutifully laugh. I've heard it before.

I hold my cold hands up to the sun as if in its praise, asking it for some of its warmth, but it is almost cold itself and cannot satisfy my request. I pull the cuffs of my thick jumper over my hands instead and wander off towards the far end of the yard.

Three sides of the court are made up of accommodation blocks, teaching rooms and administration units. The fourth side is two high wire fences separated by a metre gap. Beyond that is a road that disappears around the back of the buildings. This appears to be a perimeter road, which, at its edge, has another high wire fence that corrals everything in.

This is now my home, my secure home, but I hope to leave it soon.

I take hold of the frost-coated wire fence, ignoring its burning cold, shut my eyes and look inward. I find the link to my mother's soul and see it running out in front of me, disappearing in the darkness of nothing, the space between souls. The link is strong – I don't think she's far.

"Hey, dickhead, take your hands off the fence or security will give you some grief, yeah?"

An older boy is speaking to me. He's Asian, with long straight black hair pulled into a ponytail and a rich light-brown complexion, flawless, like a new-born conker. I don't remove my hands.

"Security'll fuck you over." He nods towards a camera nestled in the eaves on one of the buildings. He looks directly at me, unflinching, unafraid. He has clear brown eyes, and as I catch his stare, I feel an immense anger. An anger so powerful it seems his mind can barely contain it. I don't push further in case I break whatever is holding it in check.

I take my hands off the fence.

"Good move, dickhead. You don't want to lose privileges, not on your first day, yeah?" He blows into his hands. Frozen breath falls through his fingers, dropping to the ground in slow moving streams. "Fuck, it's cold."

"What is that way?" I point in the direction that the link to my mother's soul went.

The boy looks up. "How the fuck should I know? Central London, maybe. Why?"

"I need to find my mother's soul."

"Your mum's soul? What do you mean? She dead?"

"Yes, but her soul hasn't gone."

"You serious?"

"I caught it in my fire-jar and need to get it back. I need to help her die."

"Man, you're a little fucked in the head. That's crazy talk, that is. They'll put you in the bin for sure, yeah? You ought not to talk like that, you know." He shakes his head to emphasise the truth of his observation and starts to blow on his hands again.

"What are you so angry at?" I say. He stops, mid blow, his gaze staying fixed on his cupped hands for a moment. He doesn't look up.

"Why do you say I'm angry? Do I look angry, yeah?"

"Yes."

He looks up now and studies me, gives me his full attention, his spotlight eyes scanning me, recording. I'm fascinated; I've never felt so scrutinised, so observed, so analysed. I stand stock-still until he's finished.

"You're not frightened of me, are you?" he says.

"No."

Our eyes meet again and once more I can see the anger, red and black swirls of rage, spiralling up from his soul, twisting and turning in on themselves, endlessly. But at the middle of the swirl I spot something else, a glimpse before the rage covers it, a more powerful force, the rawest and most destructive of emotions: hate. True, unadulterated hate.

"Well, you should be, you crazy twat. Now fuck off." He looks away.

Dismissed, I leave him alone, but a bond has been created between us. Not like the one with my mother – something different, something in the living world, something I can't see.

It doesn't upset me, quite the opposite. It's new and fascinating. I need to think about it.

I walk slowly back to my accommodation block. The plague has done its job; the frost is corrupted, its purity soiled. But I can't blame my prison mates. They don't understand the power of beauty, its pull on their primitive selves to touch it, own it, to consume it. Their desire, unchecked, destroys it. Beauty cannot help itself; it knows the ultimate outcome, and while it makes us happy, beauty itself is sad.

But while I know this, I still, selfishly and uncontrollably, hope that the beautiful frost will heal itself in the night, so tomorrow I can take in its pleasure once again.

I consider this: although I see the dark, I live in the light, the light generated by beauty, like the beauty of the frost. But I see beauty where many do not.

I wonder if I can get a cup of tea.

Chapter Five

I pull a small piece of chalk from my trouser pocket and gently roll it between my thumb and forefinger. Its smooth, warm dry surface offers no resistance, shedding a fine white powder as I gently rotate it. My fingers, pale at the best of times, are coated in the albino dust – they look more ghost than human. Chalk is my worry beads, my addict's elastic band, a necessity. Deeply old, it masquerades as new, not unlike me, I think.

I found the chalk a few days ago nestled at the foot of a fence post. More lumps festooned the no-man's land beyond my immediate confines. I guess they were thrown up when the post was planted, violently torn from a huge ancient seabed that runs where it will beneath my feet. I imagine how the sea might have looked aeons ago. The clarity of my vision surprises me. It feels too real.

"My name is Makka," says the Asian boy.

He's appeared by me, waded silently through the old sea and caught me unawares. The vision recedes, and only the exercise yard is left. I haven't spoken to him since our first meeting over a week ago.

"You asked me why I was pissed off, yeah? Well, it's 'cause of this fucking filth that raped my ma."

I turned to look at him, but he's staring out though the fence. His neck tendons are tight and stand out like steel ropes. For a moment, he looks unbreakable – perhaps he is.

"You hate this man," I say.

"Is there anything worse I can feel?" He closes his eyes briefly. "Yeah. Yeah, hate is about right."

We stand quietly for a moment and then Makka says, "I'm going to kill him. It's simple, yeah? I just kill him." The statement is incontrovertible. I am left in no doubt that this man will die.

"Will that end it?"

He turns to look at me now. "No, the bastard isn't worth my ma's spit, but it'll fucking well help."

I nod. He looks at my hand.

"What you got there?"

"Chalk."

"Any good reason, yeah?"

I decide to tell him about me, the me I've never told anyone else about. The connection I felt at our first meeting is stronger now. I think, no feel, our futures will run together. A heady mix of blood and salvation?

He listened, said I was a crazy fuck, but I think he understood. He didn't run away.

***

Eve had already had a hard day. She rubbed her ribs and winced. Her morning client had attacked her, getting in a handy jab before she was wrestled to the ground by the assistants. The assault had unsettled Eve. She was always surprised at the randomness of such violence, but the diagnosis wasn't a challenge. The woman had a form of schizophrenia that would always leave her dangerously unstable. She would probably spend the rest of her life in a secure unit, dosed up on pills, and living in a world only she could see.

Eve moved her hand from her lower ribs as she noticed the boy taking in her pain. Now, here was a challenge, another one living outside reality. Right now, however, she could have done without it.

"Does it hurt?" asked the boy.

She ignored the question. "How are things here?"

"Confined."

He caught her eye, and she had the feeling he was trying to tell her something. She looked down at her notebook, which lay open in front of her. A barrier? She closed it and removed it from the table.

"Did you love your mother?"

"I do love my mother."

"Even though she's dead?"

"Yes. Even though I never met her."

"Perhaps you love the idea of loving your mother. Don't you think it odd to love someone you've never met?"

"No and no." The boy paused; his mouth slightly open. Eve could see he was thinking, deciding. "When I was born, she wrapped her despair at losing me around my soul, trying to hang on to me. That connection gave us a relationship so fundamental and so uncluttered that I got to know my mother better than anyone. I never had to meet her to love her."

"Like a spiritual umbilical cord of sorts?"

"Perhaps."

"Will it ever break, do you think?"

"Yes. When I help her soul to pass on. I will not hold her back this time."

"This time?"

"When her body died her soul wanted to leave but . . ."

The boy became still. Eve waited.

"I hung on to her. I didn't want her to go. I didn't let her go. I was wrong." The boy looked down for a moment. It was the first time Eve had seen an emotion register. Guilt? This was an emotion she recognised and understood.

"Do you feel guilty?" she said.

"Yes."

"Is that why you killed Mrs Johnson?"

"No, it is why I put my mother's soul in her body."

"Unsuccessfully though."

The boy nodded. "You know the rest."

"I do," she said, sitting back. She recalled the forensic team's photographs. Headless birds, feathers, leaves, ivy, blood – lakes of blood. A horror scene by any other name. A ritual killing, yet . . .

She looked at the boy sitting there passively. She looked harder, trying to see the other him, the one she felt was hidden by the façade. She saw only what the boy wanted her to see. Eve was sure of that, but not sure he knew it himself. The thought sounded messed up, but she knew it was the right one.

"Do you think of your act as a religious one?"

"No," he said. The firmness of the denial seemed out of character. He said he never lied and Eve, contrary to her professional logic, believed him. The 'no' was telling her something – not this act? Have there been others? Will there be others?

"Have you killed before?"

"No."

"Would you kill again?"

The boy was silent for a moment, and as Eve watched, flecks of golden red appeared in his eyes, barely noticeable, barely glowing. The other him?

"Like Mrs Johnson? I really don't know – that depends."

"Depends on what?"

The boy smiled; the flecks glowed brighter.

"On you, Dr Rhodes."

***

That evening, Eve went to see her mother. The dim lights of the exterior of the inpatients made a stark contrast to the bright fluorescent lights of the interior wards. The sign above the entrance read 'Nightingale House', but the occupants of the house were nothing like the beautiful voiced night-singing bird. The inpatients' songs, when they took to their imaginary stage, were mostly confused, sometimes disturbed and sometimes strangely innocent and happy. And as Eve approached her mother, she could hear her singing quietly to herself, a meaningless string of words that hung together like an odd collection of worry beads. There was no apparent beginning or end.

Psychosis had descended onto Eve's mother's life. Landing on the post-natal depression induced by Eve's birth it had thrived and grown until it became bloated with success, effectively ending any meaningful relationship between mother and daughter. Eve had reflected on this numerous times, and although she knew it was wrong to blame herself, she could not shake off a deep sense of guilt.

Guilt – such a powerful emotion.

As she sat down next to a mother that didn't recognise her, she could not help but draw parallels between her situation and the Boy's. They had both been brought up motherless, they both felt an intense guilt at their part in their mothers' decline, and they had both created alternative worlds in which to hide. But unlike the Boy, she had always known her world was an imaginary one, always knew it was an illusion for comfort and companionship. For atonement, she had opted for the real world and become a psychiatrist to help where she could. The Boy, on the other hand, had stepped into his dark imaginary world to do likewise, and the result was chilling. But Eve recognised it was love that drove his actions, as disturbing as they were, and while they were not condonable, she understood the power of this basic need.

She took her mother's hand and held it for a while. That thought, the certainty that she had always known her dark reflection world was imaginary, didn't sit comfortably with her. It felt like a tiny papercut in her consciousness. She stroked her mother's hair and put her disquiet down to tiredness.

She sat with her mother for a while, but there was no change in the woman's state, and when Eve left, her mother was still singing gently to herself.

Chapter Six

The class empties and I am the last to leave. I stand on the top-floor landing and look out of the window, over the perimeter fence, over the low-slung leafless trees and towards the distant road. Tiny flashes of car head lights flick through the washed-out grey of the winter scene. Hurrying. There is no hurrying here – just waiting. Dave tells me I have to go to court soon. A preliminary hearing, he says. I think it might be interesting.

The noise of the other boys drains away, following them down the stairs like the last of the bathwater. Where I expect silence, there is instead the low hum of voices. One is unmistakably Jenkins, but the other I do not recognise. Curious, I move to the stairwell and look down. Jenkins's head is directly below me, bobbing about as if on a spring. I pick up some words – 'Makka' and 'Paki'.

I lean out over the drop and let a dribble of saliva drip from my mouth. It falls true. Jenkins puts his hand to the crown of his head.

"Jesus fuck," he says looking up. I stare back at him.

"You prick. You'll catch it for this, freak. Right fucking NOW." In his anger and haste to get to me he takes the stairs two at a time, but his flight is interrupted.

"Jenkins," says a bodiless voice. It's Dave. "What's your problem?"

Jenkins falters, his upward rush slows and halts. I can see his hand on the banister, it's gripping it tightly.

"Nothing, Dave. Nothing," he says and reluctantly starts to retrace his steps.

"Good. Well out you go. You know the rules. You too, Bradshaw." This must be the voice I did not recognise. Dave's head appears in the stairwell and looks up. "And you – out please."

I descend, listening to the squeak of my shoes on the rubber-coated stairs. I deliberately twist each footfall to accentuate that sharp stab of sound. Dave locks the door behind me. I'm already accustomed to the clunk of the bolt dropping – a sound that barely registers now.

As I leave the protection of the building, Jenkins appears beside me. He grabs my arm. His hands and face are cherry red. Cold? Cold fury?

"What did you hear, freak? Eh?" He starts to shake me. "Fuck, I hate you. You're always watching everythin' with those puddle-of-piss eyes. Fuck, someone should poke 'em out. Get a stick and just poke 'em out. Fuck, they should." He sneers his desire into my face, enjoying the thought of poking my eyes out. The image, I dare say, is one of pain and blood for me and pleasure for him. I can see why he is in here. The thought relaxes his defences.

I give him what he hates. I stare into his eyes, lock their gaze and disappear into his mind. It's a mess of anger, pain, sadness and terror. Nothing organised. I think he is lost to his past, shaped by its events, unable to deal with them. His soul, when I find it, is turning grey, losing its beautiful paua-shell colours. It is a sad sight. I break the connection.

"Stop that shit." Jenkins pushes my face away and makes to hit me, but Makka steps in the way. I didn't hear him approach.

"Fuck off, Makka. Freak here is pissing me off. He needs teaching a lesson. He ain't right in the head. His eyes; they're all wrong. You can see that, can't you?"

"Yeah, I can see something."

Jenkins looks surprised. "Right, so let's fuck 'im over. He needs his lesson."

"No one is fucking him over. His eyes ain't wrong, they're different. They see things we don't, yeah? Now, piss off, Jenkins and leave him alone."

Jenkins takes a step back and looks between us. He points at us both.

"You're for it you pair of fucks. You'll see. You'll fucking well see."

Makka puts his head on one side. He seems to be deciding what to do with Jenkins. I step forward, step very close to Jenkins.

"I've seen your soul," I say so only he can hear. "I know your fate." His face pales. The cherry red drains away. He knows his fate too and it terrifies him. But does he know he can change it? I don't think so.

He backs off, saying nothing, and then turns and walks away.

"What was that all about then?" says Makka.

I shrug.

"Twat," says Makka watching him go. "You gotta look out for that sort. He'll do you for no good reason, yeah?" Makka is still watching Jenkins. "Who's that he's talking to?"

The boy that Jenkins is talking to is big, tall and wide. A skinhead haircut and a face that sports an angry-looking squashed nose. Like many here, it's not only his nose that is angry.

"Shit." Makka laughs. "Looks like someone hit him in the face with a shovel." The laugh was for the other boy's benefit. An alpha male thing, I think. The other boy is staring hard at us, unadulterated hate sparks and fizzes across the gap. No. Wait. Not at us, at Makka.

"He doesn't seem to like you," I say.

"Yeah? There's a thing." Makka dismisses the boy and himself by heading for lunch. "See you later," he says as he leaves. I think the boy is the mystery voice in the stairwell, Bradshaw. I'll call him Flat-Face.

***

The dark was on us again, a little later now and mixed with not only the cold, but thick fog and ghostly shadows. The high floodlights are struggling to make their presence felt. Their light is twisted and bent and fractured and lost in the labyrinth of the fog, leaving only a small amount to fall to the ground.

We are out getting the air for the last time that day, although many had chosen to stay indoors. I sit quietly on my bench, thinking. The thick mesh fence is only a few unseen metres away. I have yet to work out a plan to escape, but I feel something will come along soon. Voices, dampened by the candy-floss fog, carry to my seat. They rise in volume. An argument. Shouts and low grunts add pepper to the atmosphere. I can hear Makka.

I leave my seat and with it, my thoughts of the future, and strike out into the unseen, homing in on the voices.

"I know your sort. Dirty shits all of you. You shouldn't be allowed." The rough voice is Flat-Face's. "You're disgusting. My old man reckons we'd have to prise you off your mother before we could pack the whole fucking lot of you off back to Paki-land." He pushes Makka against the fence. "Ain't that right, boys?"

The group of boys standing around answer the call to insult.

"Paki, motherfucker, wanker, shit prick." Jenkins leads the chorus.

I'm not close enough to see Makka's face, but I can make out the steel cables bulging in his neck. There is only one way this will end, but I don't want that to happen. I need Makka. I don't want him in trouble.

Makka headbutts Flat-Face, opening up his nose. Blood pours from the split, but Flat-Face stays standing.

"Is that the best you can do, Paki boy?" He shakes his head spraying blood around and pulls a knife from his pocket. "Let's see if you bleed like proper people."

I move closer as the other boys move away. I get the feeling the knife is unscripted, and the boys seem anxious, with the exception of Jenkins.

"Do the Paki fucker, Si, do 'im." They're already on first name terms. Jenkins and the other boys leave as if on cue. Planned? This must have been the conversation I interrupted with my spit.

Flat-Face grunts as he lunges at Makka, but Makka is too quick. Taking a step to the side he catches the knife wrist with his left hand and with his right he grabs Flat-Face's throat, reversing their positions by spinning the larger boy into the fence. Flat-Face throws a punch with his free hand, catching Makka on the side of his head. Makka's ponytail swings and bobs about madly as he absorbs the punch, but he doesn't let go of either the knife hand or the throat. Instead, he retaliates with a vicious knee to Flat-Face's groin. I hear the rush of air leave his lungs as Flat-Face deflates. He drops the knife and Makka lets him go. He reaches between his legs with both hands, and we watch as he slumps to the ground and retches. Makka picks up the knife and pulls Flat-Face into a sitting position. He puts the knife against Flat-Face's throat, and I think he's going to slit it open.

"Makka," I say standing close to him now. "Makka, look at me." He doesn't, he pushes the blade of the knife harder against Flat-Face's throat. It seems that it is more or less blunt as it draws no blood, but nonetheless. "They'll take you away if you kill him. Listen to me. Look at me."

"Fuck off." The blade judders in his hand.

"Makka, please. Look at me." I touch his shoulder. Slowly he turns to me and as soon as I see his eyes, I catch his gaze. It seems Makka trusts me as the connection is easily made. I am met by a storm of anger and rage blowing unchecked through his mind. It's almost overwhelming. Violent bruised blue and purple swirls, punctuated with lightning-like flashes of brilliant white, crashing and thundering into each other. I concentrate on trying to calm the rage, to give Makka a chance to get a hold of himself. I don't think I can keep this up. It's exhausting. After a moment I break the connection, unable to sustain the effort any longer. I feel sweat on my forehead.

Makka blinks.

The rage has lessened.

I reach out and remove the knife from his hand. He resists, but only for a moment. The knife is a blunt dinner affair, but the end has been ground down to make a sharp point. A stabbing weapon. I can hear muted voices and the dull footsteps of people walking fast.

I put the knife to Makka's cheek and with the point make a quick cut. His eyes open wide in surprise as blood starts to flow from the sliced flesh.

"What the fuck . . ."

Flat-Face has rolled over onto the ground again, groaning, his head on the cold dirt. His face is pale, his eye tight shut as if he's trying to keep the pain away. He doesn't look like he's succeeding. I drop the knife into the open pocket of his coat and then distance myself from the scene.

Just in time. Ghost shapes heave into view.

"There," says Jenkins, leading a carer called Pete and a couple of warders. "Look. He's done 'im. I told you."

"Quiet," says Pete. "Makka, please step away from Bradshaw and hand over the knife."

I can see Makka has control of himself again. The steel ropes of his neck have gone, his body is relaxing, and he looks calm.

"I don't have a knife, Pete. It's that shit who has one." Makka holds out his hands.

"He's fucking lying. I saw it," says Jenkins.

"Quiet, Jenkins. In fact, you can go back to your block now. I'll speak to you later."

"Oh, fuck that."

"Now, Jenkins." Pete's tone is clear. Jenkins glares at Makka and leaves.

"OK, Makka. Step away from Bradshaw so we can check him out."

"Sure," says Makka moving away. "The fucker attacked me with a knife – cut me. I headbutted him and then kneed him in the bollocks. Twat was lucky that's all I done."

I watch as Pete kneels down next to Flat-Face and checks him out. The two warders stand facing Makka, who still has his hands out, blood running from his cheek.

Flat-Face groans.

"OK, can you two get Bradshaw to sick bay. I'll deal with Makka." Pete stands up. He has the knife in his hand.

"That ain't mine," says Flat-Face. He's barely audible. Pete ignores him.

"You sure, Pete?" says a warder as Pete hands him the knife. "One of us can stay if you want."

Pete looks at Makka. "No, that won't be necessary, will it

Makka?"

"No, Pete."

The warders help Flat-Face to his feet and between them manhandle him off into the fog.

No one seems to have noticed me, but now Pete turns and beckons me over.

"What's the story here?" he says.

"It's like I said. The fucker tried to cut me." Makka raises a hand to his bleeding face.

"Looks like he did more than try. Why would he do that?"

"'Cause I'm a Paki."

Pete sighs. "And what did you see?" he says to me.

"I don't think it is a nice thing to call Makka a Paki."

"No, it's certainly not. Whose knife is it?"

"Bradshaw's."

"Are you sure?"

"Yes."

"You saw him with it?"

"Yes. Can I go in now please? I don't want to miss tea."

Pete sighs again. "OK, let's go in. He turns to Makka. "We need to get your face looked at, but I don't think it's too bad." He hands him a tissue, which Makka presses against the cut. "You come with me, and you," – he nods at me – "go and get some tea. I'll speak to you later."

***

When morning comes it is bright and clear, and everything feels like it has been gently washed while we slept.

The bell for morning break rings out – sharp and electronic – an unpleasant sound, but a welcome one. I follow my inmates out of the block and find Makka waiting for me. He grins, a large plaster over his left cheek.

"Good move, soul boy. You fucked over that twat Bradshaw good and proper."

"Are you in trouble?"

"Bit. But fuck, you gave me a couple of stitches in my face. Improve me looks, yeah?" He grins again, but it fades quickly.

For a moment, I see the real Makka, the one without rage or anger, the one bashed and beaten by circumstances, the sad and lonely Makka.

“Thanks,” he says. I say nothing, just watch as he puts back his defences.

Chapter Seven

The dark is early. The thick cloud has bought a premature close to the day, dusk shut out before it had time to warn us night was coming. Maybe it will snow. I would like that.

I can't see Makka yet, but he will be here soon. Others mill about the yard, breathing in their last mouthfuls of freedom for the day. Five o'clock, just half an hour until we are called back inside, and the end-of-day process is played out.

I raise my face to the sky and close my eyes. I can feel the weight above me, the swollen grey-white clouds, sacks of crystal-cold grains full to bursting. The pressure is so great that a single prick would rent them open, letting their frozen load tumble to earth.

From this tranquil moment, I am unexpectedly pitched over. A sharp push from behind, and I am once again prostrate on the frozen ground.

"Hey, freak." It's Jenkins and his shadows. It seems that this is to be the greeting for me from now on. I get to my feet rubbing my sore knees through the scuffed fabric of my trousers.

"The Griffin wants to see you. B-Block basement stores, fast like." He grins at me – a watery-eyed, malicious grin. I don't move but rub my hands together to put some warmth back in them. I've never met Griffin and don't want to meet the warder now. I'm waiting for Makka.

"Now, freak, he means now, for fuck's sake." He grabs me by the neck of my jumper and drags me towards B-Block. The shadows join in, taking it in turns to push and pull me, a tag team. Jenkins opens the door to the block and the shadows, in a final combined effort, push me through.

"Off you go, pretty boy," says Jenkins and laughs. The

shadows laugh. He lets the door bang shut but stands guarding it peering at me through the small safety-glass window; an ugly portrait on clear graph paper.

It seems I have little choice so I might as well go and see what Griffin wants. I'm a little curious. Makka says he's a cunt and to avoid him as much as I can, but he never said why.

I head down the wide basement stairs and through a pair of fire doors at the bottom. A short, dimly lit corridor greets me, offering up rooms that hang off one side. There is a laundry, a small workshop and a room with an old upright piano in it. The rooms, with their backs to the perimeter road, have a single small rectangular frosted window in them, high up and barred. At the end of the corridor is the storeroom. Its door is ajar, allowing bright fluorescent light to slice out, cutting a sliver of painted concrete floor and breeze block wall from the darkness. I push it open and step in.

There are shelves and shelves of food, all tinned, boxed, jarred or vacuum packed. A palace of the preserved, the colourful and the long-lasting.

The door shuts behind me.

Griffin is there. I've seen him from a distance a few times, but he's a lot bigger close up. His bear-like stature dominates the low-ceilinged basement.

"Good. Jenkins found you." His voice is calm, but his eyes give him away. They are bright, wide, excited, anticipating.

"This way," he says, putting a hand behind my shoulder and guiding me to the far end of the store. Giant tins of cooking oil are stacked up against the back wall, almost to the ceiling, their bright yellow labels creating a vast collage. The repeated image is mesmeric, and I am sure if I stare at it long enough, I will see the hidden message, a magic eye picture. I don't get the opportunity.

"Sit," says Griffin pointing to an old wooden chair. Its high back is pressed up against the oil tins and its curved arm rests wrap around me as I sit. It feels awkward and out of place – sad. I feel sorry for it. Perhaps I can rescue it when I go.

"You know why you're here?" he says, moving to stand directly in front of me.

"No."

"I think you do. All the boys who come here – they know."

I shake my head.

"It's punishment. You're here to be punished. It's my job to see that it's done, and your job to accept it without question. You understand?" He takes a step forward. "This is all your fault. If it weren't, you wouldn't be here, right? You understand?"

"No."

"Of course you do. You may fool the others with your fruitcake performance, but I've been watching you and can see through that crap. You're an evil little shit, and you're going to get your punishment." He takes a long deep rushing nasal breath. "It's my duty, you see."

He takes another step forward and puts his feet each side of mine, pushing them together, clamping them tight. He undoes his belt and removes it, folding it in half as he does.

"A belt is a very useful object," he says tapping me on the head with it. "It can act as a restraint, or a throttle or even a whip. Oh, and of course it keeps my trousers up." As he says this, he allows his trousers to drop to his knees.

"See," he says, grinning.

"I would like to leave now," I say.

He ignores me.

"Are you frightened?"

"No."

He slaps my face gently with the belt. "What if I were to hit you? Would you be frightened then?"

"No." He doesn't seem to understand my answers.

"Sure? It makes it more fun if you are. Much more fun." He raises his eyebrows, "We'll have to start by correcting that." His eyes shine as if lacquer-coated. I try to push my way into them, to make a connection, to stop him doing this, but the coating is hard and will not yield. I cannot catch his stare; all I can catch is my own tiny reflection.

Pain erupts across my face. His belt has bit me. A leathery and stinging bite. I can feel my face redden. Griffin grabs my hair and forces my head back.

"Frightened now are we? Eh?"

I don't answer and he mistakes my silence for agreement.

"Good, good." He licks his top lip. "Now let's get started, shall we?" His voice is no longer calm, his breathing now rapid.

He lets go of my hair, grabs my right hand and pushes it up the leg of his boxer shorts. I can feel coarse hair and swollen flesh.

"Can you feel me? Yes, of course you can. I want you to rub me – hard. Do it now." He raises the belt letting go of my hand. "NOW!"

I look at the bulge of his excitement and my hand thrust in his shorts. Makka is right – he is a cunt.

I grab a handful of the coarse hair and wrench it from its anchorage with as much force as I can manage. A clump of black tightly curled hair comes away in my hand. Griffin yells in pain, a sharp cracked sound, and then hits me across the face with the belt. My head jerks to the right and before I can raise my hands in defence, he punches me on the side of my head sending me and the chair clattering to the floor. I lie, confused for a moment. A high-pitched whine buzzes in my ears while blood starts a meandering journey down my face.

I can hear shouting, a dull roar, as if the perpetrator were standing the other side of a double-glazed window. Even so I recognise the muted tones. It's Makka. I roll on to my side and sit up, snorting red snot down the front of my jumper.

Makka is on Griffin's back, his right forearm is across the bear-sized man's throat, crushing his windpipe, while his free hand tries to puncture those smoke-filled eyes. I'd like to see that happen – to watch his visual world drift away to be diluted to nothing by the vast sea of air.

Griffin's trousers are around his ankles and every time he tries to punch Makka he totters, waddles penguin-like. He looks silly. He should never have taken his belt off.

Griffin throws himself backwards slamming Makka into some shelves. Tins and jars, that moments before were sitting quietly and inanimate, explode into life. They scatter in all directions, a flurry of motion, a discordant snatch of audio –

bouncing tins and the muted smashing of jam filled jars.

Makka's yell of pain turns back to savage anger. He bites down on an ear with terrible ferocity. Now it's Griffin's turn to yell out in pain. He slams Makka back into the shelves.

Again, tins roll.

Again, jars smash.

Again.

Makka catches his head on the sharp edge of a shelf and finally slips from the bronco he was riding so well. He takes most of the ear with him.

Blood pours from the ragged remnant. Griffin puts his hand up to the torn appendage and grimaces. His scratched and weeping red-ringed yellow-smoked eyes look at me, but don't see me. But I see them, and I see what they say – Makka is going to die. I can't let that happen.

Griffin pulls up his trousers, his disadvantage gone. He turns to Makka, who is getting unsteadily to his feet.

"You fuck," says Griffin and with unexpected speed grabs Makka by the throat with one hand and squeezes.

"You fuck." He punches Makka in the face. "Fuck, fuck, fuck." With every 'fuck' he punches Makka.

And it's now, deep inside me, from a place I have yet to find, a rage burns. Wisps of the rage-smoke find their way out and urge me to my feet. I pick up a tin as I do so – chopped tomatoes. More wisps, an eruption is imminent; I've never felt like this and part of me wants to stop and work it out, but I don't have time. I feel strong and throw the tin with an accuracy I don't normally possess. There is an audible crack as the tin bullets into the back of Griffin's closely shaven head. I half expect it to remain lodged in his skull, but it doesn't, falling to the floor instead to join the innocent collateral of the battle.

Griffin sways, letting Makka fall to the ground as he raises both hands to the back of his head. He turns to face me, acknowledging my existence again. Just. His eyes are having trouble focusing – this is my opportunity, but before I can catch his stare the rage erupts.

This isn't me. I have no control. I'm swept up by the stream of molten rage and borne along; an observer. The rage flies at Griffin's eyes. There is no needle-like precision, no controlled entry, just a blunt volcanic punch that smashes the smoky eyes and pours itself into the exposed sockets. It barrels its way through the brain searing a wide path until it finds the entrance to the well that leads to Griffin's soul. It doesn't pause but plunges down the vertical tunnel scorching its walls. There is no respect for its sanctity.

Griffin's soul is engulfed, the infinite bonds that hold it suspended in place, sheared. The rage has its prey. It now retreats, pulling back through the destruction it wrought, from Griffin's body to mine. As it reaches the well to my own soul I am discarded, left to watch it disappear. I want to follow, but something bars me. I'm not frustrated. I think I'll be allowed to travel this path before long, to see what is down there, what is keeping my own soul company.

My vision returns to the basement store in time to see Griffin fall to his knees. For a moment he stays like that, a defeated body, and then pitches forward landing with a dull wet thump on the concrete floor.

Stillness.

"Cunt," says Makka after a moment. He gets to his feet and I watch as he wipes his beaten face, smearing blood across it.

"Did the fucker do you?"

"Do me?"

"Yeah, you know, make you do stuff." Makka looks anxious.

I understand what he means now. "No."

"Sure?" he says looking at Griffins trousers, which had fallen down to his knees again. "I wasn't too late?"

"No. You stopped him."

"Good," he says nodding his head. "Good." He limps around to stand by Griffin's head.

"Cunt," he says again and kicks Griffin in the face. The skull jerks back and blood sprays out creating a ragged pattern like a red ink-blot test. Looks to me like an elephant riding a surfboard.

"Shit, my face hurts. I need to sit down."

I retrieve the sad chair and Makka slumps into it. His face is swollen and there is a deep cut to his temple where the shelving caught him.

"Find us some water, will you?" he says.

I walk up and down the rows of shelves and find some bottled water. I also find some plasters and a pack of custard creams. I like custard creams; they remind me of tea at Shelly Fields.

Makka takes the water and cleans himself up a bit. I put a large plaster on his cut, but the blood soaks it immediately.

"Leave it," he says as I make to put another one on him. "We've got to go."

"Where?"

"Dunno. London someplace. But we got to get out of here now." He points to Griffin. "That fuck will be missed soon." Makka gets up from the chair and crouches down by Griffin. With a grunt he turns him over on to his back. The blood that's pooled around the body is already going sticky and it makes stringy blood beads that run from Griffin's ear and face to the floor.

"He'll have an access card somewhere," says Makka as he starts searching Griffin's trousers. He pulls the electronic key from a front pocket along with small wad of cash.

"Shit. He's still breathing. Thought we'd killed the cunt."

"His soul is gone. It's in me now. I stole it. I am sure his body will stop without it."

Makka sniffs. "Well, that's as maybe, but I want to make sure." He looks around. "Over there," he says, pointing to a small desk. "Go see if there's a knife or something."

I do as he asks, but only find a large pair of scissors. Makka grins at me, a vicious little grin.

"Yeah, that'll be right. Bring them here."

Makka pulls down Griffin's boxer shorts, exposing the unconscious man's cock. It seems to have shrivelled up. Makka grabs it, pulls it hard to stretch it and then applies the scissors. It takes a couple of goes to sever the penis, and as it comes free blood gushes from the stump and flows in a wide fall between the man's legs. Makka throws the redundant meat away.

"Got your chalk?" he says. I nod. "OK. Write 'Child Fucker' next to his head, yeah?" He hobbles off into the sea of shelving.

I do as Makka asks and write the words around the top of his head. The chalk mixes with the blood – a perverse halo sits above the dying body.

"Come on, we're out of here, yeah?"

I follow the sound of his voice and find him by an exit door. As I approach, he switches out the lights.

"Gotta be careful. There'll be cameras outside, and we don't want them snooping on us just yet." He presents the card to a reader and the door cracks open a sliver, letting moonlight drop on to him. As I look at the silver Makka, I'm moved, and I understand, for the first time, what it is to have a friend, someone who cares. But there is something else happening here that I don't understand. Some feeling that Makka and me are more important than we know. That we are carrying out a job, a mission, something spiritual – perhaps religious? I just don't know what, but the feeling is strong.

Religion – a religious act, a prophet. Dr Rhodes thought I might see my actions that way. Perhaps now there is merit in her thoughts. I'll leave her a clue. As if on cue, a lost soul drifts by, its marbled paua-shell body spinning slowly, and in the moonlight it is powerfully beautiful and sad in equal measure.

"Wait," I say and run back to Griffin's body. At his feet, I write a single word with my chalk – *Purgatio*.

"We gotta run straight," says Makka on my return. "You hear me? Straight across the road. I can see a small gate out there. See?" Makka points. I see the gate.

"Yes. What is beyond the gate?"

"Fuck knows, but we'll have to risk it, yeah? Let's hope the fucker's card works. Ready?"

I nod. We run.

We're across the road and through the gate in seconds. Our prison disappears behind the frost-coated bushes and small trees that flank the perimeter fence. The freezing night is on us drawing out our breath in icy steams as we pant from the exertion. Makka stops me and listens. There are no obvious signs of an alarm, just the distant rumble of evening traffic and the baby-like cry of a town fox.

The bushes and trees are growing on a bank, part of the barrier that hides the institute from the surrounding inhabitants. We climb it now and emerge on to a poorly lit street of forlorn and unkempt box housing. It's a cheap estate to house the poorest members of society. Looking at the state of the houses, I think we might have had it better in our prison.

We head down the street, keeping our prison behind us. Makka is limping quite badly but says nothing about it. The street turns inwards and opens up into a small recreation ground. Most of the rec's streetlights are out, but in the light of one that is working I can see a car. A Mini, idling. Its driver door is open, and four hoodies stand in its lea. One looks our way as we approach.

"Shit, look at you," he says. "You been right fucked over." He laughs. "It ain't your day is it, 'cause if you wanna get by here you gotta give me what you got left. You check?" He takes half a dozen steps towards us, leaving the safety of the car.

"That right, yeah?" he says, turning to his fellow hoodies.

"That's the way of things, Spike. Your tarmac, your rules."

Makka doesn't break his limping stride and walks up to Spike and headbutts the boy just as he turns back to look at us. Spike goes down without a whimper. I am amazed Spike couldn't see the violence and aggression oozing from Makka. It's palpable at the best of times, but now, its unmistakable. Two of the hoodies run. Perhaps they're more observant. The remaining hoodie starts screaming at Makka, and then flies at him in a whirl of arms and legs.

It is a girl hoodie.

Makka punches her square in the face and she folds, hitting the soft verge with a small crunch of breaking frosted grass. Makka rubs his fist.

"Shit, that girl's got a hard face." He kneels down next to Spike and starts to remove the boy's hoodie.

"You cold?" he says, without looking at me.

"Yes."

"Well, take the mad bitch's hoodie then."

I look down at her for a moment. I think her nose is broken.

"I've never touched a girl," I say.

Makka stands up and starts to put on the retrieved clothing.

"I didn't tell you to touch her up, just take the fucking hoodie. Come on; we gotta move."

I don't move.

"Ahh, for fuck's sake." He pulls the clothing off the girl and throws it at me.

"In the car," he says.

I get in and we're gone.

Chapter Eight

"So, what do you think?" The Inspector stood surveying the scene. The body had long gone, taken off to the police mortuary for examination. The damage of the fight still lay scattered about. Broken and abandoned tins and jars and packets of biscuits were the silent witnesses to the horror that had unfolded. To Eve, who had accompanied the Inspector to the crime scene, the air seemed to hang with a post-traumatic stillness.

"Chalk and blood. Do you think this is to be the boy's signature?" said the Inspector, turning to Eve.

"No. Well, not in this case, at least." Eve crouched down by the chalked word *Purgatio*. "Only this I would say."

The Inspector nodded. "You're probably right. There was clearly a fight here, an extremely violent one. The carers tell me they're missing another boy. An Asian lad called Makka Noorani. They say he's psychotic and violent. He'd have to be. The victim wasn't just a big man. He was more than capable of looking after himself. A bit of a reputation for aggressive defence." She seemed to be talking to herself as she circled the patches of dried blood and sprays of exploded jam. Eve wasn't listening.

"Child fucker." Eve read the chalk halo out aloud. She looked up at the Inspector. "And was he?"

"We're making enquiries."

"How did he die?"

"Probably a blow to the head. A blunt instrument trauma." She kicked a tin. "Although they cut his dick off as well, and I can't imagine that wouldn't have helped. What does *purgatio* mean? Italian?"

"No, Latin. I'm pretty sure it means something like cleansed or purified."

"Cleansed?"

"Yes." Eve stood up and stretched her back.

"Something to do with souls then. The child fucker has been cleansed?"

"Yes, that would be my guess." Eve stared at the word. If the boy hadn't written it down then the death would be a straightforward one, an opportunist killing perhaps. But the word. *Purgatio*. He believes something else went on here and wants her to know. "I think the boy believes that he's committed a religious act here."

"Really? Shit. I hate it when killing gets religious."

"Well, the insinuation is that it's some kind of religious act, a cleansing of a soul and so the purification of evil. It makes sense, particularly as the victim has been labelled a child fucker. With Mrs Johnson, it was all about the mother's soul. This word" – Eve scuffed at it with her shoe – "didn't appear at that killing. The boy made it clear to me that it had nothing to do with religion, and I have to say I believe him."

"Great. So we've got a precocious delusional juvenile religious vigilante on the loose. And he's watched over by a psychotically violent guardian angel. Shit." The Inspector straightened her coat. "This isn't making my day."

"No," said Eve. "Guess not." But it was making hers, and she only felt the tiniest bit guilty.

***

I have not been on the tube before.

It's exciting, exhilarating. I feel happy.

We abandoned the Mini. Makka said it was too obvious, but I think its Panama yellow suited it. It's a real colour, bright and burnt. Real things have real colours.

The carriage rattles along, pulled by what sounds like a mad demon, railing against its servitude, screaming and cursing, straining to escape and panting out hot breath as it tries. The feeling of speed is palpable as brickwork and unintelligible signs flash past the window, close enough to touch. I see my shadow-self in the window, my face looks puffy, but is smiling. I can see Makka, too. He's sitting next to me with his eyes shut, his broken face testament to our friendship. My shadow-self smiles some more.

The woman opposite gets up to leave as the demon slows for a station. She clutches her bags tightly to her chest as she passes Makka. He shifts his legs, which causes her to rush away in a shuffling scurry. Fear trails after her like a jet stream, dispersing into the carriage, infecting others. So many people just cannot see, blind to reality and full of assumptions.

Having disgorged the woman and consumed a couple of other passengers, the demon sets off again.

I know Makka is not asleep.

"Sorry," he says without opening his eyes.

I say nothing.

"For setting you up with that fuck, Griffin."

I remain silent. I don't understand. I think Makka might be confused.

"It was the only plan I could think of. It didn't take much to goad Jenkins into suggesting you as arse bait for Griffin. I knew what that perv did down there. Risky, but our only shot at getting close to the perimeter fence." He opens his eyes. "Sorry."

I shrug. "We're out. That's good. Are all the seats on the tube covered with this patterned material?" I point to the vacated seat opposite me. "Or are the patterns all different?"

Makka laughs. "You really are fucked in the head." He closes his eyes.

I want to know. "Are they?"

"Are they what?"

"The covers. Are the patterns all different?"

"How the fuck do I know?" He laughs again. "I think they're different, but I never really look, yeah? Anyway, this is an old shitty train, with shitty seats."

I rub the seat cover I'm sitting on. I don't think the train is shitty.

The demon slows again, and Makka gets to his feet and stands stiffly to attention. I think he is hurting, but he doesn't say anything. The doors slide open, and a woman announces that we should mind the gap. I peer down between the platform and the train on to a grubby track floor. An empty crisp packet settles for a moment waiting to be bullied again by demon breath. A soul flits by. I've seen dozens down here but cannot make out what they are saying. Their chatter is drowned out by the noise of the real world.

"This way," says Makka as he limps off towards the exit, the messenger bag he found in the back of the Mini banging against his thigh, objecting to his awkward gait. The bag contains some money and a large amount of what Makka says is skunk. 'Fucking handy' is how he described the find.

We emerge from the subterranean world on to the Euston Road, according to Makka. It is another unexpected joy. It's magical. The snarling traffic with its lights spinning off in all directions as the freezing air redirects and, in places, breaks up the sober light into colourful illuminations.

Makka sets off down a busy side road. We say nothing as we walk, but I measure our progress by the number of lamp posts we pass and by each puff of our crystallised breath, our own ice-breathing demons to pull us along.

We pass a row of shops, a fashion outlet for transsexuals, a *special* massage parlour, a fruit and vegetable store that is still open, a pub and small Thai restaurant. No one bothers with us, no one notices, or if they do, they hide any outward reaction. Perhaps beaten faces are common here.

Makka comes to a halt outside a large Victorian-fronted building. To its left is a huge gated entrance, supported by square pillars, topped by a corridor that runs from the building we stand in front of over to another similar one. They look like the gatehouse to a castle. The corridor is out of place with its big metal framed windows and flat roof. It is decaying badly and looks dejected and rejected. I can just make out the ghost shapes of long-gone letters that once sat over the gate. Their impression spells out TEMPERANCE HOSPITAL. The gate is chained and padlocked, and the windows of the two buildings are boarded up at ground level, although some have been half removed. The whole site is tired and sad and seems resigned to its fate, but it still has an air of defiance about it. I like it.

A big red-and-white sign wired to the gate says 'Private Property – Keep Out'. Someone has written 'All property is theft' over it. I point this out to Makka.

"What does it mean?" I ask him.

"It means some arty shit thinks he's makin' a philosophical point. But he's not. He's just being a pretentious twat. Come on. Let's get in."

Just left of the gate and built into the hospital's façade, is an odd-fronted shop. Its lower half is made from wooden panels with batons fixed diagonally across it. They are evenly spaced and painted red, a very faded red now. The top half is made up of wooden-framed windows, all whitewashed so we can't see inside. The whole lot is covered in graffiti. It is a surreal little shop, and I think it must have sold sweets in jars and been beautifully strange.

Makka leans heavily on the door and it opens inwards. He snorts.

"Yeah, nothin's changed." He steps inside.

I follow and shut the door behind us.

The whitewashed windows apply an anaemic filter to the yellow streetlight that seeps in through the boarding. I can hear the traffic outside, but this interior is otherworldly. Peeling wallpaper hangs like loose skin from the walls; a chandelier clings to the ceiling by an electrical thread, and a scratched and worn wooden counter stands to one side. Rubble lies around in listless heaps and the stink of defecation and damp touches everything. Despite its surroundings the counter remains proud and self-important. Reliving its past in the face of its present.

Makka makes for the rear of the shop where a hole, that looks like it's been kicked into existence, gives access to whatever lies beyond. He steps through and then calls to me from out of its darkness.

"Come on. We're in the hospital now, yeah? We gotta head up."

I'm starting to tire, and I think my face is swelling up. I'd like a tea sauna, but I am curious to see what is upstairs, so I don't say anything. Perhaps I can get a cup of tea up there.

Chapter Nine

Another cold but bright morning wanders into our room. Its light bounces off the bare walls, whose paint is peeling as if it has some nasty skin infection. Anyone that cared for the place is gone now, so the itchy patches will have to go untreated. I can't help but feel sorry for the building.

I pull myself up and off the naked mattress and, with my thick blanket wrapped around me, shuffle over to the window.

Our room is high up on the top floor of the old hospital – the left-hand tower – and I am able to see down on to the street below. It feels early, but traffic is already building up and complaining, impatient to be somewhere else. People hurry by, like the traffic – impatient to be elsewhere, but perhaps their haste has something to do with the frost. It nips at them like a Jack Russell. I can see it, and it makes me laugh.

The voices of Sadie and Bill filter through from the next room. They've been living here for almost a year, and Makka says that Bill runs the place. Makka calls him *the old man*, but he doesn't look old to me. Makka likes him and says he's 'solid'.

There are others here too: Jay, Brook, Little G and Sam make up a band and live on the floor below. They practise in the old basement operating theatre, although I've not heard them. I'd like to as I've never seen a band play expect on the TV, and that doesn't count. Bunny and Sally live across from us. Bunny looks very pale and shakes most of the time and is always smoking. I don't think he is well. Saul and Lips live at the end of our little corridor. They are always laughing and kissing each other. Lips says they work in fashion and live like this for inspiration. I like them because they seem to like everyone.

None of them have black souls. I've checked.

Across the room, Makka snorts. He is still asleep, a comfortable sleep, in contrast to the last few nights where the pain of his damaged leg has made it difficult for him to rest properly. Like me, his swollen face has reduced, leaving a violent purple bruise, but you can't see it easily under his brown skin. It must be good to have brown skin.

I stay watching my small-framed view of London for some time. From somewhere in the distance, thoughts of my mother form in the cold air and spiral towards me. Twisted ribbons of ice. I have not thought about her for several days, and it bothers me. My new world is very distracting, and I've let it draw my attention away from what is important – her salvation – our salvation.

Makka interrupts my thoughts with a loud snort and wakes himself up. He slowly rolls over to face me, yawns and scratches his head.

"Hungry?" he asks, getting up and pulling on his jeans. "Fuck, it's cold."

"A little."

"I'm starving, yeah? We'll get something from that cafe down the street, the Shag, or whatever it's called."

"It's called the Snug. It sells tea."

"Whatever, and I hope it sells more than just frigging tea." Makka pulls on his shoes and looks at me again. "Come on. I'd have thought you can dress yourself at your age." He laughs.

"Yes," I say. "I can. I have been able to do that since I was five."

Makka laughs again. He's in a good mood. "Sure. Well get a move on, my hands are going numb already." He blows on them.

I pull on my trousers. They're stiff with cold and I shudder.

"It'll be warm in the cafe," says Makka, "and the bog'll have hot water, so we can have a wash."

We pull on our stolen hoodies, and I make my bed. I always make my bed.

***

The Snug is warm and buzzing with worker drones and locals alike. Lattes and cinnamon bagels are being handed out to those on the move by a large woman in a floral dress. The smell of baked bread and frying fills the shoe-box-sized space, making me suddenly desperate to eat.

Makka and I are sitting at a table near the window so we can see the world go by.

"What you two havin' then? And it better be more than a cuppa – we're busy." A man, a match for the floral-patterned woman, is talking to us.

"Tea please," I say.

"I said more than a cuppa, lads. I aren't no charity you know."

"And two full English breakfasts an' a white coffee for me," says Makka grinning at him. The man looks a little hesitant. Makka's grin seems to have that effect, but he rallies.

"Right, OK, well. You got some money?"

Makka puts a twenty-pound note on the table and taps it.

"Just checking, no offence. Some lads will do a runner, you know, but I can see you'll be OK." He moves off and I watch as he shouts our order through a hatch. A magic breakfast food hatch. That would be great if it existed, as would a never-ending packet of custard creams.

We sit without speaking until our order arrives, great plates of hot food glistening with oil and garnished with a fading sizzle. It's accompanied by pint mugs of tea and coffee. Makka eats with purpose, but without order – everything and anything is moved from plate to mouth without much consideration. I can't eat like that.

"You gonna eat?" asks Makka through a mouthful of randomness.

I start on the bacon.

"I've gotta go and find out where The Fuck hangs out, yeah?" He waves his fork at me. "So you're gonna have to stay here because I can't watch out for you if it all goes tits up." He takes a large gulp of coffee. "Don't know how long

I'll be, but you just wait for me to get back, yeah? Bill said you can hang with him and Sadie while I'm gone. OK?"

I follow the bacon with the beans. Alphabetically ordered on this occasion.

***

Bill gives me a book to read – *Frankenstein*. He says it might appeal to me as I'm a little bit freaky. I spend the rest of the day reading it, curled up in my cold room. I don't like Frankenstein much, he's full of self-importance and then self-pity. What creator abandons his creation at the moment he brings it to life? I would have given the creature a soul.

It's dark when I finish, and I wonder if Makka is OK, so I leave my room and descend to the ground floor to wait in the dishevelled shop. I like sitting in the anaemic wash of the filtered streetlight, watching dust particles move gently in the air as I disturb the ruins beneath my feet. There are plenty of souls here too, drifting about like the dust, all very old, and beautiful and mostly unintelligible.

The shop door scrapes open and Bill slips through the gap, trailing in a fog of cold and street noise. He doesn't see me in the gloom and shouts out in surprise when I greet him.

"Jesus! You freaked me out big time. I thought you were a ghost or something. You're certainly pale enough. What are you doing sitting around in here?"

"Waiting for Makka. Do you believe in ghosts?"

"I guess. I'm pretty open minded about it, but I've never seen one. Hope not to, really." He steps over the rubble and makes his way to the hole.

"There are no ghosts," I say. "But there are lost souls. Plenty in here. Perhaps it's those that people feel and think they're ghosts. The souls here are very old."

Bill stops by the torn entrance and scratches his nose. "Well, that's interesting. You know that this hospital was built on an old medieval burial ground. In fact, there used to be a chapel here too, but it got the fuck knocked out of it in the war. It was bulldozed a while back." He steps through the hole and then his face reappears. "The crypt is still here somewhere. Come on. You can come with me and chill while you wait for Makka. Got some food and a few chemicals to try." He grins and then disappears into the dark. He shouts back at me, "You do know you really are a bit freaky, don't you?"

People have told me this since I can't remember.

***

In contrast to the bleakness of my and Makka's room, Bill and Sadie's is colourful and warm. Patterned sheets and scarves hang from the walls and ceiling, billowing out like the sides of a tent caught by a gentle warm wind – otherworldly. They share a large mattress at one end of the room. It's heaped with blankets and heavy-looking throws. Wooden boxes make up the furniture while candles are sprinkled about the place providing light and shadows. This room is made for the night, and it feels perfect.

There are several other mattresses in the room with cushions scattered about them. A black-and-white cat lies on its side in amongst these – stretched out in decadent abandonment.

Bill is boiling some water on a gas camping stove while Sadie fiddles with a music player. I stand in the doorway waiting to be invited in.

"Hiya," says Sadie. "Go sit with Alfie. He won't mind." She points to the cat. I sit down on the mattress and put two cushions behind me to prop me up. Alfie looks at me with a sideways face and miaows quietly before blinking his eyes and then shutting them completely.

Bill hands me a cup of tea.

"Try this," he says, pointing at me with a turned-up index finger. Sitting on its tip is a small translucent square encompassing a miniature red heart.

"What do you want me to do with it?"

"Swallow it. It's a tab, acid, LSD – a Red Heart. You'll trip your tiny nuts off with it. You'll see the world in a different way with this little beauty. I mean, really, like, different." Bill grins.

I look at the drug.

"I already see the world differently," I say.

"Sure you do." Bill shrugs. "But not like this you haven't." He pushes the finger towards me.

I carefully take the square and put it on my tongue.

"Me too, lover," says Sadie and takes a tab from Bill. She puts it on her tongue as Bill follows suit. We swallow together, although mine gets stuck in my throat and I need a sip of tea to send it on its way.

"Does anyone fancy some toast?" asks Sadie.

***

I've been sitting on the mattress for a while now, drinking tea, eating toast and listening to Bill and Sadie's chatter. The music from the hi-fi drifts in and out of my consciousness, each time it finds its way in it stays a little longer, all swirls and colour and mesmeric. Alfie is on my lap and I stroke his soft black-and-white fur. I can feel his purring through my lap – it's warm and reassuring. I surrender to the narcotic and let myself fall into my consciousness, into the music and its dancing visions. Outside, the chatter fades and the room melts.

But now I'm awake. Awake in the way you are when you lucid dream, and I'm being swept along by a river of colourful music. I know where I'm heading, and I'm curious to see what awaits me. The music river flows towards the well, the gateway to my soul, and tumbles over its lip. It falls in an ever-thinning spray and I fall with it.

I am here at last – my soul suspended by the ethereal bonds, a beautiful paua-shell finish glistening in an unreal light. But it's not the only soul here. Another hangs from the same bonds, but it is not smooth-edged and beautifully shaped like mine. It is bigger and spiky and sharp like a piece of broken glass. It is the shard of a shattered soul. I can see a platinum liquid moving languidly beneath its translucent surface, and although the liquid threatens to leak from the ragged edges, it does not.

I watch and, as I do, I notice distinct blotches of black and grey infection moving in the current, rising to the surface before being folded back in to the metallic fluid. The shard is sick. I am being shown its corruption. And I now remember something I never knew – this is a shard of the soul of an Angel.

I feel its age and pain, so ancient and so crippled. Tied to the earth, bought down by its selflessness, it cannot move on until all the shattered pieces are cleansed – *purgatio*.

This is the last piece.

And then I remember other things too, other important things.

I wake again, this time in the real world with a sharp slap to the face. It's Makka. His eyes are close to mine, searching, checking.

"You OK?" he says.

I nod. "I know," I say.

"Know what?"

"I know why I'm here."

"Yeah, it's the fucking acid Bill gave you. He ought to know better. That shit can really fuck with your mind, and your mind don't need no more fucking with." He taps my head. "Right?"

I don't say anything, just nod. My mind is fine and clear and there is no trace of the drug. Makka will understand another time. Right now, I'm happy. The feeling I have that I am part of something important, something bigger, is right. And not only that, I know how to save my mother.

Chapter Ten

We spend the day in the Temperance Hospital. Makka says he's been up all night and needs some sleep.

"I'm knackered, yeah? Hung with these guys from the anarchist bookshop, I mean shit, they hate the fascist cunts almost as much as I do. They know where The Fuck and his mates drink, so we're goin' to go there tonight to have a look." He pulls his boots and jeans and hoodie off and throws them carelessly on the floor by his mattress. "The anarchists say he's dangerous, they say he's got some sort of gang of Nazi head-fucks together and they've got protection." He yawns and pulls the blankets over him. "Political protection or some such shit. Well, that may be true, but that ain't gonna help him any. He'll need more than hot air to protect him."

I sit quietly for a while until Makka is asleep and then fold his clothes.

***

The day has offered little in the way of sun and so as we leave Aldgate East tube station in the gathering dark I can feel the crystallised air forming a new coat of frost even as we crunch over the remains of the last one. Frost on frost – I expect there is a Scandinavian word for it.

Makka takes us down some back streets, and we briefly pop out on to a road whose sign proclaims it as Cable Street. I can smell curry and chips. We disappear again down yet more side roads and alleyways, the contents of my bag clinking every so often. I shiver as the cold starts to penetrate my pink hoodie. Makka says I look like a girl, which apparently is a good thing – the police shouldn't bother us if they're looking for two boys.

There is no breeze tonight, and the sky is clear. We cross a railway line with a dozen tracks racing off into the night. Moonlight bounces off some whitewashed sheds by the far rails giving the scene a serene feeling. "It is beautiful," I tell Makka.

"Yeah, yeah, whatever."

On the other side of the crossing we come to a road that seems deserted. Boarded up shops face a row of terrace houses whose front doors open directly on to the street. In amongst these is a pub. Its sign says it's the White Hart. This road used to be busy and happy, I can feel it, but now it is forgotten and is itself forgetting – prey to dementia and decay. London has many such places. I think time is selfish – it doesn't stop for anything and it leaves a lot of sadness.

A bright moon casts long shadows and we stand in one projected from a shop that claims to have been "Mike's Fruit and Veg". A few feet away, a dog sniffs around a discarded kebab and seems to think twice about eating it. The odd car rumbles past with an urgency that suggests they don't want to be noticed.

"OK, that's the pub," Makka says, indicating the White Hart with a nod. "We gotta watch for him to come out and see where he goes. Yeah?" He doesn't expect an answer and I don't give him one. "Come on, we need a better place to watch from." He moves back towards the crossing and disappears down a tiny alleyway that skirts the back of the shops. I follow, stumbling in the dark. Moonlight doesn't make it in here.

Almost exactly opposite the pub, a pathway splits the abandoned shops. It's here, in its shadows, that Makka decides we should wait.

"Fuck, it's cold," he says, rubbing his hands together and looking at a side door into one of the abandoned shops. "I'd break in, but I don't wanna make a noise, yeah? The street is too bloody quiet – it's not right." Makka inches forward and peers down the road.

It is cold. I try the shop side door. It opens without a noise. I tap Makka on the arm.

"Shall we go in?" I say. He doesn't turn.

"For fuck's sake. I ain't gonna break in. Have you gone deaf or something?"

"No."

I go in alone.

The shop is warm and not entirely empty. A counter sits towards the back wall and leaflets advertising mobile phones litter the floor along with other rubbish and a swivel chair with a broken back lying on its side. Some streetlight penetrates the grubby blinds that obscure the large shop window and its adjoining glass front door. The place smells. I find the source – a plastic bag with some rotten meat in it, I think it's chicken, and next to it are several piles of excrement. They are coated in a shimmery film of blue-black buzzing. Blue bottles, dozens of them. I can feel their excitement as they feed. An old and torn sleeping bag lies nearby. I don't think the owner was very well.

Makka appears. He snorts loudly. "Fuck it stinks. Why's it so warm?" He puts his hands on a radiator and smiles. "Well, that's a bit of luck." He pulls the swivel chair to its feet and drags it to the window.

"This is good," he says sitting down and peering through the blinds. "Apart from the stink. You could have told me the fucking door was open. I was freezin' my nuts off out there."

"I did," I say. He turns and looks at me – scans me. I stand still so as not to disturb him.

"Perhaps you did," he says after a moment and turns back to the window.

I stand next to him and we look out, obscured from view by the blinds and the shadows. I watch the dog we'd seen earlier trotting its way down the opposite side of the road, stopping here and there to sniff at things. I wonder what it would be like to have such a good sense of smell. Confusing I expect. It reaches the pub just as the door is flung open and a girl runs out followed by a wiry man in a dark-green combat jacket. The man trips over the dog with both feet, and it sends him sprawling on to the tarmac. He hits the road hard. The dog yelps and then snarls at him. I can hear the man shouting from over here.

"Fuck off, you fucker, fuck off." He gets to his feet and swings a kick at the dog before sprinting after the girl. She's heading our way. The green combat jacket catches up with her just before she makes the passageway and slams her into our window. Her head cracks the glass, which opens up a cut on her forehead, but she makes no sound. Blood runs. Her eyes are level with mine – she looks straight at me and I catch her stare. I see the real her.

Then she's gone. Pulled off the glass by her hair and forced to turn and face her captor.

"Shit, you really are a piece of work ain't you?" He slaps her. "Ain't you?" He slaps her again and in response she kicks him in the bollocks. Makka laughs. The man lets her go and she dodges into the alleyway but doesn't get far. I can hear him shouting at her and then the repeated thud of punches.

"Makka, we need her," I say.

"No way. We're here to follow The Fuck. I'm not getting involved." But I can see the tension in his neck muscles. He is already involved; his body knows. He looks at the shop side door and then at me. "No."

The girl, who has made no noise during the beating, now cries out. Pain and fear.

"We need her," I say again. Makka pulls angrily on his ponytail. "FUCK." He gets up and stamps over to the side door pulling it open. The man has the girl pinned on her front in the muck and stench of the alley. He's pulling at the waistband of her thick tights. A short black skirt with lace on the hem is up over her back. He's facing away from us.

"Your old man didn't say you had to be returned unspoiled and I reckon," he tugged at her tights. "I'll take some advance payment if me fucking nuts work after the kicking you gave 'em." The side of the girl's face is pressed to the ground, but she can see us, and her eyes widen slightly. I think the man must have seen this because he turns quickly and starts to get to his feet. Makka closes the gap with one stride and aims a kick to the man's head, but it only partially connects. The man staggers backwards, trips over the girl but keeps his balance. He leans on a wall and pulls something from his pocket. I hear a click. I can't see what he is holding in the dark. Makka bends down and picks up two discarded half bricks which are lying by the girl's feet. She hasn't moved.

"Listen, Paki. You fuck off, right? This girl is mine." The man pushes himself away from the wall. I can see he's holding a flick knife. It's quite small. I don't think it is going to stop Makka. Makka says nothing, just watches the knife. "I'm telling you to fuck off and mind your own business." The man takes a step forward. "Jesus, you Pakis are thick. I'm –" But he didn't get to finish his sentence as Makka throws a half brick at him. It catches the man on the shoulder, and he bellows in pain, dropping the knife. Clutching his shoulder, he takes a couple of steps back. "FUCK YOU," he says, turns and heads off down the alley. He doesn't get far. Makka pitches the second half brick after him as if he's throwing a cricket ball. It's fast and accurate and hits the man in the small of the back knocking him over. He bellows again. It's his turn to lie face down in the muck and stench.

Makka picks up the knife, walks slowly down to the man and crouches over him and pulls his head back by his hair. He's going to cut his throat.

"Makka, wait." I step past the girl who is now sitting up nursing her beaten face. "Let me see him." I don't think Makka is going to wait, but he seems to get a grip on himself as I approach.

"Quick then. We need to do 'im and then get gone."

"Can you roll him over? I need to see his eyes." Makka hauls the man on to his back. He whimpers.

"I can't feel me fucking legs. I think you broke my back. I might never walk again."

The man seems oblivious to his predicament. He's going to die.

"Look at me," I say. He does and I catch his stare. His soul is blotchy, dirty grey and black. He has squandered the most beautiful and precious thing he has. I am ready to cleanse it, ready to see the Angel's shard that bit cleaner.

"I want his soul," I tell Makka. "I need it." Once again Makka scans me, and once again I let him. Our eyes meet, but I don't catch his stare. There is no need now.

"OK," he says, blowing through his nose. "But can we make it quick? There will be more like him about." He kicks the man.

The noise of the pub door banging open interrupts us. As we watch two men appear on the street. They each light up a cigarette and look around, but the deep shadows hide our presence.

One of them shouts. "Mitch? Where the fuck are you, you skanky cunt? Mitch?" Makka moves quickly and puts a hand over the man's mouth, over Mitch's mouth, but not before he lets out a yelp.

The men peer across the street but can't see us in the shadows. "Is that you, Mitch?" shouts the other man.

"In the shop," Makka says in a hoarse whisper. The girl pulls herself to her feet and limps in as I help Makka drag Mitch inside. Mitch wriggles and tries to scratch Makka's face. Makka punches him hard in the mouth and that seems to take the fight out of him. A tooth comes free. I pick it up. It's not very clean. I don't think Mitch has a toothbrush.

I tell Makka.

"Fuck that. Shut the door and find something to tie this turd down with."

I find a roll of packing tape under the counter and between us we bind Mitch's hands. His feet don't need binding, they don't seem to work anymore. There's a rip in the outer skin of the sleeping bag so I use it to tear off a good-sized bit and Makka stuffs it into Mitch's mouth to shut him up. The girl sits down against the back wall and pulls her legs up under her chin. She's well hidden from the windows there. It's a good spot so I sit down next to her and watch Makka pull the incapacitated Mitch over to us. Makka goes back to the window and looks out through the blinds.

"Bollocks, those guys are coming over. We gotta be quiet, yeah? You, girl. Say nothing, yeah?" She just stares at him. I don't think she can talk.

Makka looks at the door. "Shit, there's no lock."
I can hear the men shouting. They're close by.
"Mitch, you miserable fuck. Come out. You better not be fucking that bitch. Garland said she has to go back in one piece. Mitch, you listening?"
"Fuck," says Makka under his breath. He has the knife in his hand, and he's tensed, ready to fight. Without warning the girl gets up and moves to the door.
"I bet he's in here," says one of the men standing the other side of our door. "The dirty fucker."
The girl flicks a small latch just under the handle.
"Nah, it's locked," says the man rattling the now unmovable handle. Makka and the girl stare at each other for a moment. Makka nods and the girl sits down.
That's good. I'm feeling happy.
The men shuffle about the alley for a moment, shouting for Mitch, but then wander off back to the pub.
"Right, let's get on with it," says Makka, dragging Mitch into the centre of the room. I clear away the fliers and other rubbish and set to work. I'm pretty certain there isn't going to be a repetition of what happened to the Griffin – I don't have any of the volcanic sensations I had then, so I'm going to use the same method for extracting the soul as I did on Mrs Johnson. I'll store the soul for now and will figure out how to feed it to the Angel later.
I pull the chalk from my trouser pocket and draw the circle and the square around Mitch. He rocks himself back and forth and grunts into his gag. His eyes are wide now and I think he's realised he's going to die. I pull a jar, a night-light and some matches from my bag. Lighting the candle carefully, I place the now glowing jar by his head. Mitch watches my every move. He's stopped grunting now.
"I need some bees and dead birds," I say to Makka.
He rolls his eyes. "And where the fuck am I supposed to get them from? Can't you just do it without the ritualistic bollocks?"
"No. I don't think I can."
"Well, shit. You'll just have to try. We've really got to get

out of here. I'm guessing this twat and the girl will be missed soon." Makka sighs. "Shit, we didn't even find out where The Fuck lives."

The girl gets up again, undoes the latch on the door and walks out.

"Hey, where are you going, girl?" says Makka, moving to the door and looking out. He immediately retreats as the girl re-enters clutching a dead crow.

"I saw it in the alley," is all she says as she drops it at my feet. Makka looks at me.

"She speaks. Will it do?"

I think it will. It's bigger than the finches I used on Mrs Johnson and should be stronger, but I still need bees.

"I still need bees."

"What about these little fuckers buzzin' about?" says Makka. He takes a swipe at a few bluebottles, who are more interested in us than feeding.

I look at them, imagine the scene, imagine them working with the crow – grabbing the soul as the body dies and pulling it into the real world. Now I see it, better, more appropriate. Dark collectors for a dark soul.

Chapter Eleven

The night feels even colder as we re-cross Cable Lane, and my pink hoodie is losing the battle to keep the frosted air away from my body. Somehow, the cold gives the dark above our heads a velvety texture. I want to touch it.

I can see Makka is unhappy.

We are passing a shop whose sign announces that it is Bagel Bake and that it is open twenty-four hours a day. Light and the clatter of tins and the smell of baking spills out on to the street, and we're caught in its sensory mix. Held fast for a moment.

"Shit, I'm hungry," says Makka, breaking the silence we've walked in since we caught Mitch's soul. "You hungry?" he says to the girl and me. We both nod. "Cream cheese and salmon? Yeah?" We both nod again. I have no idea what he means by that. I have never eaten a bagel before, but from the smell of it, I know I am going to like it.

We stand outside the bakery and eat. A little of the cream cheese melts from the still-warm bagel and runs down my hand. I carefully lick it off. This really is wonderful. I add bagels to my top five things I like to eat. I place it second, behind custard creams.

We eat in silence.

"Right," says Makka, finishing his last mouthful and screwing up the now-empty bagel bag. He throws it at a bin, but it catches the lip and bounces off, landing in the gutter. He turns to the girl. "Right, you can fuck off now, yeah? Good luck and that. We've gotta go."

"Makka, she has to come with us," I say. "I need her."

"No."

I say nothing.

"NO."

I say nothing.

"What the fuck for?" Makka's anger is out. It leaps from him. A bright-eyed panther. "I can't look after two of you. You're bad enough. Yeah?" He runs his hands through his hair and down his ponytail.

"I don't need looking after," says the girl.

Makka turns on her. "Yeah, right. So you lying face down in the shit an' about to get fucked by some halfwit Nazi is what you call looking after yourself is it? Yeah?"

"Fuck you," says the girl.

I like her.

Makka looks at me. I'm tempted to catch his stare and calm him down, but I don't. I think it better that he comes to his own decision about this. I know it will be the right one.

"And I never even found out where The Fuck lives. And now it's going to be a sod sight harder to find him." Makka rolls his head trying to get the tension out of his steely neck muscles, but fails.

"Who's 'The Fuck'?" asks the girl.

"None of your business. Really, none of your fucking business." He pushes past her and marches off.

"Is it Garland?" the girl shouts after him. "Is it?"

Makka stops.

"If it is," she continues, "then I know where he lives. Take me with you, and I'll tell you."

I can see Makka thinking. His head rocks backwards and forwards making his ponytail dance. He turns and walks back to us and puts his face very close to the girl's. She doesn't shy away. I can see him scanning her like he's scanned me before.

A long moment passes.

"OK," he says, rolling his head again. "OK." This time his neck muscles start to relax. "You're a crazy bitch, you know that, don't you? I'm going to kill The Fuck, Garland. Just so you know." He stands back. "He's my father." Makka spits the last word out. I watch it fall to the pavement and fade to nothing. "You sure you wanna be part of this, yeah?"

The girl nods. "Will you kill *my* father for me?" she asks quietly, her eyes never leaving Makka's face.

A bond is made.

Now we are ready.

I pick up the bagel bag from the gutter and drop it in the bin.

***

"You can sleep here or find yourself another room," says Makka. We have returned from our night trip, but the cold darkness is still hanging in the morning air. "Won't bother us either way."

"Here," says the girl. She looks at the two mattresses.

"Sure, I'll get you a mattress, yeah?" he says. "But don't expect much, They're pretty shit."

I sit on my bed while Makka goes and finds a mattress. The girl comes and sits next to me.

"You saw me through the window," she says. "You know – earlier. You have strange eyes, beautiful and, well, they seem very old, and," – she pauses and brushes some dirt from her tights – "what did you see when you looked into my eyes?"

"Pain," I say.

The girl nods. She pulls up her knees and lays her forehead gently on them. Her short chestnut-brown hair hangs down over her cheeks. I think she might be crying. I am not sure what to do, so I say nothing.

Makka returns, dragging a mattress. It looks a lot better than the ones we have. The girl sits up and carefully rubs her tears away.

"What's your name, girl?" he says as he throws the mattress on to the floor and kicks it into position.

"Vee," says the girl.

"Do you want some tea?" I say.

"I'd prefer a rollie."

***

"So, what do you think?" asked the Inspector as she pushed a photograph across the table to Eve. Eve picked it up. The fluorescent light that illuminated the afternoon dusk of the Inspector's office flooded the print, exposing the scene in all its gruesome – and if Eve was honest with herself, fascinating – glory. The photograph had been taken through a large shop-window whose vertical blinds had been pulled back on either side. Perfect framing. A body lay within a chalk circle that contained a square that touched the circle at its corners. Blood had pooled about the corpse, and what looked like hundreds of large flies were feasting on the spillage. Many more were clustered around the man's throat and mouth. A headless bird sat like the devil's own halo above the figure, and scrawled at its feet was the word *purgatio*.

"So, what do you think? said the Inspector again, this time tapping her fingers on the table.

Eve looked up. "I think," she said slowly, "that you have a serious problem. When did this happen?"

"Two days ago."

"This is a ritualistic, religiously motivated killing." Eve stared at the photograph again. "It's an evolution from the earlier murders. Johnson was killed using the ritual. The boy claims it was to do with his mother's soul being restored. Griffin was killed without the ritual but with *purgatio* written at his feet. I think the Griffin killing wasn't planned. Certainly not by the boy, but something happened there, something that triggered what he perceived to be a 'cleansing'. This one." She tapped the photograph. "This one is different – deliberate. He's found what he's looking for.

"His *modus operandi*?" asked the Inspector.

"Yes, I would say so. I take it the victim wasn't well regarded?"

"Correct. Bit of a scrotum actually." She leaned forward and read from a sheet of paper on her desk, "Belonged to a group called the New England Movement. A grandiose title for an obscure far-right bunch interested in the politics of the bigot, misogynist and racist. Quite frankly, you couldn't get a more stereotypical jack-booted Nazi-type if you tried." The Inspector straightened up. "They aren't going to like it. Your boy is in a barrel of shit over this. If we don't find him before they do, we probably won't find him at all."

"My boy?" asked Eve.

"Your boy," confirmed the Inspector. "I made a request to have you join the team. A child that kills? Well, that's gold-plated crap to the press. I'm afraid I need a professional on the team to help figure this out. Thought you'd be a pig in muck about it. Just your thing, no?"

"Not keen on the metaphor," said Eve. "But yes, it is my thing." She was feeling pretty much like a pig in muck, but she kept that to herself. "So we've two killers here. I would guess that –"

"Three killers," said the Inspector. She slid another photograph across the table to Eve.

"Three?" Eve looked at the new still. It was low quality, grainy and in black-and-white. She peered at it. "A girl. Looks about what, fifteen?"

"It would seem so. We grabbed the photo off the railway CCTV. We've no idea who she is, but she was picked up by our crusaders somewhere around the scene of the killing. We've an earlier picture of the boys crossing the railway bridge and she's not with them. So, it looks like your boy has a couple of helpers now."

Eve stared at the picture. "Helpers," she said quietly. Yes, helpers. Now that triggered a memory. The chalk drawings, helpers, *purgatio*, but what? Something in the shadows of her mind moved, stepped forward into the half-light, but she couldn't quite see it.

"Yes, helpers," said the Inspector. "If it wasn't already truly screwed up, it is now."

There was a knock on the door and a uniformed officer entered.

"You'd better have some good news for me, sergeant. I'm not feeling overly charitable at the moment." She glared at the man.

"Well then, Ma'am," said the sergeant who, to Eve's mind, didn't seem at all worried by the implied threat. "It's my good luck that it's good news."

***

The stairs that lead from ground level are wooden and wide. Banisters ascend in rounded grandeur disappearing into the darkness that haunts the first floor. I am sitting on the fifth step watching souls dance over the Victorian tiles that make up what I take to be the entrance hall. I catch them in the beam of my torch, a spotlight on their performance. Despite the dirt and broken pieces of masonry, there is an elegance to this stage. I observe carefully, opening my mind to the scene, and imagine. And there it is. The past pulls itself forward to show me what once was. Light streams in from the stained-glass porthole window that sits above the oak doors. The black and white tiles are clean and whole, and dance with the rainbows of reflected colour.

A nurse in a starched blue-and-white uniform passes me on the stairs, and to my left I can hear the clatter of wheels and urgent voices. A trolley appears. It is a thin-wheeled bed being pushed by a porter. The hard heels of his shoes strike harsh notes on the tiles. Somehow, they feel clean. Harsh but clean – a reflection of the hospital. Two nurses accompany him as he steers left, into an alcove. A young girl lies on the bed, a blanket tucks her in tightly – safe but secure. She looks straight at me; deep green eyes catch my stare. They want me to watch.

I do.

At the end of the alcove there is a set of double doors. The procession heads through them, offering me a glimpse of a dimly lit, stark-tiled corridor. As the doors swing shut the scene fades, pulled back to the past leaving me in the present.

She had beautiful eyes.

I watch the poorly lit souls dance for a moment longer and then pull myself up. I descend the last few steps and carefully pick my way across the broken floor, souls pushed away by my gentle bow wave. I follow the girl's route and enter the alcove, but there are no double doors at its end. Just a grimy beige wall with a torn poster on it that says 'Cover your cough'. As I watch, a soul appears at the base of the wall and moves off into the room. Another appears and goes the other way. I put my hand on the wall. It feels wrong, out of place, and I think the building resents it. It is also very damp. Using a fingernail, I scrape the surface. It peels off like a gritty paste, soft and wet and barely able to stick to itself. I shine the torch around the alcove and its hard-white light picks out a broken wooden chair leg that lies discarded and lost in amongst the dirt. I pick it up, wondering where the rest of the chair is. It has a spiky torn end that I use to stab at the wall. The plaster comes away, falling to the floor in wet slaps. It doesn't take long to open a me-sized hole of cold darkness. I shine the torch in and the light bounces about the dirty white tiles of a steeply dropping corridor that appears to turn into a tunnel. The tunnel disappears in a slow right-hand bend. I can feel the air move, so I do not think it is a dead end.

A sharp scraping noise pricks the silence, and I hear voices. I turn off the torch. The sweet shop door scrapes shut.

"Fuck, it's dark in here," says a voice.

"And it stinks of shit," says another.

"Shut the fuck up," says a third.

Light drifts through the entrance hole.

"Use your phones." A fourth voice grunts, and now there are a number of lights flicking about. I position myself by the entrance to the alcove, tight up against the wall so I can see, but cannot be seen.

"This way," says voice three. I guess he is in charge. A leg appears through the portal followed by its owner. He takes two careful steps into the hallway, shining his phone light about him.

"Come on," he whispers loudly. Three other men follow, their lights crisscrossing. Now I can see the aliens, and I recognise two of them from the White Hart. I think they have come for Mitch's soul. I watch as they move up the stairs. They are not very quiet.

Makka and Vee will be down in a moment.

I stand in the dark and wait.

But not for long.

They appear, descending the stairs quickly and quietly and I think I give them a fright when I turn my torch on.

"Shitting hell! Turn the fucker off will you, yeah?" says

Makka.

I turn off the torch. Makka has his messenger bag slung over his shoulder and Vee is carrying mine.

"Let's get the fuck outta here." Makka heads for the portal to the sweet shop, but as he reaches it, the shop door scrapes open again. Makka retreats. "Fuck," he mouths, and motions towards the alcove.

We scuttle into its thick darkness.

A number of policemen step through the portal carrying torches. They are followed by a woman. It is Ma'am from the police station.

"Up," she says. "Quick and quiet."

I wonder if they know the White Hart men are here.

***

Eve sat in the back of the police car. The Inspector was insistent that she stayed put until they had secured the boy, but Eve had other ideas. She watched the Inspector and half a dozen policemen disappear through the door of the derelict shop and then left the car and followed suit.

The interior of the shop was gloomy, damp and smelt of decay, but the atmosphere seemed somehow friendly. She saw a ragged hole in the back wall, so she headed for it and carefully stepped through into the darkness.

Above her she heard muffled shouts and thumps and was about to ascend the stairs when a light caught her attention.

It was the boy.

He stood in the entrance of an alcove, a torch pointing up illuminating his face. He smiled and then moved out of sight.

"Wait." She stumbled after him almost tripping on the uneven floor. "Please, wait." She entered the alcove and found the boy standing a short way from her with his back to a large hole in the wall behind him.

"Hello, Dr Rhodes," he said.

Eve composed herself. "Hello." She looked about the darkness. "Are you on your own?"

"No."

"OK." She took a deep breath. "We need to talk. Really talk."

"Yes, I agree, but I cannot at the moment. I have to leave, but first I want to give you something." He stepped forward so the light shone up between their faces. Eve looked into his eyes and felt as if she had been caught, as if gentle hands encircled her mind. And from the half-shadows of her memory stepped the thought she could not see earlier.

"Janenssen," she said. "The case of Charles Janenssen." She blinked and felt the gentle hold gone.

The boy smiled again.

The light went out.

Eve felt herself grabbed from behind and pushed face first up against a side wall. Hands were around her throat.

"Who the fuck are you?" asks a coarse male voice. "Police bitch?" Eve's forehead was bounced hard against the wall. The attacker pulled her around to face him.

"No," she choked.

"Liar." The hands tightened around her throat. "Who were you fuckin" talking to?" The man now bounced the back of her head against the wall. "Who?"

Eve scrabbled at the throttling hands trying to relieve the pressure. Her vision faded and she felt herself about to pass out.

"Who?" asked the man again.

"Me," said a voice, punching its way out of the darkness. A light came on. There was sound of tearing flesh and then Eve felt a warm liquid spray across her face. The strangling hands left her throat. She gasped and slumped against the wall. A torch beam lit up her attacker who lay on the floor, a wooden chair leg stuck fast in the side of his throat.

The torch beam closed in on the man. She watched in detached horror as a boot pinned his head to the floor and a hand reached down and pulled the chair leg out in one clean movement. Blood pumped out in gushes, splashing on to the floor, mixing with the dirt and decay. The man, with his hands to his throat, shook in noiseless spasms of shock.

The light shifted its focus on to Eve.

"You OK?"

Eve couldn't see who it was but guessed it must be Makka. She nodded, unable to speak.

"Just as well the boy likes you, yeah?" And with that, the light disappeared.

Eve's legs gave way and she sank to the ground. She sat in the dark and sudden stillness with only the slowing gurgles of the dying man for company. She could smell the blood, taste it in the air.

Likes? She let that word bounce around her disassociated mind. Had he been in her head? It felt like it, but her overriding feeling was not that he liked her, but that he needed her.

A voice drifted out of the wall.

"Find my mother's soul, Dr Rhodes. Find her for me."

Chapter Twelve

The tunnel is narrow and quite low. I think it is just big enough to wheel the beautiful-eyed girl's bed through. Makka is carrying the torch, and in its jumpy beam I can see the Victorian tiles extend up the walls and over our heads in an arch, forming the roof of the tunnel. Here and there the ceiling bulges downwards causing the tiles to pull apart. They look like ripe cocoons of some giant insect about to rent themselves open and drop their hungry contents on us. I jump up and touch one. It is cold and lifeless. Shame.

After a minute or two, the torchlight picks out a small alcove to our right. It must be a passing bay so trolleys coming each way can pass one another. The light moves on, but I stay. I am curious. There are a lot of souls here in the tunnel, and many of them are appearing and disappearing through the wall of the bay. I move carefully through the dark to the wall and touch it. It's stone. And I can feel what's beyond.

The light reappears along with Makka. "What the fuck are you doing?"

I rub the stone. "We need to get in here," I say.

"What?" He points the torch at the wall. "It's a fucking wall. What? You want me to kick it down?"

"Yes, please." I can feel rather than see Makka shaking his head. I don't think he believes me.

"Sure, whatever. But right fucking now we gotta split. Come on." He sets off down the tunnel again checking that I'm with him. I am sure we will be back.

Vee is waiting for us a little further on. The tunnel starts to rise and a moment later we come up against a rough rendered wall. Makka taps it with his foot.

"Soft," he says. "Here, hold this." He gives the torch to Vee and takes a step back. A noise interrupts him. He holds a hand up and we listen. Voices ride the still air – muffled but audible.

"Shit," says Makka and lays into the wall with his feet and hands. The wall capitulates with little resistance and we are soon through into the second hospital building.

To our left is a short corridor that leads to the main hall. It is much like the building we left. We follow another corridor taking us to the back of the building. At its end is a fire door. Makka pushes against it. It moves, but then sticks.

"Come on, push," he says to Vee and me. We do as we are told and lend our weight to the battle. The door moves some more, and the gap is now big enough to squeeze through. Makka switches off the torch and we disappear into the night.

***

A police car rockets by, a flurry of light and sound and purpose. I watch it manoeuvring its way through the evening traffic, the violence of its blue light battering everything it passes.

I don't think it is searching for us, but Makka isn't so certain. I can hear another siren crowing somewhere further down Camden High Street. We are standing in the entrance to a Chinese tea shop, and I can just make out the faint smell of the teas. I go in and let the aroma of spice and smoke and sweetness and other scents I cannot distinguish tangle in my hair and clothes. I can almost see the snaking tendrils of tea wrapping themselves around me, gently pulling me forward. Makka breezes past me and the eddy currents of his movement blow the tendrils apart.

"Good idea, yeah? Get off the street for a bit and have a think." He heads for a table near the back and sits down. A young waitress looks at him, anxious, but relaxes a little as Vee and I follow suit.

There is a menu of all the different teas with descriptions of their taste and their province of origin and it is arranged in alphabetical order by name of tea. I would have arranged it by province, I think, but I would have to see what that looks like on paper first.

"Do you think they should have arranged the teas by province?"

Vee says nothing.

"Don't give a shit," says Makka. "Just pick something."

I pick the first one on the list – *Anji bai cha*. Makka and Vee do the same, which is good because the description says it helps with stress.

We sit and wait for our tea in silence. Makka is thinking. He's looking directly at me, but I don't think he is really looking. I think I'm just the cue for his thinking. I can see the steel muscles of his neck flex as ideas come and go. Vee watches Makka. I think she can see he is struggling to come up with our next move, but I am not worried. Between them, they will think of something.

The tea arrives. Makka insists on some milk, but the beautiful white tea needs no addition. I take the chance to bathe my face in its rich steam.

"I know a place we can go," says Vee as she blows on her tea. "It's not far."

"Yeah?" says Makka, looking across to her. "Safe is it?"

Vee simply nods, but Makka wants more.

"You sure, girl? Don't fuck with me 'cause I'm not in the mood."

"It's fucking safe, right? It's safe." She snaps the answer back, and it says more than she means. I don't have to look into her mind to see something is wrong. It's not missed by Makka either. "Trust me, we'll be safe," she adds, and looks out across the cafe avoiding our eyes.

Makka doesn't respond, just slurps his milky tea and makes a face. "Shit. This tastes like pissy twigs." He pushes it away and sits back. "OK, I haven't a better fucking idea at the moment, so we might as well check out this place, yeah? Where is it?"

"Just up the road."

"Right, let's go." Makka gets up. I don't move. I am going to finish my tea first.

***

Vee's safe place is a flat above a row of shops on Camden High Street only a few hundred metres away from the Chinese tea shop. We climb a metal fire escape at the back of the property out of sight of the well-lit street. Vee says this is how her father and friends get into the flat when they don't want to be seen. The stairs are black and stippled and ring if you kick them. Vee reaches behind the last metal rung and retrieves a key. We step through the doorway and into the darkness of a small kitchen. Vee switches a light on.

Makka nods, walking out of the kitchen and into a hall. "How many rooms does it have?" Vee doesn't answer but stays in the kitchen. She seems reluctant to go any further. She turns and looks into my eyes.

An invitation.

I pause for a moment and then accept. Her mind is full of storm, of purples and dull reds and flashes of white like lightning bolts. It is pain rolling over and over on itself. It is more intense than the first time I looked. I withdraw.

"Here?" I say. Vee nods.

"Yes, here. This is where the pain comes from."

"What you mean?" says Makka, who has returned from exploring. Vee goes into the hallway and nods at one of the bedrooms – its door is slightly ajar.

"There," she says. "That's where they did it. In there." She pauses. "That's where they hurt us. Me and others."

I look at the room. Pain radiates out from the open door and prickles my skin. Makka is silent for a moment, but I can tell he is thinking.

"OK, we should go. We can find somewhere else, yeah? We don't have to stay here."

"No," says Vee, turning to face us. "We need to stay. It's safe. No one comes here now." Her face is expressionless, but her eyes are glazed with tears, although none fall. "Just promise me you won't go in there and I'll be all right."

I can see Makka is not convinced, but he nods. He turns and goes over to the bedroom door, shuts it and then in one violent movement snaps the door handle clean off.

"No one goes in there. And when we find your dad, I'm goin' to fucking kill him."

Vee crosses her arms. "Good," she says.

***

I am lying on the cold metal floor of the fire-escape landing. My left cheek is pressed against its stippled surface and I am hoping that the small raised domes will make a beautifully regular pattern in my flesh – a temporary tattoo. From my vantage point, I can see out across the back yard of the flats. A plane tree stands more or less in the middle of the garden, tall and aloof, its branches held high out of the dirt and the grubby air that drifts around its base. It is pretending not to be here.

The ground is a patchwork of tangled weeds, dirt patches and rubbish. Carrier bags, like flocks of ground-dwelling birds, cluster in social groups occasionally raising a handled wing in acknowledgement as the light mid-morning breeze ebbs and flows. The sun is still as weak as it was at the detention centre, like the weepy eye of an old man, but it drops small packets of light on to the scene. I can see a cat taking advantage of the transient warmth. The cat is a beautiful Bengal. I know this because one used to come into the gardens at Shelly Fields. It had no fear and would roll around in the dirt by the swings on dry days, only leaving when it felt like it, despite the hissing and protestations of our carer who said she had an allergy to cats. I think the Bengal's size and arrogance frightened her. This Bengal's lazy demeanour belies its attentive eyes. A large blackbird hops about amongst the plastic birds, flipping over leaves and crisp packets in search of food.

It is about to die.

It hops too close to the statuesque predator. In a beautiful arching move, the Bengal strikes. It holds the bird in its mouth, its sharp teeth clamping around the feathery neck. The bird flaps its wings, beating the air in terror, desperate to escape. The air ignores its pleas. After a moment, the wings stall as the engine that drives them turns over a few last times and then stops. I can hear its silence.

The Bengal senses the bird is dead and lets it fall from its mouth, all interest gone.

I would like the bird.

The Bengal sits by the dead bird for a while and then looks up at me as if it knows I was there all along. Our stares connect and I ask it for its kill. The Bengal looks away, deciding, and then picks up the bird, and in a series of easy bounds ascends the fire escape. I sit up and take the gift and in return spend ten minutes stroking the soft stripy fur of the small tiger. Without warning it leaves. Better things to do, I expect.

Makka and Vee are sitting in the kitchen when I come in.

"What's up with your face, yeah?"

"Stipples," I say.

"Shingles?" says Vee.

"Stipples," I repeat. I don't think I need to say any more. It is obvious. They both look blankly at me. I hold up the dead bird. "Have we got an airtight bag I can keep this in, please?"

Vee gets up and pulls out a roll of cling film from a drawer. "Will this do?"

We wrap the bird up in the clinging plastic and put it in the fridge.

"Where'd you get the thing from anyway?" says Makka.

"A Bengal cat. He didn't have any use for it, but we might want it later."

"Yeah," says Makka, nodding. "A certainty."

I wonder about getting hold of flies and Vee tells me I can get them from some pet shops. Apparently geckos eat flies, and people keep geckos as pets in tanks.

I have never seen a gecko.

Chapter Thirteen

Eve hadn't slept well that night. It wasn't the image of the dying man that had kept her awake, and she felt some guilt at this, but the thought of Charles Janenssen. She was up early and had made herself some tea before taking it over to the bay window of her lounge to look out over the public gardens. She let the steam from the tea wash over her face, an experience she had always enjoyed as a child. From her top-floor flat she watched as the dawn pushed its way forward, fracturing the night sky, opening up the darkness with slivers of light. She could just make out the garden's tennis courts and flower beds beyond, although her reflection obscured the view. She closed her eyes and took a deep breath through her nose exhaling through her mouth, relaxing, letting her thoughts go wherever they wanted. They wandered about carelessly for a while and then settled on a word – *schizophrenia.* And she now remembered – well, at least she remembered where she'd heard Janenssen's name before. It had been in a first-year lecture at university on the history of schizophrenia, but the detail eluded her. Did she still have her notes? No, of course not. That was what the internet was for. She took a sip of tea and retrieved her laptop.

After thirty minutes of searching she had found only two references to Charles Janenssen and schizophrenia. One was an article in a Victorian journal called *Natural Philosophy and Psychic Endeavour* on a 'remarkable case of dementia praecox', while the other was a reference to a book: *Dualistic Religions: Good or Bad?* by Steven Doyle, a Cambridge University academic.

The Victorian journal was not online, but a copy was lodged in London University's Senate House library, which she had access to. She decided to head over there as soon as it opened. She searched for Doyle's book as well, but no one on the internet seemed to know about it, let alone stock it. That wasn't unusual for an academic work. She suspected only about ten had ever been printed and half of those probably sat on the shelf of the author. A bit cynical perhaps, but she didn't care.

A little buzz of excitement flitted about her mind. She somehow felt more alive than usual this morning, despite yesterday's violent encounter. Or perhaps because of it. She gently rubbed her throat – yes, because of it.

***

Eve pulled her scarf a little tighter around her neck as she left her flat and headed for Maida Vale tube station. It was a cold morning, but frost hadn't bothered laying down its fine, chilling veneer. She couldn't shake off the feeling that this was all somehow supposed to happen, or that at least the boy was directing events. She thought about yesterday's encounter; the look he gave her and the way her mind felt just before she remembered Janenssen's name, as if . . . No, this was ridiculous. People can't manipulate minds like that. She should know. Of course, he could be getting into her mind in the psychological sense, but she felt she'd have spotted that, that she would be able to judge whether his projected innocence was truthful, or that his assertion that he didn't lie wasn't itself a lie, and that his rationalisation for his behaviour was not simply a manipulative trick. She blew out her cheeks and her breath misted for an instant before vanishing. Wouldn't she?

When she reached the tube station she took the Bakerloo line to Regent's Park and then walked the mile or so to the Senate House library. It would be good to have a slow day, a little time to recover after her near strangulation. The Inspector hadn't been entirely sympathetic at her experience and had even gone as far as to grumble that she'd let the Boy get away. Eve's defence that Makka had stabbed a man to death in front of her and was clearly psychotically violent hadn't cut any ice.

Eve stopped in front of Senate House for a moment to admire its construction. She was a fan of the art deco style. Its cubist features, modern for the time, felt to her as if it belonged to an altered reality, one that diverged in the 1930s, one that had retained its identity in the face of time and change, one that she would like to have lived in.

She entered through the wood and brass revolving door to see what secrets it could spill.

***

It was Eve's turn to push a photograph across the Inspector's table. The Inspector picked it up.

"When was this taken?" she asked.

"1889. That's a vaulted room down in the underground. Amazing, isn't it?"

"It looks just like the shop-front killing. Unbelievable. Where did you find this?"

"In a volume of *Natural Philosophy and Psychic Endeavour*. A short-lived Victorian academic journal. That's actually a police photograph – pretty rare for the time. It was included as part of a paper written by a self-styled gentleman philosopher called Alfred Stern on the case of Charles Janenssen. Janenssen was convicted of a number of ritualistic murders in the 1880s and duly hanged for his crimes. Those he killed belonged to a rather nasty eugenics cult. It reads all a bit Sherlock Holmes-ish. Stern claims that Janenssen said he could see the lost souls of the dead as well as those of the living, just like our boy."

"Right," said the Inspector scratching her forehead. "Right." She looked up and raised her eyebrows. Eve continued.

"And, that the ritual element to the killings was there to enable Janenssen to collect the eugenicists' corrupt souls."

"What the hell did he want them for?"

"No idea. Either Janenssen never said, or Stern didn't see fit to write about it."

"Bloody hell. So we're buggered for a motive then, even an insane one," said the Inspector as she looked back at the photograph.

"Not necessarily," said Eve. "Stern did say that Janenssen was carrying out a task set him through his connection with an ancient Persian religion called Banuism. Stern suggested that this was part of Janenssen's *dementia praecox* – premature dementia."

"Am I supposed to know what you're talking about?"

"Schizophrenia to you and me, and that Banuism was just part of the complex, actually extremely complex, delusional world Janenssen inhabited. In other words, Banuism was a fictional religion."

"Aren't they all? So?"

"So, Janenssen didn't dream up Banuism, someone else did around 200 AD. There's not much on the internet about it, but there is a reference to it in a book written by a Cambridge academic called Stephen Doyle, who, and it's almost certainly not coincidental, also references Janenssen."

"Great. What did the lovely Doyle have to say about, erm, what did you call it?"

"Banuism. No idea. I can't find a copy of the book. But he's still alive and teaching in Cambridge, according to his college's website, so I could give him a shout and see what he has to say."

"Right. Do it."

Eve nodded.

"This begs the question," continued the Inspector as she pushed the photo back towards Eve, "how the hell does the boy knows about all this stuff? It's clearly not something you can lay your hands on easily. It's not only extremely disturbing – and frankly bonkers – it's also complicated, and the kid is only thirteen! How in God's name does he understand it all?" She waved an arm around to emphasise her disbelief.

Eve smiled. She liked the word oxymoron and the irony of her thinking this hadn't escaped her either; it seemed to sum up the basics of the Boy's understanding of his calling – kill to do good.

"It is pretty incredible, and until we can get our hands on him, we won't know," said Eve. "But it's fair to assume he is following in the footsteps of Janenssen."

"Well, it needs to stop now," said the Inspector. "Quite frankly, this is all too damn freaky." She looked up. "Do you get the feeling we're in some kind of B-movie?"

Eve shrugged. "Can't say for sure that we're not." She stood up and walked to the window. It was always dark outside when she visited the Inspector. Some ironic reflection on the case?

"So where does his mother's soul come into all this?" asked the Inspector.

Eve didn't turn to answer. She was caught by her reflection in the window. She could see the struggle in her eyes before she registered it in her mind. Damn it. She should tell the Inspector about the Boy's request. But . . .

"I don't think it's particularly relevant," she heard herself saying. "Probably an early attempt to understand the world that he was creating in his mind. I suspect that's forgotten now that he's found his real purpose." Her reflection's jaw was tight. She tried to relax it.

"Hmm, well, it seemed important to him at the time, but OK, if you think it's out of play now then we'll put that aside for the moment. What next then?"

Eve turned back to the room. "I'd say he's going after the Nazi gang just as Janenssen went after the eugenicists. It's a characteristic of the psychotic. Once they perceive you as part of their reality, whatever you say or do they'll make you fit into their world view. And in the boy's case you'd be . . ."

" . . . buggered, right?" said the Inspector as she got her feet and went to the door. She opened it. "Sergeant, where are our Nazi fuckwit boys? Do we still have them in custody?"

"Nope. Released this morning, Ma'am."

"What! Who the hell gave that order?"

"Came from the top."

"The Chief Constable?"

"Yes, Ma'am, came down here himself this morning with some kind of political. I think he said he was a special adviser to the Minister of Justice, or something like that. Apparently, he'd hired the buggers to find his daughter and was more than a little agitated about the situation. Suggested we needed to get our priorities right."

The inspector was silent for a moment. "Daughter? What's the political's name?"

"Duncan Parks. Said his daughter ran away a few weeks ago and if we hadn't interfered, he'd have her home now. Said her name's Victoria."

"And you didn't think to tell me this when I came in this afternoon? Buggering hell. Why am I always the last to know?"

"Sorry, Ma'am."

"I don't believe that for a moment," said the Inspector as she shut the door with only a hint of a slam.

"So," said Eve, "we now know who the girl is."

"Yes, I guess so, and that just messes it up some more. Pouring politics on to this cluster fuck of a religious fire is not what we want. We'll all get burnt if we're not careful. Seriously, Eve. We have to catch these children – and I can't believe I'm saying children – and put an end to it. If all of what you've said is right, and I can't see why it isn't, we're going to see a murder fest, and the Nazi fuckwits are going to regret their career choice." She paused and then added, "As might we."

Chapter Fourteen

King's Cross station was surprisingly busy, given it was post rush-hour, so Eve had to carefully pick her route through the host of commuters who had congregated under the departure board. No one was really paying attention to each other as they either craned their necks trying to see which platform their respective trains would leave from, or were busy looking at their phones.

She made her way down to platform 9, past the long queue of tourists waiting patiently to have their picture taken under the Platform 9 3/4 sign. The Cambridge train was pretty much full, but Eve found an empty pair of seats, a tabloid paper lying on one of them. She took her coat off and stored it in the overhead luggage rack and then eyed up the two seats. She preferred to sit by the window so she could look out and lose herself in her thoughts, but she also hated the feeling of being trapped if someone then sat next to her. She opted for the window seat and hoped to hell no one did.

She hadn't meant to pick up the paper but found herself reading it anyway. The headline story was a detailed account of some irrelevant misdemeanour of a celebrity. She gave up reading it after the first few sentences and was about to abandon the paper when she noticed the small side story: *Ritual Killer Makes Sacrifice*. It mentioned the shop-front killing and described the scene pretty well. It then let itself down by suggesting it was a voodoo killing by immigrant East Africans before it confused things by switching its attack to Satanism, which it blamed on Eastern Europeans and then, rather half-heartedly, on Swedish death metal groups. If only they knew, she thought. Although perhaps the facts would make little difference in this post-truth environment. She dropped the paper back on the seat.

So, now the media were on to it. Looks like the children's luck had run out as had hers, she noted with resignation, as a large man in a tight-fitting pink jumper picked up the paper and then sat down on the seat it had vacated and began consuming the post-truths.

The train eased its way out of the station and into the bright, clear late morning of north London. Eve watched as the graffiti-covered railway arches drifted past before being replaced by houses and flats and shopping centres and eventually countryside. She caught her reflection in the window. She always looked for her reflection. Not because she was vain, particularly, but because seeing her other self was comforting. The lost mother thing again and, if she were honest, the alienation of her father who seemed to silently blame her for his wife's mental decline. She still spoke to him occasionally, but even now it was distant, and conversation was never more than skin deep. She knew she had emotional issues and had long ago buried them deep in her consciousness. Wrong? Yes, but she seemed to be able to deal with them better than most.

Her dark reflection reflected – well, it was better than sucking her thumb.

The tight pink jumper man farted. *This* was why she hated being trapped in the window seat. Perhaps the post-truths were causing him gastric problems.

***

Eve found the cafe Professor Doyle had suggested for their meeting. It sat on a narrow backstreet, its black façade and gold lettering proudly announced it as Clowns an established Italian café-cum-restaurant. Eve had hoped to meet the professor in his college rooms. She would have liked to look around the grounds and medieval buildings, but he had quashed that idea. "Bloody college is festooned with academics. No place for a serious conversation." She was a little disappointed, but rather liked his observation.

Clowns was packed, warm and friendly. The clientele appeared to be a mixture of students and locals, both English and Italian. Eve stood at the counter and waited to be served. A well-dressed, confident woman was chatting in Italian to a man holding a small child as she busied herself with making coffee and slicing cake. The rapid fire of their conversation was astonishing and quite mesmeric, so much so that Eve almost missed the woman turning to her to say, "*Ciao*, my darling. What would you like?" The woman spoke English with an Italian accent, a soft lisp and sparkling eyes.

"Oh," said Eve. "Yes. A cappuccino please."

"*Certo*," said the woman. "You looking for the professor, *si*?"

"Stephen Doyle? Yes." Eve must have looked a little surprised at this assumption because the woman laughed.

"He said he would be meeting a lovely lady at about now. I told him he was *folle*, mad, but here you are. *Si*, *si*, here you are." She turned and started to make coffee. "The Professor might as well live here you know. He's always here drinking coffee and telling me I should marry him. I say to him – *non*, you naughty man, you are already married, but most days he still asks me. He also asks my sister. *Si*, a naughty man, but *dolce*." The milk frother hissed into life and killed off the one-sided conversation.

"Here you are, my darling, *un cappuccino*," said the woman a moment later. "You want chocolate on that, *si*?"

"No thanks," said Eve pulling her purse out of her bag.

"*Non*. Already paid for. The professor is upstairs,"

"Really?"

"*Si*, *si*, upstairs."

"Right, thanks." Eve picked up the coffee. "What does he look like?"

The woman thought for a moment and then settled on, "He's wearing a red woolly hat and he dresses a little like a *vagabondo*."

Eve raised her eyebrows and smiled and then headed up the stairs.

Professor Doyle was sitting at a corner table adjacent to a

large sash window, which overlooked the street below. He was staring through the glass actively watching the ebb and flow of the street life, his red hat bobbed about in the process. He wore glasses, was clean shaven and dressed rather haphazardly, not in an eccentric way, more in a couldn't care less what he put on kind of way. Eve navigated over to him.

"Professor Doyle?" she asked. He looked up, smiled and stood.

"Stephen, please," he said, indicating a chair opposite him. "Only the students, pompous academics, and Maria and her sister call me professor." He sat down. "The Italians love a title."

"Thanks," said Eve. She put her coffee on the table and took her coat off. "And thanks for the coffee," she added as she sat down.

"Pleasure." He rubbed his hands together. "Banuism then," he said cutting out all the usual small talk a first meeting might be expected to generate. "Not many people show an interest in ancient religions, and just about nobody is interested in Banuism. The odd academic here and there, but no normal functioning person." He pulled off his hat revealing a receding crew cut and scratched the top of his head. "Scratchy hat. You don't mind me calling you normal, do you?"

"No. I'll take that as a compliment. Psychiatrists are rarely considered normal."

"Good, good. Might I hazard a guess that your interest in the religion is in some rather direct way connected to the ritual murder reported in various ways in the press today?"

Eve took a sip of her coffee and nodded. "Yes."

"Excellent. Tell me all." He sat back, crossed his arms and stared at her.

She told him all, with the caveat that the Inspector would almost certainly castrate him if any of this found its way into the press.

"OK, let's start by filling in what few gaps I can in your knowledge of Banuism," said the professor. "But I'm afraid it really is only a few gaps."

"Fine, given that I only know its name and that collecting

corrupt souls seems a key ingredient, I'm sure whatever you add will be helpful."

"Well, the first thing to point out is that it's not, in itself, a religion, more an esoteric movement of an early Persian religion called Manichaeism. Manichaeism takes a dualistic cosmology approach to its theology, centring as it does on the balance between good –essentially the light, spiritual world, and evil – the dark, materialistic world." The professor scratched his chin and looked out of the window. "Hmm, it's interesting to consider that even then, well before this age of materialism," he waved a hand about expansively," Manichaeists considered materialism to be a dark and corruptive force." He looked back at Eve. "A bit prophetic if you ask me."

"Not a fan of materialism then?" asked Eve.

"Not really." He sighed. "But my anti-materialism stance doesn't stretch to coffee or almost any Italian food."

Eve said nothing, hoping the professor would get back on track. She didn't really want a lecture on anti-materialism. She liked her creature comforts and thought that an annoyingly well-argued position on the subject would just make her feel bad.

"Anyway," said the professor, "Manichaeism was so called after the man who established it in early 200 AD. A chap called Mani. He had a couple of revelations and from that, and his upbringing in a Jewish Christian Gnostic sect, he developed his anti-materialistic theology. This is all well-documented. But what isn't well-documented is the emergence of the Banuistic movement from within Manichaeism."

Eve took another sip of her coffee. "Don't tell me – Banuism was founded by a man called Banu."

"Close," said Stephen, smiling. "Artabanu actually, which roughly translated means righteous or truthful light. We know this because of a page of text from a Manichaean scripture that gives us the briefest of overviews of the occluded movement of which Artabanu was the divine head. Artabanu claims to have had a revelation, which he said completes the triad of holy visions of Manichaeism. His revelation was that the King of Honour, an angel and the guardian of the seventh level of heaven, the realm of light, shielded mankind from a wave of evil sent to bind them to the realm of darkness. The angel absorbed the evil, but its soul shattered in the process, with a multitude of soul shards falling to earth."

A student had come and sat down on the table next to them while the professor was talking and was busy trying to listen without appearing to do so.

"Private conversation, Cramer," said the professor addressing the young man. "Now push off." He gave the boy a thin-lipped bugger-off smile to make sure he got the message.

"But it's fascinating stuff, professor. Can't I just listen in for a bit? I'm sure it would be extremely helpful in the essay you set last week. I've never heard of Banuism."

"I'm sure you haven't, but that's why I wrote a bloody book. Now, off you go. Chop, chop."

"My coffee, professor . . ."

The professor raised his eyebrows to an impressive height.

"Oh, OK, I'll take it with me." The student picked up his coffee and headed off down the stairs.

"You've got to have eyes in your arse around here. There are students and fellow academics in every pub, coffee house and brothel in Cambridge. Occasionally you'll even find one in a lecture."

"Brothel?" said Eve.

"Hmm, oh probably, just a figure of speech really, although there is certainly a tradition of that kind of thing. One of the colleges was originally a nunnery, but was closed down in the fourteenth century due to the almost complete absence of said nuns. Most of the poor ladies that remained were classified as whores."

"Interesting," said Eve. "Relevant?"

"Not that I know of," said the professor. "But that doesn't mean it might not be. The problem we have with Banuism is that we know so little about it. To be fair, it probably doesn't involve prostitution, but then again, I wouldn't have thought it would have involved ritual sacrifice either, but it appears that it does."

"Charles Janenssen?" asked Eve.

"Yes, good old Charles Janenssen has certainly staked out a claim for that. At that time, no one had ever heard of Banuism so people thought it was simply the imagination of the insane. Even once we knew Banuism had existed we could still dismiss the rituals themselves as the work of an unbalanced mind as there was no reference to such activities. However . . ." the professor paused and took off his glasses before cleaning them with his hat. Eve smiled to herself – a dramatic pause? He was in lecture mode. "A new piece of information has come to light that suggests Janenssen's rituals are indeed a practice of Banuism. Last year, an archaeologist from the other place . . ." he looked up at Eve, who looked back blankly. "Oxford," he said. "Anyway, this archaeologist finds what he believes to be a monastic ruin on the Afghanistan–Iran border bang on the old silk route, but it turns out to be a Manichaean temple. However, he discovers an anteroom, or the floor of one, which has a circle carved into it encompassing a perfectly fitted square. Now, we could, if we weren't the enquiring sort, dismiss that as coincidence. A circle with a square inside isn't a unique symbol after all. However, also carved into the floor is a set of images, sort of stick men. It appears to be an instruction manual, and you'd not be surprised to hear that it documents the process of sacrifice. That is not a Manichaean practice."

The professor retrieved an old plastic bag that had been sitting next to him on a spare chair. He pulled out a folder, opened it, and handed Eve a photocopy of a picture.

"Now, if you look carefully you can see that the second to last frame shows what looks like a twisted object coming out of the immolated figure's chest. And the final frame shows the same twisted object in what I take to be a container of sorts."

Eve looked. "The soul?"

"Well, if you believe Janenssen's account of things, then yes, the soul. And like Janenssen, the manual here seems to show the soul captured in a container."

Eve put the picture down and drank the rest of her coffee.

"One obvious question," said the professor picking up the

photocopy and peering at it, "is why would any self-respecting Banuist want to collect souls? Its alignment with Manichaeism would suggest that any form of violence would be the last thing we should expect. Still, here it is in black and white."

"Colour," said Eve.

"Precisely," said the professor, nodding. "Here is the evidence in black and white in full colour."

Eve smiled – academics must have the last word. She thought of the Boy's message left at the scenes of his sacrifices. "Something to do with cleansing of the soul?"

"Possibly," said Stephen, waving a finger about. "But whose soul? The victim or the perpetrator?"

Eve shrugged.

"This boy of yours, any idea how he knows about all this?"

"No, but he clearly does, and I would hazard a guess there is more to come. Any other thoughts?"

"Hmm. Well, a few years ago, ten I think, the bursar of one of the colleges came to see me. He said he had a very old parchment that his father had told him was some description of an ancient religion called Banuism. To be honest, I wasn't sure I believed him. He had a reputation for being a bit of wanker with the truth. We talked a little about Banuism, and he promised to show me the parchment and an old stone bowl that he claimed was a Banuistic artefact. However, he never came back to me with it, and I left it because I couldn't really stand the bullshitter." The professor went to take a sip of his coffee, but the cup was empty. He peered at the mosaic of milk froth and sticky chocolate powder that clung to the cup's edge. "More coffee?" He didn't wait for a reply. "Maria, two more of your delicious crapuccinos please. *Adeso, per favore*," he shouted, which turned quite a few heads in their direction.

"You think I'm your slave. You think again," came back the disembodied reply.

"Right," he said to Eve. "They'll be here in a moment. Where was I?"

"The bullshitting bursar."

"Oh yes. But, a couple of years later he was 'let go' by his college – paid off. In effect, he was sacked as colleges are incapable, or were at the time, anyway, of actually sacking anyone, as it never occurred to them that they might have to. Now, the thing is he was sacked for wanting to 'feel a female undergraduate's soul'. Well, that didn't go down well for him, not unsurprisingly, really, but given what we've talked about this morning it rings some alarm bells."

"So, do you now think he did have a parchment and somehow translated it and it revealed some disturbing suggestions for ritual sacrifice?"

"Well," said the professor, using a forefinger to scoop out the froth from his cup. "Yes."

They sat in silence for a while. It was an uncomfortable thought.

"Bursar's name?" asked Eve.

"Richard Trapt. He must be in his mid-seventies by now."

"Any idea where he disappeared to?"

"London. Apparently, he had a family house there. Camden I think."

Maria appeared with the coffees and a couple of biscotti.

"You're an angel, Maria," said the professor.

"*Si, vero*, and you are *un peccatore*."

Chapter Fifteen

The street has terraced houses on each side with a few trees dotted about the place like tired guards. Their lower branches are missing, and they droop as if they have their chins on their chests. Last night Makka had gone out into Camden town and had come back with a beer mat and an address. He was checking the back of it now. It is green and has Staropramen written on it and underneath that is says 'est. in Prague'. The scribblings on the back ruin it. It was not designed to be scribbled on. Makka looks up and then makes for the end terrace on the left hand side. It has a heavy, dirty blue door and grimy grey windows. The house looks as tired as the tree guards. In fact, the whole road looks tired. Everything just wants to sleep the sleep of those who have had enough. That is sad, and I touch the broken brick wall that partitions off what would have been a tiny front garden. I offer my sympathy. Makka bangs on the door.

"Right, you two, keep it shut, yeah?" He looks at me. "No weird stuff, right? I reckon these guys will spook easy."

The door opens a crack. "What the fuck do you want?" asks a disembodied voice.

Makka steps forward and opens the courier bag he is carrying so that the mystery voice can see inside. That seems to do the trick.

"OK. In," directs the voice, and door opens. We step over the lip into the mouth of the sad house.

The mystery voice is a young man with a beard and hair that falls about his head in long plaits that look like lengths of rope. I whisper to Vee about them and she tells me they are dreadlocks. I don't know what that means, but I like the look of them. Perhaps I'll do my hair that way.

We are shown into the front room, which contains a television, a low wooden table and two sofas. One sofa is covered in faded and wrinkled brown leather and looks like the frowning face of an old man, while the other appears to be made from an assortment of rugs. I don't think I'll be able to sit on it – it is too chaotic. The wooden table is full of cups and cigarette packets, beer cans and small tins of lighter fluid and a small soft toy that looks like a camel with one eye. There are other people in the room too – another young man and a young woman are sitting on the leather sofa. They barely look up from watching the television as we enter. Makka and Dreadlocks sit on the empty sofa and Makka gets out the skunk from his bag, which brings the other two to life.

"You wanna try a smoke first, yeah?" asks Makka.

"Sure," they say, pretty much in chorus.

Vee sits on the floor while Makka constructs the smoke. Dreadlocks' initial hostility has gone now and he's chatting about some band he says are 'sick'. Makka lights up the joint, and the rich, sweet smelling smoke permeates the room. I watch as the joint gets passed around. Vee shakes her head when it's her turn and Makka intercepts it before it reaches me. I know he doesn't want me to take any more drugs, and I am quite happy not to. The atmosphere in the room is relaxed and people seem to sit a little more comfortably on the sofas.

Vee picks up one of the lighter fluid tins and a Zippo lighter with a skull on it. She shakes it. "Can I fill the lighter?" she asks no one in particular. Dreadlocks shrugs. Vee takes that as a yes, so I wander out of the room while she busies herself. I am curious to see the rest of the house.

The hall floor is covered with black and white tiles large enough for me to stand on without stepping on the joins. They are laid out in chequered pattern, a pathway for chess pieces. I am careful to move as a knight would because that's what I think I am, although I have no armour or a sword.

As I pass a door that sits crouched under the stairs I simultaneously have two visions: one of my mother's soul, quiet and content, happily suspended in the ether of a soul well, waiting to pass on, and the other of dark souls being consumed, devoured by the Angel's soul. The visions are linked by an artefact, an ancient Noachian stone – the Soul Stone. I can see it clearly and stand motionless admiring it.

The visions fade and I am left with an unusual feeling in my chest, as if a thread of impossible thinness is wrapped around my heart, tugging at me, urging me to allow it to pull me to its source.

I do. I think I know where it leads.

The thread disappears through the wood panelling of the little crouching stair door. I open it. Concrete steps descend into a pool of darkness, and I can smell the musty dampness of lime and brick and paper and other cellar inhabitants. There is a switch by the door, and I flick it on. Light rushes in from wherever it has been hiding and condenses on the light bulb throwing a blanket of pale gloom over the place. Shadows leap about in surprise as if caught unawares.

I carefully shut the crouching door, adjust my bag and head below ground.

The cellar is divided into several large alcoves fronted by brick arches. There are boxes of old newspapers, an exercise bike, empty beer bottles, a soiled duvet and a tired sofa without its cushions or covers – its springs exposed in naked embarrassment. I walk between the alcoves which are littered with more detritus heading for the far wall. Here there is a ragged hole big enough for me to squeeze through. The thread pulls impatiently.

I push myself from one cellar into another. This new one is much like the one I have just left except it is full of furniture and smells of polish and wood and age. I can just make out the shapes of chairs stacked upside down on table edges. The thin light from the ragged hole tries to fool me into thinking they are grotesque upturned beetles, kicking their legs in annoyance as I disturb their illumination. I'm a little disappointed they aren't real, but the illusion is enjoyable.

The gaps between the furniture create a path, which I negotiate carefully as the light grows dimmer. The path ends in a brick wall, the boundary to the next cellar and a dead end, but the thread pulls me again. It wants me to go through the wall. I run my hands over the rough masonry and find the lime cement. It has more or less turned to dust. I take my knife from my bag and scrape at the joints. In a matter of moments, I've removed a brick and with it comes a flood of bright white light. It pours through the gap as if in a hurry to explore the new-found space.

I look through the tiny glassless window, but cannot see much, so pull at the exposed bricks. They come away without much resistance and I'm soon standing in a third and very different cellar. This one does not have the smell of dampness or of long-forgotten items from the upstairs world. It is clear and clean and is distinguished by three features; a cage that could contain a large animal, the ritual symbols I use to collect souls cut into the brickwork of the floor, and a jet-black roughly hewn stone bowl sitting at the exact centre of the engraved circle and inner square.

This is not a happy place. It is easy to read the story of this room. Wisps of fear are tangled in the cage bars like candyfloss spun from terror. No animals have been incarcerated here. Just people.

Stored.

I squat down and touch the brick floor. It pulses pain, both from the branding of the symbols on its surface and from what has gone on here. Although the floor's wound has been cleaned, there are traces of blood, dried and dead.

Sacrificed.

"Well now. What do we have here?" says a papery voice. "A young . . ." The voice pauses, and I turn to look at its source. "Girl?"

I think the pink hoodie has confused him. His eyebrows rise together, suggesting he doubts his own suggestion. I had heard him enter the cellar. He was not very quiet.

He is old. The little hair he has is combed across his age-spotted head. His skin thin with a transparent quality like that of a greased paper bag. I can see the blood vessels and bones and tendons of his hand. He is almost naked with age. The man looks at the hole in his basement wall.

"Hmmm. What sort of thief are you?"

I don't answer.

"A soul thief maybe?"

I don't stand up, but touch the scarred floor again. Pain.

"Watch, you see? Watch the people coming and going. Make notes and that. Especially the young people. It's important, you see, to watch and wait." He picks at the frayed cuffs of a cotton shirt just poking out from under his brown jacket.

"Bursar you know. Meet people – royalty and what have you. Important people." He waves an arm about and nods. "Need to know if they are important. Connections, you see. Important." He stops waving his arm and focuses on me. "Not from round here, are you? No. Not an important young lady, are you? Hmmm? Won't be missed I expect. Hmmm?"

I am not sure which question to answer, so I don't answer any. "Are those chickens?" I ask, standing up and pointing at his tie.

"Good heavens, no. Cockerels, young lady, cockerels. Important bird. Was a bishop and, um, founded a college you know." He pauses and seems to be a little unsure of what he has just said. "Yes, that's right, a college." He strokes the tie, smooths it deliberately, slowly. He seems reassured.

"The Bursar has lived a long time, you see. Hundreds of years. That's right, hundreds of years. Amazing isn't it? Do you know how that's done? Hmmm? How to stay alive? Hmmm?"

He looks at me and I catch his gaze. His mind is a spinning vortex of bruised purples and streaks of ochre, sucking any sane thoughts down its spiralling throat and spitting them out beaten and broken and wrong. The Bursar is hostage to this creation, his own creation – a desire so strong it has become all-consuming. It has one goal, one insatiable desire. It corrupts and transforms and presses every thought into its service. It wants immortality.

Although the vortex spins and howls like the wind in a chimney it cannot hide the emptiness of its surroundings. The Bursar's mind is like a deserted city: all the structures are in place, but there is no life. The Bursar is all but gone. I navigate to his soul well. Its rim is blackened as if there has been a fire, scorched and soot covered. Like his mind, the well looks abandoned.

I descend.

I find the Bursar's soul. It is tar-black and only a fragment remains, hanging on to life by a single ethereal thread. I think I know where the rest is. I break the connection.

"Well?" asks the Bursar. "Do you know?"

"Yes," I say, going over to the stone bowl and picking it up with both hands. "But you are wrong."

He laughs. "Don't think so. Souls, you see. That's the trick. Young souls." I hold out the bowl.

"This is the Soul Stone," I say.

He looks surprised. "Well, yes. Yes, it is. And the Bursar uses it to feed on souls. Yes, that's how it works." He pulls a pistol from his jacket pocket and points it at me. "Now give me the stone," he says, with a voice that is burnt and charred and cracked with corruption.

I look down at the Soul Stone and into the depths of its polished black bowl. I see a shadow flit by, a soul so dark it barely registers. It is the Bursar's soul. I think the stone has been collecting it bit by bit, preparing it for consumption. For every life the Bursar took, the Soul Stone took a part of his soul. There will be no immortality for the Bursar. There will only be oblivion.

I hold out the stone. "The symbols on the floor are wrong too," I say as he takes it from me.

"Poppycock. Now get in the cage. Things to do before high table." He smiles. "*Benedic, Domine, nos et dona tua, quae de largitate tua sumus sumpturi.*"

I have been watching Vee for the last few moments, since she carefully stepped through my hole in the wall. She is now directly behind the Bursar. He waves the gun towards the cage. "Father's you know – the pistol. Had it in the war. Kept it. Works. Shot someone once. Burglar, I think, or it might have been a rabbit." He seems confused again.

I haven't moved. Vee waits for him to become aware of her presence. I help him by looking over his shoulder directly at

Vee. He turns his head slowly.

"Ah, another young soul to feed on. Excellent," he says, but I don't think it is excellent because Vee squirts lighter fluid in his face and in one coordinated move flicks the skull-embossed Zippo into action igniting the fuel.

The Bursar's face goes up in flames. He tries to take a step back to bring the gun to bear on Vee, but his legs are in the wrong place and he stumbles. The gun goes off. It is so loud that I think my ears have exploded – blood splatters my face. But it's not my ears that have exploded it is the Bursar's head. He seems to have accidently shot himself. He falls with ironic accuracy into the dead centre of the floor-carved symbols, his arms outstretched, his burning face looking up. Blood flows from his head, the missing part of the skull making it easy for it to escape, seeping out towards the carved channels. The symbols start to fill with rich red liquid.

Vee squirts some more lighter fluid on to the Bursar. Flames now leap from his chest too. The Soul Stone lies next to the burning body.

"Let's go," says Vee, and grabs my hand.

"Wait." I drop to my knees and pick up the Soul Stone. It is warm and vibrating slightly, and as I watch the last fragment of the Bursar's soul is pulled from his body and assimilated into the stone. His soul is prepared and ready for oblivion.

I stand up and Vee takes my hand again.

"Ready?" she asks. I nod, but as we are about to go, Makka comes crashing through the hole. He takes in the scene.

"Who the fuck is that?" he says motioning towards the burning Bursar.

"The Bursar," I say. "Vee set his face on fire and then he shot himself."

"What? Why?"

Vee says nothing.

"He wanted my soul," I say.

"Yeah?" Makka looks at the cage and then at Vee. "Well, fuck him then. But why did you come here in the first place?"

I hold out the Soul Stone. "It's the Soul Stone."

Makka looks at it. "You need it, do you?"

"Yes."

He nods. "OK, but we'd better get the fuck out of here. Yeah?" He turns and heads back through the hole.

Vee lets go of my hand and empties the tin of lighter fluid on to the Bursar. "Fucker." Flames leap again.

I take out my chalk and leave a message for Dr Rhodes at the feet of the Bursar.

He wears very hairy socks.

***

It is late and it is time.

We need to feed the Bursar's soul to the Angel and must prepare the ritual. We decide the second bedroom will do. It is more or less empty, so offers us enough space.

"I need to draw the symbols on a floor," I say to Makka.

He rubs the floor with his foot. "Well, it's fucking carpeted. How about using flour or something like that?"

"No. It must be chalk," I say. "Although I think blood might do."

"Really? You want me to pull up the carpet?"

"Yes please."

He looks at Vee, who shrugs.

"OK." He sighs and starts picking at the carpet where it meets the door. He works his fingers under its lip and pulls. It comes away from the floor. He pulls some more and the whole edge pulls up with a tearing sound. The teeth from the carpet gripper don't give up their prey easily.

"Come on. Give us a hand."

Vee and I grab the raised carpet and pull. It comes away from the sides now and we pull it all the way back to the window. The floor is skinned leaving exposed chipboard – perfect for me to draw on. I take some chalk from my pocket, kneel down on the boards and draw out a large circle. Inside that I draw a triangle. I make sure each of its points touches the edge of the circle. In the dead centre, I draw a small circle just big enough to enclose the Soul Stone. And finally, I draw three lines, each one starting at the centre of the large circle and flying out to the points of the triangle. These are important. I have drawn a two-dimensional prism. Everyone connects to everyone else.

Makka and Vee look on. I place the Soul Stone in the small circle, pour in some lighter fluid and then ignite it with Vee's Zippo. It flames immediately and within seconds the fire has pulled the stored soul of the Bursar out of the stone. It now dances on the end of the flame, the orange tendrils flicking, licking and caressing its black, infected surface.

"What can you see?" I say.

"Nothing," says Makka. "Just the stone. I thought you'd lit it, but it isn't burning."

"Nothing," says Vee.

I turn out the light and sit down at one of the points where the circle, triangle and radial lines meet. The moon looks in through the window. A powerful symbol – white and pure.

"Sit," I say, and indicate to the other two points.

They sit.

Makka on my right. *Rage*.

Vee on my left. *Pain*.

Me. *Judgement*

They are *Seers* and I am *Arta – Righteous*.

I look first at Makka, catch his gaze and remove the filter, as I did with Mrs Johnston, that stops him seeing what is really there. I now look to Vee and do the same. The filter will return after a while, but for now they can see the world of the Dark Chorus. My world.

The dancing soul has their attention now. I focus on it too and feel their presence. We are now connected, a single entity. Assimilation starts.

The Angel's soul stirs.

Pressure builds. Energy flows. Rage of injustice and Pain of innocence power the process. The chalk lines glow. The flames grow in the Soul Stone and the soul twists and turns and tries to break free. It seems to know what is coming for it.

Oblivion arrives.

It erupts – firing barbed white flames of celestial energy. They pierce the Bursar's soul hooking it like a speared fish.

The Soul Stone flames go out and for a moment the black soul resists the pull of the line, straining for freedom. But it cannot escape its entanglement. In an instant it is gone, pulled to the depths of my soul well and consumed.

The glowing chalk lines go out.

Makka and Vee sit back, breathing heavily. Their faces glow with the effort. We stay in the room for some minutes, washing in the moonlight, recovering. Nothing is said.

Tomorrow we will assimilate Mitch's soul.

Chapter Sixteen

Eve stepped over the threshold of the mid-terrace house and into a narrow hallway, made almost impassable by stacks of old papers and books and vinyl records. She picked up a record – Pop Hits 1970. Long, wavy hair, flares and vomit-yellow jumpers leapt out at her. A classic fake of its time, poorly executed bland covers of the year's best pop songs. Simply wrong.

She sniffed the air. That's how the house felt – wrong. She recognised the atmosphere of a space whose owner had lived in a reality distorted by what she thought of as a mental filter. She'd felt many such spaces in her professional career.

"This way," said her police escort. Eve dropped the best forgotten bit of recording history back on the pile and followed her companion through a small doorway hidden under the staircase. It took her down into a well-lit cellar and straight into what, to Eve, looked like a scene from a TV crime drama. White-overall-clad forensic types were going about their business, while standing thoughtfully at the foot of a white-plastic-sheeted body was the Inspector.

It smelt of burnt hair and disinfectant.

"Ah, Dr Rhodes," said the Inspector as Eve came and stood alongside her. "Sorry about the lateness of the call, but I thought you might want to see this iteration of your boy's killing spree in the flesh, or rather burnt flesh, in this case."

"That's OK," said Eve looking at the floor symbols carved into the brick floor and the worn brown brogues and hairy socked ankles poking out from under the white covering. "Can I hazard a guess as to the victim's name?"

The Inspector took a sideways look at Eve with her eyebrows raised in what Eve now understood was one of the

Inspector's preferred methods for a silent response.

"Richard Trapt," said Eve as she crouched down to touch the carved floor. "He was a Cambridge college bursar." Her fingers brushed the cut floor and she had a sudden and overwhelming feeling that the Boy had done much the same.

"Hmm, correct," said the Inspector. "And I'll take a guess that you found that piece of information up in Cambridge."

"Correct," said Eve. "I'll tell you about my visit in a moment, but first . . ." She left the sentence unfinished, stood up, faced the Inspector and raised her own eyebrows.

"A few hours ago the neighbour reported that he'd found a new hole in the wall of his cellar, and then, when he took a look through, he saw this mess." The Inspector waved a hand over the scene. Eve turned to look at the Boy-sized hole in the far corner of the room. "First attempts to place the time of death put it at about two days ago. He was killed by a shot to the head."

"Sorry," said Eve, snapping her gaze back to the Inspector. "Are you saying the Boy, or more likely Makka, shot him?"

"Actually it appears he shot himself." The Inspector moved over to the body and pulled back the cover. Eve could see the damage the bullet had done to the side of his head and the large quantity of rich deep-red dried blood that had presumably gushed from the wound. The Bursar's face was also badly burnt, but still recognisable as a face. It had a startled look about it. He probably hadn't expected to die.

"Why do you think they burnt his face?"

"Well, I was hoping you might have some idea about that." The Inspector pulled the sheet further back to reveal that the Bursar's clothes were also burnt. The remains of the tie caught Eve's attention. It had what looked like chickens on it.

"You mean you think it might be ritualistic? It's possible." She looked around for any evidence of flies, bees, or beheaded birds, but there was none. What there was, and she'd seen this when she first entered the cellar, was the chalked word *Purgatio* scrawled in the Boy's writing at the foot of the body, and at its head a new set of words: *Oblivio salvationem Angelis opperitur* "Oblivion awaits the Angel's salvation," read Eve. “If we take that, the reference to cleansing, and the absence of other ritual artefacts, then I’d suggest that the Boy has developed another method for soul extraction. He’s possibly adapting his behaviour, his rituals, to suit the environment. You have to understand that someone with his heightened sense of self, and his belief in the world as he sees it, will have no problem assimilating any experience into his reality. He’s effectively shuffled the two realities like packs of cards, integrating them. This allows him to operate in both spaces simultaneously.

“OK, we’ll make that assumption for the moment. But what do you make of the fact that the symbols are carved into the floor? Clearly the Boy didn’t have the time to do that, which suggests that they were already here. So, spill the port. What do you know about Trapt?” The Inspector pulled the covering back over the dead bursar as she spoke.

“OK. First I’ll give you a quick summary of what Professor Doyle told me.” Eve recounted the salient points of Manichaeism and the emergence of Banuism, the archaeological findings on the silk route and the discovered reference to soul extraction.

“Lovely. So Banuism is indeed a murderously orientated religion – that’s not a surprise. And Trapt?”

“Trapt, as I said, was the bursar of one of the colleges. He contacted Professor Doyle some ten years ago asking him about ancient religions and Banuism in particular. Trapt told Doyle that he was in possession of part of an old manuscript that his father had picked up in the Middle East during the war. He also claimed to have a crude stone bowl that his father was told was an important Banuistic artefact. Trapt promised to show Doyle the manuscript. But he never did. Doyle said he pointed Trapt to the Janenssen article, and after that he heard no more from the man. He emailed him a few times, but gave up, assuming he was making it up. Apparently, he had a reputation for over-stated self-promotion, and Doyle assumed this was one of those “bullshit” moments.” Eve paused. She looked from the carved symbols to the cage in the corner of the room. “But, well . . .”

"Quite," said the Inspector. "The cage is a little disturbing, and I have a bad feeling we are going to be a little more disturbed than we might like."

"Yes," said Eve slowly. "I think so too. Doyle gave me two other pieces of information concerning Trapt. The first was that about eight years ago Trapt was paid off. According to Doyle that's the equivalent of being sacked in Cambridge college terms. His departure was over some bother with a young female student. The incident was reported as sexual harassment, but the interesting thing about the student's statement was that she reported that Trapt had kept saying he only wanted to 'feel her soul'. It seems this was interpreted as a sexual euphemism. The second note of interest is that Trapt emailed Doyle with a message just before he left that simply read that Banuism was the key to eternal life."

A plain clothes detective descended the stone steps in a rush of urgency. "Ma'am, you need to take a look at this."

"At what?"

"We found what we think is an old air raid shelter at the bottom of the garden. It's been . . . repurposed." The detective stuck his hands in his overcoat and stared at her, tight-lipped.

"Into what?" asked the Inspector.

"A crypt."

"Shit." The Inspector turned to Eve. "The used vessels of eternal life?"

Eve nodded. "I'll give this one a miss if it's all the same to you."

"Sure," said the Inspector, who looked like she would quite like to give it a miss too. Eve felt sorry for her. There are plenty of shitty jobs in the world, but heading up a murder team must be one of the shittier ones – emotionally at any rate. "I'll be back in a bit," said the Inspector and turned to the detective. "Lead on then." They disappeared up the stairs and out of the cellar.

Eve returned her thoughts to the Bursar's death scene. She re-read the Boy's message – Oblivion awaits the Angel's saviours. But that didn't make sense. Why would anyone help restore the Angel to its rightful place if their reward was oblivion?

"*Purgatio*," she read out under her breath. "Cleansed."

The two messages must be connected. Is he talking about himself? No, he collects the souls of the people he considers corrupt, so it would be reasonable to assume these souls are the helpers he's talking about. But how do they help? Maybe the answer was somewhere in the house – the Bursar's parchment seemed a likely source.

Eve left the cellar and the activities of securing the dead. She stepped out through the squat door into the cramped hall and then poked her head into the front room. The curtains were drawn, and she had the impression that they hadn't been open in some time. The room smelt of damp and disuse; the expensive looking leather sofas that had once been a beautiful polished brown were now dry and cracked. Dust and time sat heavily on all the surfaces. Eve didn't enter the room. She felt certain that to do so would cause it to crumble in on itself. The parchment wasn't here.

The back room was much the same, although at some time in the near past boxes had been dumped there and, like meteors hitting the moon, their impact had radiated out dust in fine circular waves.

Eve appreciated the art of this, but understood that for all its interest it was only there as a result of an environment that mental illness had created. The Bursar was undoubtedly an extreme case, but abandoned environments like this were common to many afflicted people, including her own mother.

She took the wooden stairs to the next floor and noticed the elegant brass stair rods that pinned the carpet to each step. This had once been a beautiful Victorian residence. As she reached the landing, a police officer emerged from the first-floor front room. Eve stepped aside to let him pass. He nodded and headed down the stairs clutching a laptop in a large plastic bag. That must be the study.

She ventured in.

Again, the curtains were drawn, but this room was lived in – or had been. A number of standard lamps cast the room in a warm orange glow. The main ceiling fitting had no lampshade and no bulb. The Bursar clearly liked the shadows.

The back and side walls hosted floor-to-ceiling bookcases. Eve inspected their contents: books on architecture, military history, philosophy, ancient Greek and numerous other academic-related tomes. There were novels too, all literary and classic, and like their academic brothers and sisters they looked unread. Eve had the impression these were all for show, and that thc audience was the Bursar himself. Self-delusional. She expected he had come to believe what he thought he was – an intellectual, an academic, a man of importance. Perhaps working in an academic environment had made him feel that way.

An old-fashioned desk dominated the floor space, with a worn captain's chair as its accomplice. To the right of the curtained bay windows was a small spindly legged occasional table, the sort that Eve had always thought pointless. However, the Bursar must have thought differently as he had placed a number of objects on it. Above it hung a large framed picture covered by a gold-flecked cloth. Eve pulled the captain's chair away from the desk. One of the casters was stuck and complained as it was dragged across the floor. She sat down with the intention of going through the drawers and wondered if she ought to be wearing latex gloves or some such thing, but her attention was drawn back to the picture. She stared at the cloth, which to her mind's eye now looked like a shroud, and then at the table with its oddments. Was it some kind of shrine or worshipping set-up? Curious. She pulled herself out of the chair and approached the shrine, or whatever it was. There was an old bone-handled knife, a leather-bound notebook, a small porcelain cup and a tiny bell. But, what was more noticeable was the ring of faded varnish in the centre of the table's surface – a missing artefact. The mythical stone bowl maybe?

Eve raised her eyes to the shroud. She had a feeling that she now knew what was hidden behind the gold-flecked fabric. She pulled the cloth away to reveal what looked like a very old parchment, torn at the edges and discoloured with age and neglect. Still, much of the text looked readable – although not to her, and probably only to a handful of people in the world.

This must be the script the Bursar had mentioned to Professor Doyle. And if the parchment existed then the stone bowl probably did too. She took out her phone and snapped a number of photos. Doyle was going to be more than a little excited when he received these. She would have smiled at the thought if things hadn't been so grim. She pressed send and off the pictures went, fired out into the digital ether.

The leather-bound notebook caught her attention, so she picked it up and flicked it open.

Time blurred.

The face of a young girl stared out at her from a Polaroid photo, vivid and real. Her beautiful brown eyes glistened with tears of terror and desperation, her face was pale, and her blonde hair stuck to her forehead. She was clearly in the cellar cage, caught in the act of pleading.

Her name was Mary. It was written next to the image and below were details of the girl, her height, age, hair colour, eye colour, the clothes she was wearing, the date she arrived and the date of her sacrifice.

Eve couldn't look away. She felt herself pulled into the moment by those eyes, pulled into the picture, pulled across time and into the horror, stunned by the crashing wave of her own despair and helplessness at Mary's fate.

When she was a young girl, she would have moments when she knew she was entering a different world, her world of dark reflections, and she recognised this shifting feeling now. The difference here was that she did not want to make the transition, did not think she could recover from it if she let it take her, but the horror-greased edges of reality offered her mind no grip.

She fell.

A hand gently tugged the book out of Eve's grasp and the connection was broken. Eve gasped and stumbled forward as reality returned. She had been holding her breath and felt light-headed.

It was the Inspector.

"Eve?" she said, touching her on the arm. "Perhaps you should go home." She looked at the picture of Mary and flicked through the other pages. More desperate faces flickered briefly in the dim light. The Inspector shut the book.

"Perhaps it is time for us all to go home," she said.

"Yes," said Eve, trying to control her voice. "The crypt? Children?"

The Inspector sighed but said nothing.

Eve's phone rang. It was the professor's number. She wasn't sure she was ready for his enthusiasm, but her curiosity asserted itself.

"Ah, Dr Rhodes, it's Stephen Doyle here. These pictures you sent me are unbelievable. Where did you find the parchment?"

"In Trapt's house. I'm looking at it now. What are you doing up at this time?"

"Insomnia. I'm marking undergrad essays in a bid to send myself to sleep, but some are so dreadful that they're making me laugh and that is keeping me awake. So, Trapt has let you see the parchment, has he?"

"He had no choice. He is extremely dead, and I can't say I'm feeling any sorrow at that fact."

"Ah. Hmmm. Is the stone bowl there?"

"No. The Boy has been here. My guess is he took it. Have you any thoughts on the text?"

"Yes. I've managed a quick translation, but I'll need to study the parchment in more detail. Don't hold me to what I am going to tell you now."

"The Inspector's with me, so I'll put you on speakerphone. She'll want to hear this."

"Ok, no problem. I'm guessing Trapt was burnt to death. Yes?"

"He was certainly set on fire," said the Inspector. "But appears to have somehow shot himself, which is what actually killed him."

"Really? Oh well." Eve could almost hear Doyle's shrug.

"Why did you think he would have been burnt to death?" said the Inspector.

"Well, the text has something to say on that, but we're jumping ahead of ourselves. Now, the parchment enlightens us with several key facts about Banuism. The first – and this, Dr Rhodes, answers the question you asked me when we met up – is that dark souls are collected to cleanse the shards of the soul of a fallen angel. By doing this the shards can be pieced back together and thus the angel restored. It seems only corrupt souls will do the trick – the more corrupt the better, which is a bit ironic. The existence of this document may well be the proof needed to pin down the aetiology of the shattered soul story which pops up in other early religions . . ."

The professor paused for effect.

"And . . ." said the Inspector.

"Oh well, it's exciting to a sad old ancient religion professor like me." He took a deep breath. "The second fact is that these fallen shards reside in, literally inside, individuals called Arta." Eve could almost hear him adjusting his glasses now. "It doesn't say how that is supposed to happen, but it appears to be a necessity. Artas are the holiest of the Banuists and are supported by two seers. The closest translation I can come to for the seers' named roles are Rage and Pain."

Eve looked at the Inspector who raised her eyebrows.

"So," said Eve, "the Boy thinks himself Arta and he has collected Makka and Victoria as Rage and Pain."

"Quite possibly," said the professor. He now seemed to be eating something. "The third fact," he mumbled, "is that the stone bowl Trapt mentioned is called the Soul Stone and is the key artefact in the cleansing of the angel's soul. It holds souls and represents the angel in the acquisition process. It makes up the fourth point in the Banu Prism, a declared holy shape, which allows each member to connect with each other and so facilitate and power the process." There was a pause and then the professor added, "I think."

"And the fire?" said the Inspector.

"Fire pulls the soul from the body. It's part of the collection process. Once out, the Soul Stone captures it. I would guess Trapt was set on fire before he shot himself, that way, as he died his soul would be pulled from the body."

"So what's with all the dead birds and bees and flies?"

"Well, the parchment doesn't say, but I would guess it's

another way of acquiring souls. It would allow other Banuists to work at collecting corrupt souls. We can only assume that there would have been a lot of shards to cleanse so a lot of bad souls would have needed collecting."

"So why would Trapt kill innocent children using the rituals the Boy uses to kill his victims? Why would he think these children would have corrupt souls?"

"What?!" The professor was choking on whatever it was he was eating. His disembodied coughing bounced around the room, reminding Eve that she was still amongst the horror. "Trapt's been killing children? What an absolute fuck. Shit. I knew he was mad, but a child killer . . ."

"Yes," said the Inspector. "And if this gets out to the press, you probably won't live to regret it."

"No, no. Yes, quite, understood," said the professor who sounded shaken.

"So, any ideas why Trapt would kill like this?"

"I can only assume he tried to translate the parchment himself and misunderstood it. There aren't many people in the world who can read this sort of ancient script and read it accurately. Words can have multiple meanings, but can also represent an idea, or even a complex action. For example, the line documenting the feeding of the angel's shard could be translated as offering eternal life to the fed soul. My guess is he assumed that by feeding souls to himself he would live forever."

"Sounds plausibly insane," said the Inspector.

"It would explain his last email to me. If he did come to that conclusion then Trapt thought he'd worked out the text and didn't want to share his knowledge of eternal life with me or anyone else," said the professor. "I would guess that's why he went quiet on me." He coughed again. "What a complete fucker," he added.

"Is there anything else the parchment has to tell us?" asked Eve.

"Well, there are a couple of lines I couldn't translate. The image you sent wasn't clear enough. If I could get my hands on the actual parchment, then I can see if it has anything else to reveal."

"OK, I'll see if I can ship these unholy words down to you," said the Inspector.

"I'll wait to hear from you, then."

Professor Doyle rang off and the room was quiet again.

"Go home, Eve," said the Inspector. "Enough is enough, eh?" She left the room.

Eve looked at the parchment. This was all becoming so real. Everyone talked about it as if it were real. Perhaps it was? She closed her eyes. *Get a grip*. Her mind wondered about the Boy. She hoped he was OK.

Looking down at the leather-bound book, she thought of Mary again and allowed a few silent tears to flow.

Chapter Seventeen

We have been in the flat now for three days. Makka says we need to stay out of sight for a while to let all the shit settle. It has been raining all day today and a cold wind is blowing it up against the window, so it hits with an audible thud before sliding down the pane. The rain is confused, it does not seem to be able to decide whether it is snow or simply drops of water. I don't mind this confusion. In fact, I have enjoyed watching it trying to make up its mind.

The flat is quite cold. The heating is not working, but there is electricity. We have set up our base camp in the living room, which houses a TV, an azure-coloured settee and matching armchair (there is a label on the sofa telling me its colour), a coffee table and a thin standard lamp which looks as though it is made from brass. There are also some faded floral-patterned curtains to pull across the window. We have made beds out of blankets, cushions and some curtains taken down from other rooms. Makka says he's often slept wrapped in curtains. He didn't say why, but perhaps he just likes it.

We also have a small fan heater that Vee found in a cupboard, so the room is pretty warm.

Yesterday, Makka and Vee went out to buy some new clothes. My pink hoodie is covered in the Bursar's dry blood and Makka says we need to throw it away. I am not happy about this. I like it, but Makka insists. I now wear a long-sleeved T-shirt with S*hit Happens to Others* written on it. And I've got another hoodie, green this time, with a picture of a man smoking a joint on the front. Makka tells me it is cool because it's Bob Marley, but he never said who Bob Marley is. I also have a coat. It's a green parka with a furry hood, but the fur isn't real. Both Makka and Vee have some new clothes too.

Vee is dressed all in black: black leggings, black skirt, black top, black jumper, black coat with a hood and now black lips too. I think she likes black. Makka has a long brown trench coat. He looks like a cowboy, but he needs a hat. I tell him this.

"Fuck off," he laughs. "This is cool. Sorta like the coat Morpheus wears in *The Matrix*. Yeah? It's nothing like a cowboy's coat. And I'm not going to wear any fucking cow-wanker's hat. Yeah?"

I don't think he knows what a cowboy's coat looks like.

I am in the living room with Vee watching the rain again when Makka comes in. He has been in the kitchen making a lot of noise with what sounded like pots and pans banging against each other.

"Can you cook?" he says.

"Cook?" says Vee.

"Yeah. You know? Cook with ingredients and stuff."

"You think I can cook because I'm a girl? Do you? Because if you do, you can shove that thought up your arse." Vee is sitting on the armchair. She crosses her arms, pushes herself further back into the cushions and stares angrily at Makka.

"Easy, yeah? *If* I was thinking that, which I'm not saying I was, I'm definitely not thinking that now. Was just hoping you could 'cause I can't and I'm fed up of pizza and the like."

Vee says nothing, but continues to stare.

Makka drops himself down on the settee and sighs. A reflective silence falls over him. "My ma used to cook," he says. "A lot." And he nods. The fan heater hums. "I can't really remember her now, yeah?" He picks at his jeans. "I just remember her cooking."

Vee unfolds her arms.

"You got a ma?" he says to Vee looking up.

"Dead," she says. We wait for more, but she only shrugs and adds, "Just dead."

Makka runs both hands over his head and through his hair, his brief reflective moment gone. "Fuck it. Pizza it is then," he says and gets up and leaves the room. Vee sits still for a moment and then follows him out. A minute later, Makka shouts at me from the kitchen.

"Me and Vee are just goin' out to look for some food, yeah? Don't leave the flat. Right?" We won't be long." I hear the kitchen door open and close, and I am left to the stillness of the room. I suppose that Vee is fed up with pizza too. I turn out the lamp and sit by the window watching the last of the day's light blow away in the drizzling wind and think of my mother.

The vision I had of my mother before I collected the Soul Stone has given me the reassurance that my idea for saving her from the Dark Chorus will work. I am happy at the knowledge. However, before I can do this, I need to help Makka kill his father.

I promised him I would.

The Angel will have his soul and Makka will have his revenge, but I don't think that will quieten his rage. I think it is his burden, as is pain for Vee and the Angel's soul for me. Perhaps when the Angel's soul is cleansed, we'll all be free.

Perhaps.

The darkness of evening arrives, and I close my eyes and listen. I can hear the rain on the window, the muffled sound of traffic and the comforting hum of the fan heater. I tune into the hum and let myself ride its harmonic currents until I end up where I was hoping to be – in the hall of memories. These are not my memories, they are those of the Angel, but it is only in the last month that I have understood this. In this other world, hall doors form a circle around me, a carousel of memories, with numerous carousels just out of sight that can be loaded and spun. A vast number of untold memories. Most of the doors are closed to me, but I am sure they'll open when, or if, their content is needed. I am looking for a particular door, one of the few that are open to me. I spin the carousel. It seems to know which portal I am after, and when it stops spinning, I am presented with a beaten dark-oak door. I push it open and enter.

The scene before me is now a familiar one. I have watched this a dozen times, first as an unprovoked lucid dream and later as an explicitly retrieved memory as I am doing now. A brick-vaulted room lies exposed, lit by yellow smoky lanterns that throw long-legged dancing shadows about the place. To my left an opening offers me a glimpse of a steam engine, small and compact, sitting on a track that disappears into the blackness of a tunnel. This world is sooty. In front of me, on the ground, tied up with coarse rope, is a man. He is gagged with a dirty cloth. His face is pock-marked, and his eyes are wide with fear and hate. His clothes are not modern, and I now know they are late Victorian. He is lying in a chalk square, which is enclosed in a circle. The two shapes touch at the square's corners. Lit candles are in place at these junctures. It is the ritual, and the prisoner is about to be cleansed. I watch as a well-dressed man wearing a beautiful long cashmere coat sets down a jar with a small flickering candle in it. He stands over the trussed-up man and takes several deep breaths before he busies himself with collecting the man's soul. I watch the soul emerge, dark and ruined. It hangs in the air for a moment and is then grabbed by the fire-jar.

Collected.

The well-dressed man picks up the jar, turns and looks straight at me. I like this bit the best. I think he can see me. He has deep green eyes and a full, rich-black moustache. He smiles.

My memory is interrupted by the drumming sound of feet on the metal fire escape and the air moves as the kitchen door is thrown open. I can hear heavy, rapid breathing. Makka enters the front room like a howling storm.

"Get the fuck up. Now. We gotta get out of here."

Vee pushes past him, grabs her new black rucksack and starts stuffing it with bits and pieces. Makka is darting about the place. "Pigs everywhere. Someone must have seen us."

"Pigs?" I say. "What sort of pigs?"

"Na, you numb nut. Police."

"Did you get any tea?" I am hoping for a cup of tea as I am feeling thirsty.

"What? Fuck, no. Get up." He shouts the last part at me, so I do as he says and get up. I retrieve my courier bag from behind the azure settee. I always keep everything in my courier bag so it's tidy. I don't like things to be in the wrong place. Especially my things. I pull on my parka, zip it up, pull the hood over my head and sling the bag over my shoulder.

I am ready.

Vee is ready,

Makka is ready.

We leave the flat via the kitchen, go down the fire escape and out on to a quiet back street. I see the Bengal sitting statuesque and luxuriant on the pillar of the garden wall. He ignores me. I remember I have left the dead blackbird in the fridge and consider asking Makka if we can go back for it, but the steel tendons of his neck are taut. He is in fight mode, so I won't bother. Anyway, now I have the Soul Stone I can use fire instead of dead birds and flies to draw out souls. I think it will be easier.

Makka leads us into an alleyway between two sets of terraced houses and we stand in the dark lea of the passageway. A police car glides up the street and parks behind the flat – no blue light or siren to warn us. It sits there, a menacing presence, waiting to pounce like the Bengal cat. It looks like they've found the flat. Makka taps me on the shoulder and nods towards the far end of the alley. We move quickly, pausing at its end waiting to see if there are any police on this new street. There aren't, just a few people heading wherever, actively minding their own business, so we cross the road and set off down a side street to make good our escape.

***

"OK, in here," says Makka as he pushes open the door to an all-night cafe called The Full Bacon. It has a picture of a smiling pig for a sign. I am not convinced the pig would smile if it knew what was in store for it. The room is warm and full of fluorescent light and vinyl tablecloths. The windows are steamed up and hot air currents waft about, blowing a heady scented mix of fried foods, cakes and coffee. My stomach rumbles. There aren't many people in The Full Bacon, and those that are seem preoccupied with whatever they are eating. We sit down away from the window. I notice that the vinyl tablecloth is mustard coloured with blue and grey cockerels printed on it. The Bursar would have liked this.

A tall man with a well-trimmed black beard, rich-brown eyes and wearing a grubby apron comes over to our table.

"What are you going to have, eh?" He smiles. I like him. Makka is looking at a plastic menu and blows out his cheeks as he reads it.

"Fuck knows. Erm, all day breakfasts all round?" He looks at Vee and me.

"Yes please," I say. "And a cup of tea. Do you have any Chinese tea?"

"Sure, little buddy. I think all our tea is from China," says Black Beard, smiling some more.

Vee nods. "Chocolate milk too," she says.

"Wait," says Makka. "I'll have mine in a bit. I just have to pop out. Get these two theirs, yeah?"

"Sure, buddy. We'll knock yours up when you get back." Black Beard smiles again as Makka takes out a twenty-pound note from his bag and gives it to Vee.

"See, we can pay, so don't skimp on the portions, yeah?"

Black Beard laughs. "Hell, buddy, I wasn't thinking you weren't going to pay, but appreciate you letting me know you can. Good sized portions for you tribe, eh?" Black Beard heads to the back where the kitchen must be and disappears through a jangly bead curtain.

"Right, back in a bit. Gotta sort this out." Makka waves the phone we took off Mitch at us and then leaves. Vee and I sit in a comfortable silence. I can hear the sizzling of fried foods coming through the jangly bead curtain and my mouth starts to water.

"Do you have a mother?" says Vee.

"Yes. She's in a jar."

Vee traces one of the vinyl chickens with a forefinger. "In a jar?"

"Yes. Her soul is in a jar. Her body is dead."

Vee nods. "A father?"

"No. I don't have one."

Vee smiles. "You mean you don't know who he is. I think

immaculate conception may be pushing even your weirdness a little too far."

I think about this. "If I have a father, then I don't know who he is."

Vee gives me a hard stare, but I am not going to add anything to this statement. It is as true as I can make it.

"Your mother is dead," I say.

"Yes, she's dead. Drank herself to death. Bitch." Vee doesn't look at me now but goes back to tracing the vinyl chicken with her forefinger. "She couldn't stand my father, but she couldn't leave him either. I don't know why. At least when she was alive she stopped him from using me."

"Do you love her?"

"Stupid bitch," she says quietly. I can see that she loves her, but she is angry at her. We return to our silence, but it is now more contemplative.

Our drinks arrive. I sip my tea. It is not Chinese. I will have to tell Black Beard when he comes back. Vee drinks her milkshake from a tall, scratched plastic glass. It looks cold.

"We'll get caught, you know," she says. "And we'll have to go to prison."

"Probably, but we have no choice now. You have seen the world of the Dark Chorus. You know we have to do this, have to cleanse the Angel's soul. We have been chosen."

"I don't mind going to prison. I don't mind dying. I'm already tired of this life." As she says this, she rubs a forearm gently. I have seen her do this before.

I say nothing, but look at her and sip my tea. She notices me looking.

"None of your fucking business," she says, abruptly removing her hand from her forearm.

I say nothing, but wait. It is as good as a question.

"I said it's none of your business. Don't you listen?" She glares at me defiantly for a moment and then seems to sag with the effort. She rolls up a sleeve. Along her arm are scars from numerous cuts. I count them. Twelve. One of them is fresh and raw.

"Why?" I say.

"To take the pain away. Because I deserve it. Just because."

Pain dulls pain. One form overrides the other, but the physical pain will ease as the body heals. The mental pain, however, takes much more time to heal, if it ever does. Vee's mental pain is deep. It takes a lot of courage and physical pain to endure it.

I wonder if I could take her pain away, and if I could, whether I would? I need her pain to be able to cleanse the Angel. I consider this as we sit in the false light of the café and decide not to try. I promise myself that as soon as this is over, I will do everything to help Vee.

I feel sad.

The Angel asks a lot of us, but we must endure. We must restore the Angel and save the Dark Chorus.

The food arrives, and I complain about the tea.

"Sorry, little buddy, I was pulling your leg. We've only got good old builders' tea, I'm afraid."

Vee and I eat. I decide to consume my food according to its size. It is quite difficult to decide which is bigger, the sausages or the fried eggs. In the end I go for plate coverage and so start with the eggs.

Just as we finish, the door bangs open and Makka is back. He drops down into the seat next to Vee.

"Good news, yeah? I got a pay-as-you-go sim card for the phone and called Bill. He says he's sorting out somewhere over in Deptford where we can crash, yeah? Says to meet him at the Crypt on the high street at midnight on Saturday. It's where the band are playing." Vee and I say nothing. "It's a venue, you pair of nadgers." He waves at Black Beard who puts his thumb up and disappears into the kitchen.

"OK, I've gotta good feeling about tonight. I reckon it's time to kill The Fuck. Yeah?"

I nod. I wonder what nadgers are.

"I don't think we should risk you coming along, Vee. If it goes tits up, The Fuck will hand you back to your old man and that's not gonna happen."

Vee starts to object, but is cut off mid-breath.

"No fucking arguing, Vee." He looks directly at her, his face fixed. He isn't going to budge in this, and Vee can see it. She blows out her breath of objection.

"OK," she says. "I'll head across town and take out some cash with my dad's card. He'll probably notice and think we're heading south."

"Yeah, good idea. Fake trail and that. I like it."

Makka's food arrives and he attacks it in no particular order. I really don't know how people can do that. He is silent for a few moments as he concentrates on his late-night breakfast.

"We'll meet at the Crypt in Deptford tomorrow night, yeah?" says Makka as he stabs at a mushroom. He waves it around on the end of his fork. "And, like I said, Bill's sorting a place we can crash for a while." He eats the mushroom and grins at us. He looks happy. I think it's at the prospect of killing his father.

***

The sergeant flicked the light switch. A fluorescent tube coughed into life like a tar-afflicted smoker. Eve didn't think it had long to live.

"The jars," said the sergeant and waved an expansive hand through the air as if he were introducing a famous rock band.

Eve looked at them. "And which one contains the Boy's mother's soul?"

"Ah, well. There was a bit of an oversight with that. The specific jar is here, but was put back without a label. I don't think anyone thought it that special." He gave an apologetic smile. "They are almost all exactly the same, all empty but for an unlit night-light."

Eve sighed a quiet 'bloody hell'.

"It's almost certainly one of the ones at the front here." The sergeant picked up a jar. "This one perhaps?" He had chosen a jar from the table in front of them. It was covered in jars, dozens of them. There were two other tables in the room, one to the left and one to the right and they were also covered in jars.

Eve was amazed at just how many jars there were and at the

dedication the Boy had shown to collect so many souls. She corrected herself – imaginary souls. He had said it had taken him months; he had listened and captured each one, soul by soul until he had heard his mother. Such a bizarre love. A displacement activity to allay his perceived guilt? A schizophrenic aberration? A psychotic reality? The Boy's words flicked across her consciousness – 'Find my mother's soul Dr Rhodes'. Or perhaps reality? Oh, for goodness' sake.

The sergeant's radio blossomed into chatter. He played with the volume control, as if mimicking his job-sakes from the films, and then made some unintelligible police noises into its transmitter.

"Apologies, Doctor Rhodes," he said once he had finished. "I'm needed elsewhere for a bit. You'll be OK on your own for a moment or two, won't you?"

Eve nodded. "Sure. You do whatever it is you need to do. I'll be here when you get back."

"Good," he said as he headed out of the room. "Won't be long." He disappeared in a cloud of crackled acronyms and polished squeaks. The door clicked shut behind him.

It was now just Eve and the jars. Souls?

How the hell was she supposed to know which was the Boy's mother? She relaxed herself, tried to open her mind and then as quietly as possible she looked, really looked.

But did not see.

Damn it. This was ridiculous. What was she thinking? Why was she even here? This was all the making of the Boy's psychotic delusion and she had, foolishly, let herself be manipulated. She had persuaded herself that it was professional curiosity that had bought her here, but that was rubbish – utter rubbish.

She made to go, and switched off the terminally ill light. Darkness was welcomed back, but before she could turn the door handle a light flared up behind her and flicked shadows across the walls. She let her hand fall to her side and closed her eyes. She already knew what she would see when she turned because she could feel it, hear it – the dancing chatter of a soul.

She turned and opened her eyes to see a jar on the front row of the main table alight. Its night-light burnt bright and captured in its flame was a paua-shell-coloured soul – the mother's soul.

Eve picked up the jar and held it close to her face. It was so beautiful that it made her tremble. And then, as if its revelation were a catalyst, other jars started to light up, other souls revealed themselves. One by one they flicked into life until the room was saturated by the celestial light of the Dark Chorus.

She felt tears fall from her eyes, tears of astonishment, of joy, and of despair.

The door opened. The Dark Chorus disappeared.

"What are you doing in the dark?" said the sergeant from behind her. "You all right?"

With minimal fuss, and out of sight of the intruder, Eve put the jar into her oversized handbag. The sergeant switched the light back on. Its cough was even worse this time.

"I'm fine," she said. "Just trying to see things the way the Boy might see them." She turned and looked at the policeman. "He's as mad as a box of broken cheese crackers, you know. That's a shrink's technical term, by the way." She smiled. There was no hint of the earlier tears. Like the lit jars they belonged to the other world.

"Well, you said it." He laughed and looked at the table. "Do you reckon you know which one is supposed to contain his mum's soul?"

"Not a clue," said Eve as she zipped her handbag shut. "Shall we go?"

Chapter Eighteen

The bus hisses at me angrily, annoyed that it has had to stop. It folds away its batwing doors, daring me to enter. I accept its challenge and step up into its warm body.

"Can we sit upstairs?" I say.

Makka rolls his eyes which I take as a 'yes', so ascend the curved staircase. I want to sit at the front, but those seats are taken so I choose one three rows back on the left-hand side. I slide into the seat by the window. The seat covers are patterned, blue and orange, different from the tube seats, but comfortingly similar. I stroke the fabric.

Makka drops down next to me. He hasn't said anything for a while now. I think he is wondering what it will be like to kill his father. It is not something I can imagine as I don't know who my father is.

The bus moves off in a series of short growling accelerations accompanied by the percussion of vibrations playing out unique rhythms as resonance frequencies are reached and passed through. No sooner have we set off than we are slowing, the bus readying itself for the next stop. More sounds. I expect them to be backwards, a reflection, the opposite to those of acceleration, but they are not. They are their own sound, proud and different and independent.

The darkness of the evening emphasises the illumination of any light. As the bus moves down street after street I am able to look directly into people's lives. Their curtain less windows offer me snapshots, a moment in their time, frame after frame: a boy with wide eyes stares at me from an empty room, a family sit on a sofa watching television and eating crisps, an old man is writing at a desk, a couple are cooking and drinking wine, a girl does her make-up, an old lady sits looking at a clock, two men are playing a video game – I see so many people, doing so many different things. Being on a bus at night is the most interesting of things to do. I tell Makka this.

"Some might consider that a bit pervy, yeah? Voyeuristic." He runs his hand over his face. "Still, people are interesting I suppose, but they're also twats. I don't trust most of them. They'll let you down big time." He turns to look at me. "Just when you need the fuckers to stand by you, the selfish bastards will piss off and leave you in the shit. Yeah? That's what people do." He turns to look forward again. "Twats."

He says nothing else. I think he will tell me more eventually. Like me, he is a product of two worlds, neither of which he fits into. Not yet.

I look out of the window again and catch a framed shot of a girl getting dressed. I don't think it perverted, just a matter of curiosity. A voyeur by circumstance.

The girl has beautiful chestnut-coloured hair.

***

The street is very still, as if it's holding its breath, afraid that someone will notice it. Makka is also worried about being noticed.

"Listen, we gotta keep invisible. Yeah? This is not a good place for someone like me to be seen in. You understand?"

I don't.

"No," I say.

"I'm a Paki to the people that live round here. They'll do me if they notice, so let's keep the hoodies up. Yeah?"

We keep walking. Makka has his head down so you can't really see his face, but his body is taut, ready to fight. A savageness radiates from him. I count the door numbers. "Twelve, fourteen." A car whistles past us. "Sixteen, eighteen, twenty." A motorcycle pours down the street vomiting noise as it goes. "Twenty-two." We stop, facing a small end-of-terrace house. Its unkempt dirt-brown door is set right on the street, two brick widths from the corner of the house, which forms part of an alleyway. Light leaks out from a gap in the curtain, dripping on to the street. Someone is in the front room. A door opens further down the street, and Makka pulls me into the alleyway. We wait quietly as a couple of voices, one low and rumbling and the other sharp and barking, exchange undefined words. They drift away from us, off into the night.

"Listen," says Makka. "We'll knock on the door. As soon as The Fuck answers it, I'll kick it in, punch him hard in the face and then stick him with this." He pulls a six-inch-blade kitchen knife from his pocket. It looks like the one that lived in a drawer in the flat. "It won't kill him straight away, so you'll have time to set up your stuff. Then we cut his throat and set fire to him and you can collect his soul. Yeah?"

I nod.

"Ready?"

I nod again and pat my bag.

I follow Makka out of the alleyway and once again stand in front of the dirt-brown door. Makka bangs on it. I can hear someone coming. Makka tenses himself. The door opens a fraction and a face peers out, but before they can register who we are Makka kicks the door open with the flat of his foot. It hits the peering face between the eyes and the person rocks backwards. Makka is through the doorway in an instant, punching the face hard. I can hear a dull thump as his fist makes contact. The victim falls backwards into the hallway. I step into the house and quietly shut the door. It's all over in seconds.

Makka pulls out the knife and gets ready to stab the fallen man.

"FUCK," he says, looking down on a woman. "FUCKING FUCK." I think Makka is going to explode in anger and despair. He leans down, grabs the woman by the front of her jumper and pulls her up so her bloodied face is inches from his. "Who the fucking hell are you?"

I can see the woman trying to focus on him, but she is having problems. "Stacy," she says. "What the fuck do you want?" The words are a little slurred.

"Where's Garland?" Makka shakes her. "Where the fuck is he?"

Stacy tries to push him off. "Not here. He's out. Now fuck off. When he hears what you've done to me he'll kill you."

Makka lets her go and she falls back to the floor.

"A Paki in his house. He'll kill you."

Makka kicks her in the ribs. She grunts and curls up into a ball.

Makka pulls at his ponytail. "Fuck," he says again.

Stacy starts to whimper. I think her beaten face is hurting.

"Shut it," says Makka, but doesn't kick her again. "OK. We can't stay here until tomorrow 'cause we'll get caught by the whole fucking Nazi neighbourhood." He paces down the hall and then back. "So we'll leave The Fuck a message, yeah? And then get out of here." He points at Stacy. "Look at her and tell me."

I know what he is asking.

I crouch down next to Stacy. She uncurls and looks at me. Tears drop from her eyes.

"Tell him what?" she asks. Her speech is halting. I catch her gaze and enter her mind. There is pain and anger and hate and love.

A small but bright-blue spinning cloud of love.

It is beautiful.

I take a moment to enjoy its radiance and then hunt down her soul. It is as expected, infected, grey with large black blotches. However, I can see a tiny bright paua-coloured dot floating in amongst the darkness. Resistance? Maybe, but I think it will soon be lost.

I exit.

Makka looks at me.

"Almost black," I say.

"That's good enough." He grabs her by the collar of her jumper and drags her into the front room. She squeals and tries to hit him, kicking her legs this way and that trying to free herself. Makka dumps her on the floor and puts the knife to her throat.

"Shut the fuck up," he says.

The room contains a worn-out sofa, a cheap wooden coffee table with a pile of magazines, an overflowing ashtray, and a half-drunk cup of coffee sitting on it, and a large-screen TV. The beige walls have no pictures hanging on them and the carpet looks threadbare.

The room is neglected as, I think, is Stacy. This is not a happy place.

"Find me something to tie her up with," Makka says.

I head down the short hallway to a kitchen and look in the cupboards and drawers. There isn't much to find, but in an old ice-cream carton I locate, amongst some nails and screws and some rusting keys, a roll of green insulating tape. I give it to Makka. He binds up her hands and feet.

"Please," says Stacy. "What are you going to do? What do you mean 'good enough'?" Her hair, which was pulled back, has come loose and some of it is stuck to her bloodied face.

Makka rips off three pieces of the tape and sticks them together to make a much wider piece.

"We're going to kill you," he says as he sticks the tape over her mouth. "And he," nodding towards me, "is going to steal your soul."

Stacy's eyes go wide in terror. I can feel it pouring of her, drenching the room. She starts to shake and mumble into the tape.

I crouch down beside her again and look at her and wonder at the tiny paua shell dot and the bright blue of her love. Perhaps they are connected. And as I think this, I have the strongest of feelings that I am being watched. And whoever is watching me feels familiar.

I turn and look to the doorway.

"Get the fuck on with it," says Makka. "We gotta get gone, yeah?"

I get up and walk out of the room.

"Where the fuck are you going?"

I don't answer, but stand at the bottom of the stairs looking up. Looking down at me is a young girl. I think she is about four or five. She is carrying a faded-grey toy rabbit. I catch her gaze just for a moment, long enough. And now I know.

"What is your name?" I say.

She looks at her rabbit and then holds it up. "This is

Rabbit," she says.

I nod.

She clutches Rabbit to her chest. "My name is Holly and I'm almost five."

"What the fuck are you doing?" shouts Makka. "The bitch is going mad in here."

I can hear thumps and the banging of feet on the floor. I ignore the noise.

"Come down," I say. "I want you to meet someone."

Holly comes down the stairs carefully. "I don't want to fall," she says. "I fell once. It hurt, and daddy was cross."

I put out my hand, and she takes it. I lead her into the front room.

"What the . . . who the fuck is this?" Makka seems exasperated. He's got Stacy pinned to the floor. She is wriggling and kicking, but stops when she sees Holly.

"This is Holly," I say.

"Who gives a shit?" says Makka letting Stacy go and standing up.

"She's your half-sister." This is not what Makka was expecting. There is a moment of unexpected stillness – his anger is stunned.

Holly looks at her mother lying on the floor and then at Makka. She goes over to him and holds out her little grey rabbit.

"This is Rabbit," she says. "You can hold him if you like. He'll make you feel all happy." She waves Rabbit at him and its floppy ears leap about. Makka reaches down and with exaggerated care takes the toy. I can see him looking at his hands, one holds a knife and the other a toy rabbit. I suspect he is quite surprised by this.

Holly crouches down by her mother. "Mummy, you're crying red tears again." Stacy makes a muffled sob and closes her eyes. Holly peels away the green insulating tape from her mother's mouth.

"Please," says Stacy. "Please don't hurt her. Please." Holly sits down beside her mother.

Makka says nothing. We wait. A car goes by, its engine

misfiring. We wait.

Makka takes a deep breath.

"Right. You live," he says looking down at Stacy. "You live because of her. Yeah? Only because of her. The boy here can see your soul and he says it's almost black. I don't know if you can change that, but you better fucking try 'cause we're going to come back and if it's still black we'll take it. You understand?"

Stacy nods.

"Did Garland tell you about me?"

Stacy shakes her head. "No."

"Yeah, well that's not a surprise. He raped my mother, yeah? And she killed herself because of that. Because of him." Makka points at Holly and himself. "We will be fatherless soon 'cause I'm goin' to kill The Fuck so she'll only have you, right? And that's why you live for now. I don't want her to have no one. Yeah?"

Stacy nods again. "Yes, I understand."

Makka looks at me. "We're going." He waves his arm at the room. "I think The Fuck will get the message."

He walks to the doorway, puts the knife in his pocket and turns back to Holly. He throws Rabbit to her.

"Thanks," he says.

"Bye-bye," says Holly, and we leave.

The street is not as we left it. It now feels brooding with menace. Makka is walking at a furious pace and I have to trot to keep up, the Soul Stone banging against the other contents of my bag. His mind is elsewhere. I think it was right not to kill Stacy, but I had to let Makka make that decision. This part of our story is his, and that is why I didn't tell him about the beautiful blue in Stacy's mind.

A man stands in the entrance to a house talking to someone while the sound of a television drifts out from the open door. We walk by without Makka registering their presence, without even a sideways glance. He doesn't have his hood up.

We walk past the next house before a voice shouts after us.

"Hey, you, Paki. Who the fuck do you think you are? Gandhi or somethin'?" The voice laughs, but there is no humour in it. "Oi, I'm talking to you, chapatti. What the fuck are you doing down this street? Cocky cunt or somethin'?"

I look back and the man is starting to walk after us. Two men come out of the house. One is carrying what I think is a baseball bat.

"Makka," I say pulling on his sleeve. "Do we play baseball in this country?"

"What?" My voice seems to bring Makka out of is reverie.

"Do we play baseball in this country?"

"Oi, you fucking Paki. Come 'ere," says the voice.

Makka turns. I can see him come back to the present, his neck muscles tense, his eyes take everything in.

"No," he says to me. "It's not a fucking sport. Now RUN!"

So we do. But I can't keep up with Makka. I follow him down a side road that ends up by a canal. As I round the corner, Makka grabs me and more less throws me on to a canal barge. It has a tarpaulin over it and Makka forces me under it.

"Don't make a fucking noise. Meet me at the Crypt in Deptford tomorrow night." He slings in his bag pulls down the tarpaulin and runs. Almost immediately, I hear the men come round the corner shouting, their voices all mixed up – angry and excited. They blow past me like a siren on a police car. No one stops.

I am at the back of the barge, sitting in an entrance well. It smells of oil and dirt and rotting vegetables. The boat hasn't been used in a long while, and it seems to have given up on doing anything other than dying by slow decay. I raise the tarpaulin slightly to see what I can see, and what I see is Makka standing in the middle of a footbridge over the canal. The Voice and his two friends have blocked off one end and are posturing, pointing, shouting, but not going in for the kill. Makka, has his back to them, ignoring them. He is concentrating on a man walking towards him from the other side.

Makka is radiating overpowering rage and hate. I think the man must be The Fuck, must be Garland, must be Makka's father. The Fuck walks up to Makka and only stops when they are face to face. I don't think they have said anything to each other up to this point, but it is hard to say as I am too far away to hear. The Voice and friends move to surround the pair. I don't like what is going on. I need Makka to help me cleanse the soul, but the tight knot in my stomach also tells me that it is not only this that makes me worry, but that my friend will get hurt. I want to help. I try to summon the Angel to tear the soul out of The Fuck's body as it did to the Griffin, but it remains stoically unresponsive. Perhaps it has been sated by its recent feeding.

The Voice is standing behind Makka, and as I watch he takes a step forward and pushes him violently in the back. Makka staggers, but it is a controlled stagger, as if he was expecting the push. He barges into The Fuck, grabbing him by the throat and driving him backwards. With legs pumping Makka forces The Fuck at speed. They hit the low railing of the footbridge and pitch over it in one continuous move. A howl of pain reaches me. It is The Fuck, but the howl is cut off as he and Makka hit the cold, dark water of the canal and disappear.

The Voice and his friends peer over the railing shouting for The Fuck. I watch them run across the bridge and disappear behind its façade. A moment later they appear with The Fuck. He has his hands on the small of his back and appears to be in some pain.

Good.

The others then start to run up and down the canal bank looking for Makka, but there is no sign of him. After five minutes they give up. They cross the bridge and walk past my hiding place.

"Do ya think he's dead?" asks the Voice.

"I fuckin' hope so," says one of the other voices. It could be The Fuck.

"I dunno," says another voice. "Pakis are hard to kill. The fuckers never know when to give up."

Their voices trail off as they disappear down the side street and back to their homes. Traffic makes a distant noise, but I am listening to the silence of the water, straining to hear anything that breaks its acoustic banality, but there is nothing.

I feel pain, the same pain that I felt when I failed to bring my mother back to life.

I am at a loss. Lost.

I need maternal help and so focus on my mother's soul. I can feel the ethereal thread joining us and I sit back in the dark of the tarpaulin and let this connection calm me, comfort me, hold me.

After a time, I feel a little better and find myself reflecting on the comment of one of the voices – *Pakis are hard to kill. The fuckers never know when to give up* – and I have to believe, however defamatory, that the statement is true. I must believe Makka is alive. In fact, I think I would feel it in my soul if he were dead. Once again, I realise that I am feeling sorry for myself and that won't do.

I sling Makka's bag over my shoulder and scramble out from under the tarpaulin and head for the bridge. I cross it and turn left following the canal path. I don't know which way the Crypt is so I think I will head for the noisy road. Someone there will be able to tell me the way. Every so often I stop and crouch down to see if I can see Makka. I call out his name in a quiet shout, but the dark water ignores me.

Something is prodding my mind. I let the something tell me what it is and nod to myself. So, my mother has moved. Dr Rhodes must have her now and, despite the situation I find myself in, I smile.

Chapter Nineteen

I am not sure how long I've been walking as I don't have a watch, but I think it must be about an hour. As I pass a large, dirty Victorian brick building, a bell rings. I stop and take a proper look at the building. It is a Baptist chapel and I know this because it says so above the door. As I look higher up, I can just make out the faint ripple of the air as the single 'bong' radiates out from the hidden bell. I am in two minds as to whether I can actually see the ripple, but there are so many ways to see, feel, and hear the world that it wouldn't surprise me if I could. If it is self-deception then I'll go along with it because I can't see that it does me any harm. The ripple fades away.

Adjacent to the chapel is a small garden. A gravel path leads to a wooden bench over which presides an ornamental lamp post. It is barely lit and seems to mimic the damp light of a Victorian street gas lamp. I like that. It is a bench set in an earlier time. I think I'll sit on it for a moment and do a bit of time travelling.

The bench is the colour of pollution, its original hue long since gone. There is a dull brass plaque screwed to the seat's back that reads *Arnold Layne – a musical gardener*. I wonder if this means Arnold was a gardener who was a musician or whether he was someone who gardened music. I like my second thought – it has interesting imagery.

I put my hands flat on the seat beside me, pull my knees together and let myself relax. I have not done this for a while. I know I am lost, but also know that if I sit here quietly a solution to this problem will find its way to me. I close my eyes and gently breathe in through my nose and out through my mouth and let my mind wander.

I become aware of a second breath, breathing in time with my own. I open my eyes slowly. Sitting facing me, is a fox. Her bright eyes reflect the dim light and she is looking straight at me, straight into me. I let her and wonder what she sees. She is so beautiful. After a moment she gets up, takes a few steps towards me, turns, and then sits down again at my feet with her back to me. Her tail is fluffed up and she wraps it around her more like a cat than a dog.

We sit together for a while and watch the traffic flit by. The interval between each burst of noise and mechanical muscular motion becomes less, and the sound that is the background to the city becomes our shared silence. Eventually she gets up, stretches, and with the briefest of looks acknowledges our time together and trots off.

I stand and stretch too. I have a strong feeling that help is not far away.

I step back into the now and head off down the street leaving the chapel to its thoughts. The road opens up. Shops and office blocks fall away, and the vista broadens offering me the dark waters of the Thames whose rippling surface is adorned with flakes of light bobbing up and down on its surface.

A large sandstone road bridge with thick vase-shaped balusters spans the river. I venture out across the bridge, and the further I go the further I can see up and down the river's vast twisting body. I reach the middle and peer over the edge, watching the water flow underneath, watching to see if Makka should float by, perhaps spat out into the Thames from a tributary. He doesn't. I am beginning to feel he might be dead, and the thought starts to numb my brain. I stand back and look up at the sky. It's clear and sparkly and beautiful. I banish the thought as an unworthy one and set off to finish crossing the bridge.

As I do so I come across a man leaning against the bridge's balustrade. He is not looking out into the water but moves his gaze from one end of the bridge to the other and back again. He stops as I draw level with him. He seems interested in me and gives me a curious look – a holistic stare is the best I can describe it. His eyes narrow a bit and I think he is a little confused by whatever it is he sees, but he says nothing. I smile at him and keep walking. The world is full of interesting people.

As I reach the bridge's far end I notice a set of wide steps leading down and then under the structure. I hear a dog bark and the voice of a man rising up on its own hot thermal.

I descend.

I am curious to see what is going on. There is a large concrete landing halfway down tucked beneath the edge of the bridge. An old man, holding on to a dog's collar, is sitting in a sleeping bag surrounded by plastic bags and bits of cardboard is being shouted at by a well-dressed young man. I think the young man is drunk. He sways about, rolling this way and that as the force of his abusive language almost knocks him off his feet. Two other similarly dressed men are laughing and encouraging their friend to greater verbosity.

". . . and you're a fucking loser. You think I'll just give you money. Well, loser, fuck you, think again. Get yourself a job like any decent person. But you're not decent are you, you're just a cretinous hobo."

The old man says nothing, but keeps tight hold of the dog's collar. Its ferocious barking adds to the noise of the scene, which is in turn amplified as it bounces around the concrete-walled landing. The dog is a small animal with floppy ears and brown patches on a white coat. I have seen a picture of a cow with the same markings. It is called a short horn.

"Shut that fucking mutt up." The young man swings a foot at it but misses. The old man pulls the dog back and hugs it protectively, shielding it from further attack.

"Leave 'im alone. I don't want no trouble," he says.

"Too late, you pissy old shit," says the young man and he leans forward. "You stink." He grabs the man by the front of his coat and punches him. He's too drunk to make much contact but the old man's head still jerks back.

"Come on, you old fuck. Fight back." He rabbit-punches him again. "You coward. Come on."

The old man just hugs the dog tighter. "We just don't want

no trouble," he says. "Please."

The young man stands up, swaying badly. He turns to his friends who are now leaning against the wall and look like they are having trouble staying upright. He points to the old man. "What a loser." As he looks back, he notices me.

"Oi, spaso, fuck off."

I don't move.

He takes a couple of steps towards me. "Are you a retard or something? I told you to fuck off." He manages to focus on me, and I catch his drunken stare. A mix of arrogance, self-obsession and fear whirl around in dark reds and burnt blues. I look at his soul and allow him to see it too.

He takes a step back as if I had slapped him. "Fucking hell. You're some kind of freak," he says. "I'm right, you are a spaso retard." He says this for his own benefit. He is frightened by what he saw but hides it with bravado so his friends don't notice. "Come on," he says to them. "Let's leave these pair of fucking losers to their shitty worthless lives." He stumbles off and his friends follow.

The dog stops barking, and the old man lets him go. The dog walks over to me. I let him sniff my hand and he wags his tail. The old man rubs his beaten, bearded face. "He seems to like you," he says. "He don't like many. You must be a good 'un."

"Does your face hurt?" I ask.

"A bit. I've 'ad worse." He sniffs loudly. "What you doin' out so late? Runaway or summat?"

"Summat," I say, and he laughs.

"Well, you sit down for a bit. You look tired, lad."

I nod.

"I got some cardboard here," he says, and puts a large piece down next to him. "That'll keep a bit of the cold off your backside."

I sit down and the dog comes and sits between us.

"Here." The man hands me a blanket and I tuck it in around me. It smells of so many different things I can't really distinguish any of the them individually. The overall effect isn't that pleasant, but it is warm.

I scratch the top of the dog's head.

"He's called Crisp on account of him liking to eat crisps, although he's not too keen on the cheese and onion. I reckon it's the onion he takes against." He rubs Crisp's back, and the dog flops down, head on paws. From inside his coat, the old man pulls out a tired-looking, dirty leather pouch tied securely with a piece of string. He unties it and fumbles about inside producing a cigarette paper and tiny amount of dry-looking tobacco.

"Vee smokes," I say.

"Vee?" He rolls the tobacco inside the paper and licks it shut.

"She is my friend, and she likes to smoke."

"Oh, right. Well, I bet she don't smoke stale old dog ends like me, eh? Just as well, 'cause they're as rough as an elephant's arse." He offers me the pouch. "Smoke?"

"No, thank you."

"Well, that's probably a good thing. They can give you cancer and stuff, but I ain't worried. I enjoy a smoke an' there ain't many things left to enjoy from where I'm sittin'."

I look about. "No."

The old man lights the thin little cigarette and inhales deeply and with considerable pleasure. "Ah, that's good," he says letting smoke pour from his nose and mouth. He closes his eyes and puts his head back and we sit like that while he slowly inhales his way through what Vee would call a 'rollie'.

"Why didn't you fight back?" I ask when he has finished.

"Ah, well, I don't take much to fightin'. Not now."

"Why?"

"Why? We'll it ain't good to fight. A lot of bad comes from it. A lot of bad." The old man strokes Crisp and stares into a memory. I say nothing but sit in silence. Silence has its own time and its own space, and I can see the old man is elsewhere.

I wait.

The drumming sound of a diesel engine climbs the stairs from the lower road, investigates our landing and then moves on up and away, disappearing into the night. A food wrapper stained with what looks like red and yellow sauce from whatever it had enclosed drifts down from the bridge above and settles amongst the many plastic bags the old man has around him. Crisp yawns.

"Do you think it's good to fight?" asks the old man.

I don't know so I say nothing. He looks at me. "Well, it ain't." He rubs his sore face again. "I used to think it was. In fact, I used to enjoy goin' out on a Friday or Saturday night lookin' for a scrap. Yeah, I did enjoy that." He nods. "I was pretty good with me fists and that. Too good as it turned out." He clenches his right hand making a fist. "Killed him, you see. Only took one blow. They say he was dead before he hit the ground. Weak skull, see." He looks at his fist and then relaxes it. "Well, I went to jail and that was right. I didn't mean to kill 'im, but I did, and I was punished." He looks around the cold, dirty concrete landing. "And all this livin' on the street is my continued punishment." He sighs. "I can't shake the guilt, and I suppose I'm not supposed to." He turns and looks at me. "To kill a man is a terrible thing." He continues to stare, and I meet his gaze, but don't catch it. "A terrible thing."

He strokes the dog again. "Who's a good boy, eh, Crisp?" At the mention of his name, Crisp thumps his tail on the cardboard flooring.

"What if you knew the man was evil?" I ask.

"Ya can't know that. There's no way to measure a person's badness."

"I can."

"Naa. No one can, lad. We just think we can."

"I can see their soul."

The old man strokes Crisp some more. "Ya can, can ya?"

"Yes."

"And how can ya tell if a soul is a bad un?"

I pull my legs up a bit and make myself a little more comfortable. "They change colour. They go from a beautiful mix of blue and turquoise and silver and green, the colour of a paua shell, to black – tar black."

"I dunno what a paua shell is, but it does sound beautiful. How black does a soul have to be before you reckon you could take a man's life then?"

I think about this. Stacy's soul was black but not completely black. She was almost gone, and it would only have been a matter of time before it would have succumbed to the inevitable. Inevitable? I think so, but I don't know so. Maybe it would have been wrong to have taken her soul. She did have that beautiful paua shell dot of love buried in amongst the tar. Could that have saved her?

"I reckon," says the old man as I haven't replied to his question, "that whatever anyone 'as done, they deserve the chance of redemption. I suppose I *would* say that, but I do really think that is right. Even that posh twat that punched me."

The posh twat's soul was pretty black, but it still had some way to go. I wanted to take his soul anyway. I didn't like him. Part of me feels this is a perfectly good reason to have taken it, but I can see this is not logical; it isn't an empiric rule. Crisp licks my hand.

The old man smiles a lopsided smile as his right cheek is swelling up.

"My advice to you, lad, if in doubt do the kind thing, eh?"

I like Crisp and I like the old man, so I think I'll believe that it is possible for a soul's redemption if that soul is not pure black. I'll make a rule. I will only take and feed pure black souls to the Angel. I'll call it Crisp's Law.

"OK," I say. "Can you tell me how to get to Maida Vale?"

Chapter Twenty

Once again, Eve was awake early. She was a little annoyed; it was a Saturday and she deserved the lie in.

She was about to make a cup of tea but then changed her mind. Why not treat herself to a cooked breakfast this morning? As soon as she thought this, her stomach rumbled and she felt her tastes buds reacting to the virtual egg, bacon and toast they had conjured up.

She took Professor Doyle's approach to getting dressed and selected clothes on the basis that they came to hand first and not whether they went together in any way. The result was more than a little alarming, but she rolled with the self-inflicted punch. She was in that sort of mood.

The day was overcast and surprisingly windy. The trees on the avenue were having their branches flicked about by petulant gusts. Twigs broke off in a random shower of dead wood, landing on any car parked up on the street for the night, before being bundled along in mischievous encouragement to collide with anything that dared to get in the way. Eve enjoyed the tussle.

She made it to the cafe and its calm interior. Black-and-white photos of coffee beans, men serving coffee in the 1960s, and beautiful young woman in miniskirts adorned the rough brick walls. Solid wooden tables with tiny tin buckets that held teaspoons and forks were neatly arranged along each wall. It was a generic boutique coffee shop with one distinguishing feature that the other coffee clones didn't have; it served cooked breakfasts, proper cooked breakfasts.

"Windy out," said an old lady sitting by the window.

Eve felt obliged to answer. "Yes. Very."

"But only in one direction," said the old lady. "That's a bit of luck in't it?"

Eve looked out of the window. Christ alive – it was her day off. "Yep, very lucky." She went and sat several tables down and away from mad old lady chit-chat.

She ordered an egg, bacon and mushroom breakfast, a side order of toast, and a cafe latte – two shots. She found a copy of *The Week* magazine in the newspaper rack and got stuck into that while she waited.

She was so engrossed in an article on the effect of global warming on the polar bear population in the Artic that she nearly leapt out of her seat when the Boy said, "Hello Dr Rhodes."

She breathed in deeply through her nose and steadied herself.

"Hello," she said.

"You said you wanted to talk to me."

"Yes, I did, didn't I." Eve looked around. "Where are Makka and Victoria?"

The Boy looked slightly puzzled. "Victoria? You mean Vee, I think."

"Is that what she calls herself?"

"Yes."

"OK. Well, where are they?"

He didn't answer. Eve tried again. "Are they about somewhere?"

"Yes." He smiled. "About is right." A strange answer, but then he was a very strange boy.

"Sit down," said Eve. "I expect you'd like a cup of tea. Would you like anything else?"

"Can I have some toast as well?"

"Sure." Eve caught the attention of the girl behind the counter. She ordered the extra food.

The Boy's appearance was markedly different from when she had last seen him properly at the youth detention centre. Then, he'd been dressed in clean clothes, his blond hair washed and cut, and his face clear and pale. Now he was dirty. His parka was stained, his face and hands grubby and his hair had grown and needed a wash. He also looked tired.

He sat down opposite her without taking off his parka or removing the two courier bags whose straps crossed over his chest giving him the appearance of a Cromwellian New Model Army child soldier. And she supposed in his own and disturbing way he was a child soldier. He sat still while she took in his appearance. She looked into his eyes. Had he changed at all? Unlike the rest of him they were clear and bright. She felt caught in their gaze, and a sudden urge to help him, to believe in his fantasy welled up in her consciousness and then, as quickly as it had arrived, it disbursed itself, ebbing away to leave a faint but persistent echo.

He smiled at her.

"You've been busy," she said.

"I expect you disapprove."

"Yes, but I now understand why you do it. I know about Banuism and Charles Janenssen."

"Good. I hoped you would understand. I left those messages for you. It's important that you understand."

"Really? Why?"

The Boy looked down at his hands, which he had placed palm down on the tops of his thighs. She could see that he was struggling with the question. The vulnerability he'd displayed at their detention centre interview was back again. Guilt? Guilt about his mother?

"I will tell you at our next meeting." He looked up and the chink in his emotional armour disappeared.

Their drinks arrived. The Boy put his face over the mug of tea and let the tendrils of rising steam caress his skin. Eve had the urge to do likewise, but the steamed milk of her cafe latte was a poor substitute. As she watched, his face relaxed and for a moment he looked like the child that he was and as far removed from a serial killer as you could get.

"You will get caught you know, and soon. So our next meeting may well be at the police station."

"Yes, I know we'll get caught, but not before we have completed the tasks we have set ourselves." The Boy took a sip of tea.

Damn it. More people were going to die. Perhaps she ought

to grab him now and call the police because asking him to stop was pointless; his world was just too real to him. No, not too real. It *was* his world.

"So, are you going to collect more corrupt souls to help restore the fallen angel to heaven?"

"Yes. It is the last shard of the angel's soul."

"And you have this soul inside you somewhere?"

"Yes. It sits alongside my own soul. I can't put it aside and forget about it. It's with me until I die or until I can cleanse it. I have no choice in the matter." He paused to take another sip of tea. "I am what Banuism refers to as Arta – the righteous."

"As was Charles Janenssen?"

"Yes, and many others before him."

"Can anyone be Arta?"

"No, but you could have been."

"Me?" Eve was a little taken aback. "Why me? What is it that makes someone open to being Arta?"

"When you were young, Dr Rhodes, I think you saw another world, one of reflection and shadows. I think you have seen it recently, but your mind has put it aside supposing it to be a figment of your imagination. I told you that I removed the filter that stopped Mrs Johnson from seeing my world. Well, you removed that filter yourself when you were young, when loneliness and guilt absorbed you. You don't have a filter, but you have trained your mind not to see that world anymore. This is why you could be Arta. You can see other worlds, and I think you have caught sight of mine. You have seen the Dark Chorus."

She tried to stay calm. There was no way he could know that she had seen, no, *thought* she had seen. albeit very briefly, the lit candle and flickering soul of his mother.

"Most people during childhood have imaginary friends or see imaginary worlds," she said. Especially those with attachment issues as she had. The Boy nodded.

"Of course, but you know your world was different. It was real. It still is – as is mine."

Their conversation was interrupted by the food arriving. The Boy cut his toast into precise quarters and then buttered one piece, making sure the butter covered the whole of the toasted surface and was evenly spread. He took a bite.

Eve wasn't sure if she felt hungry now. Of course, what he said was delusional, but at the same time it felt true. *No*, she told herself, *he's messing with my head. Get back in control.* She took a mouthful of breakfast.

"To you," she said, after swallowing the food, "I'm sure that's how it is. But to me and most other people that is simply not the case." She was careful not to say 'delusional' or 'insane' or any other antagonistic or labelling words.

"You mean you're not prepared to accept that it is the case."

"No, it's not a matter of acceptance. There is no case. I understand that as you see it the world of the Dark Chorus exists, but that element of reality is exclusive to you. However, a normalised view of reality is that it is one where the majority of the experience is shared. Even from your standpoint you share a great deal of your living experience with others. Me for instance, the man over there ordering coffee, the children you shared a home with. It's not me who needs to accept the situation you find yourself in, it's you. You need to accept that the Dark Chorus is not a reality but an illusion. Even if you never shake off that illusion, you need to accept that it is not real so you can avoid its influence. You cannot spend the rest of your life killing people." Eve sighed. "To say it's not socially acceptable is an understatement."

The Boy had been listening thoughtfully, and at the same time had buttered another quarter of his toast. He looked at her again with his flawlessly clear eyes. Eve once had a Siamese cat that looked at her in the same way – stared directly into her eyes, looking past them and into her mind, or so she had always thought. However, unlike the Boy, the cat never seemed to stop talking. True to form, the Boy said nothing in reply but smiled at her and concentrated on eating. Oh well, she might as well join him.

They sat in silence while they ate.

"I have to go now," said the Boy once he had finished his tea and toast. "I have to meet up with Makka and Vee." He pushed his chair away and stood up.

Eve thought she ought to make an effort to stop him, but for some reason that thought felt wrong. Well, it was the police's role to do the catching, and anyway, with the threat of Makka somewhere close by she'd be mad to try and physically detain him.

"Thank you for the tea and toast," said the Boy. "You need to remember what it was like when you were a child. It is not something to hide from. It's a gift." He made for the door, and as he reached it turned back to her.

"We'll see each other soon, but in the meantime look after my mother, won't you, Dr Rhodes?"

Chapter Twenty-One

I find the church and it is bathed in white light, thrown up from two ground-mounted floodlights. The soft stone looks old, but it has been cleaned recently and seems proud of the fact. The spire pricks the night sky and the whole building has a sharpness about it that gives it a startlingly three-dimensional quality. I am quite transfixed. Inside the gate that guards the large grounds are parked a number of cars and a battered old brown Transit van. Music pulses at me from across the road somewhere. I think this is the band from the Temperance Hospital – Double Zero.

Five people are over by the impressive stepped entrance. Three are standing while the other two are lying on one of the broad steps looking up at the cold clear night. They are smoking, talking loudly and laughing. As I watch, they pass the smoke between them. I think that they are taking a break from the music so I will ask them if they have seen Makka or Vee. As I move past the brown Transit van, the rear door opens.

"Oi, get in here." It is Makka. He is alive.

"You didn't drown," I say.

"Yeah. Good, isn't it. Now, quick, get in the friggin' van."

I do as I'm told and climb past Makka into the dark interior. It smells of oil, coffee and cannabis. I give Makka his courier bag.

"Did you float out to the Thames? I looked for you when I crossed a bridge but didn't see you."

"What? No." The rear door has a window in it, and I see his silhouetted head shake. "You are a mad fucker. I hid between two canal boats. I didn't float off anywhere." He looks out of the window. "I got fucking cold, I can tell you that. Those dickheads came back and went up and down the canal for ages looking for me." He turns and looks at me, although I can't make out his expression. "Sorry I couldn't get back to you, but it was too risky. Yeah?" He wants me to say something, so I do.

"That's OK. I met a dog called Crisp, although he doesn't like cheese and onion crisps on account of him not taking to the onion."

"Right. Well, good. I was worried you wouldn't make it here."

"Where is Vee?"

"Dunno. Still waiting for her." He resumes his lookout. "I hope she's OK," he says to the window.

We sit in the still air of the van's interior. It is a metal cocoon – safe and secure. I can feel carpet under my hands. I am about to ask Makka whether the carpet is patterned or not, but he springs to life before I get the chance. He opens the door and calls out to Vee. She runs over to us and quickly climbs in to join me on the carpet.

"Hello, Vee," I say. She is breathless.

"I'm being followed," she says. "I tried to lose him, but I don't think I managed. I'm sorry."

"It's OK," says Makka. "Yeah? It's OK. We'll deal with it. Any idea who it is?"

I can feel Vee sit back against the side of the van. She catches her breath.

"Yes. He's a journalist. I don't know his name, but he . . ." she shifts her position and I get the impression she is twisting the sleeve of her coat, rubbing the cut on her arm, hurting herself. ". . . was one of my father's friends. He particularly liked me."

"Liked?" says Makka.

Vee is silent.

Makka growls. "Right. We'll kill the fucker. Here. Now." Makka's rage flies out of containment. I don't think I am going to get the chance to apply Crisp's Law in this case, although I suspect it will be unnecessary anyway. Makka prods me. "You got what you need? Yeah?"

"Yes," I say.

Makka once again resumes his lookout and almost straight away says "Is that the shite?" He points out of the van window. Vee takes a look.

"Yes."

"OK. Let's do it." Makka makes to open the door, but Vee stops him.

"Wait. It would bc better if we kill him out of sight. We don't want to get caught."

"What? No way will I get caught. Yeah?"

"Makka, there are people walking up and down the street. Of course you'll get caught. Come on."

I can feel Makka's annoyance. The animal in him wants to strike now, the panther wants to make a kill.

"Yeah, OK. You're right. I just want to smash his face in – right now." He looks out again. "Where's the fucker heading? To the gig maybe?"

"I'll go and get him. I'll take him to the back of the church." Vee sits back in the dark and I can't make out her face.

"How are you going to do that?" says Makka. "I mean, he's a fuck sight bigger than you."

Vee says nothing, but moves to the door and lets herself out. "Trust me, he'll come."

"Oh, wait. No fucking way." Makka doesn't seem happy with the unspoken idea. I don't understand why. "No. I don't want you to, you know . . ."

Vee looks at him. "Just be there, Makka. Be there, and don't let him hurt me."

He takes a while to respond. "I'll be there. I promise. Yeah? I'll be waiting."

Makka opens the door for Vee, and without looking back she walks out of the churchyard and disappears down the street.

The Dark Chorus is singing. I get so used to it I sometimes forget they are about. There are plenty of the poor souls here, and I wish I had time to collect them so they could at least find a little peace.

But there is no time. Makka jumps down from the van. "Come on. We'd better get hidden."

I follow him, and as I shut the van door, I can just make out the pattern of the carpet. It's a very dirty, blue-paisley affair.

"The carpet is paisley," I say. "Is the van yours?"

"What? No. It's the band's. Now stop fucking about and let's get going."

The group of five people are still there. We give them a wide berth, but I can see there are two women and three men. They don't look much older than us. I often wonder what it's like to be someone else. To think differently, to live differently, to be different, to have a different story. I suppose it's impossible to know because if I were that person, I wouldn't be me. Of course, it may be that I can't be anyone else because everything I see, feel, or smell is simply a construct of my own consciousness. Everything is a projection of my thoughts. I decide against this as we hurry along the far side of the church, mainly because that seems dull. I can't prove it isn't the case, but actually, I don't care. I think I'll continue to wonder what it's like to be someone else. I enjoy the thought.

I run into the back of Makka, who I hadn't noticed had come to a halt. "Sorry," I say.

He ignores the bump.

"OK, over here." Makka circles around a large tomb that is overhung by some branches of a very old yew tree. It creates a deep darkness into which he disappears – undetectable. I follow. From our vantage point, we can see the dimly lit open space at the rear of the church. It's a stage waiting for a performance, and I think it will get an unexpected one tonight. Makka kicks something with his foot. It clanks against the tomb. He picks it up, weighing it in his hand.

"This'll do," he whispers.

I think it is a rock of some sort. We wait.

The night is clear and a little cold, but my parka keeps most of the chill out. I can hear sporadic traffic noise, the chatter of the people still smoking at the front of the church and the odd creak from the yew tree as the light night breeze catches it. The bark of a town fox bounces back at us off the church wall and is returned by a second bark further off. I am trying to trace the engraving on the side of the tomb. It's badly worn, but I think it's some kind of serpent. It is long and twisting. Maybe it's a dragon.

Makka puts his hand on my shoulder and shakes me gently. I look up and out and see Vee walking around the church with a man. He must be the journalist. Vee looks different. She hangs her head and seems subservient. He stops her short of our stage and says something to her. She doesn't respond so he taps her hard on the head twice. She then undoes her jacket and the man puts his hand inside it and starts kneading her breasts. Vee manages to break her trance for a moment and says something to the man. He nods and they walk further around the church and on to small paved area, on to our stage.

Makka has gone, and the play unfolds.

***

". . .and then she threw back her head and screamed. I mean really screamed. I nearly shat myself." The young demonstrative man turned to his friend. "Isn't that right, Addy?"

"Yeah, yeah, that's right. Dave nearly shat himself. I have to say that I'm not sure I didn't actually shit myself. I'm not feeling too well."

"Wait. Hold up a minute. None of that makes any sense," said the Inspector. Eve, who just walked up behind her had only caught the tail end of the conversation. She had once again found herself at the scene of a murder, and once again it was late. In fact, so late that it was probably early. Darkness still hung in the air, but it was the last of the real night. Eve enjoyed the feeling of a new day arriving. The Inspector spotted her.

"Ah, good. You're here." She turned her attention back to the two young men. "This is Dr Rhodes. She's a psychiatrist working with us for the moment. Now, tell us what happened again, and this time speak slowly and try not to leap around like a frog with a fire cracker up its arse."

"Sure, sure. Sorry," said Dave. "I'm a bit fazed by it all really. Isn't that right Addy?"

"Yeah, we've been tripping our bollocks off for hours and what we saw." He looked at Eve – "Well, it isn't the sort of thing you need to see at the best of times. Do you know what I mean?"

"No," said the Inspector without a shred of empathy. "Now, if I were you, I'd be more worried about me busting your bollocks than I would be about you tripping them off." She leaned in towards the pair. "Get on with it."

Dave coughed. "Erm, Doc, you aren't going to put us in the loony bin are you? 'Cause we're not mad, you know. We really saw some weird shit. Really."

Eve crossed her arms, looked at the Inspector and then back at the young men. "Probably not," she said.

The Inspector grinned. "Now, if you wouldn't mind, get on with it."

"OK, so me and Addy here go out for a bit of a smoke just as the band were coming to a bit of a break. They're bloody good, aren't they, Addy?"

"Yeah, yeah. Awesome."

"I mean the bass lines are kicking and –" The Inspector slapped Dave.

"Focus, for fuck's sake."

"Right." Dave rubbed his cheek. "Is that police brutality? I mean . . ." His complaint petered out under the intense stare of the Inspector.

"So, we are sitting on a grave thing, stone box with a lid, you know."

"A tomb," said Eve.

"Yep, that'll be the thing. Anyway, it's set back from the church quite a bit and in the dark. A good place to have a smoke you see."

"No one could see really," said Addy.

"That's right. So, we're sitting having a smoke when we see this man and a girl all dressed in black come around the back of the church and stand pretty close to us. He says to her, you know, like, she should erm play with herself."

"You heard him say that, or was that just your wishful thinking?" asked the Inspector. Eve was watching the pair carefully.

"No way. That's not fair. We heard him say that and then he said he'd missed her doing that," said Dave.

"The girl didn't want to do what he said, you could tell." Addy pulled off his beanie and ran his fingers through his long hair. "And then he gave her a bit of a slap."

"And then what happened?" asked the Inspector.

"She pulled up her skirt," said Dave. "And me and Addy were about to, you know, help her out 'cause like it was wrong and a bit creepy, but fuck me if this, like, demon figure didn't suddenly turn up." Dave rubbed his face. "He was wearing a long coat, like the Morpheus guy in *The Matrix*."

"More like Blade I reckon," said Addy.

"Anyway, the man turns to face him and, yeah, you're right Addy, more like Blade he was. So, the Blade guy hits him in the face with a stone." Dave throws an arm out.

"Yeah, like whack, straight in the face," said Addy.

"The guy falls over and Blade is on him, literally, you know. He sits on his chest, holds the guy by the hair and smacks him in the face with the stone..." Dave is now jumping about putting his words into actions, "...again and again and again, whack, whack, whack."

"All right. Calm down now," said the Inspector.

"I felt ill," he added.

Addy took up the narrative. "Then this spooky little guy appears and says something to Blade and he stops beating the shit out of the guy on the ground. To be honest, I don't think Blade wanted to stop." Addy thought about it. "Naw. He defo did not want to stop, but the small dude persuaded him."

Dave cut back in. "Anyway, Blade goes over to the girl, and I think, right that's over, but the small dude then draws a circle around the perv on the ground and then inside that he draws a square. It all looked satanic to me. The small dude then puts a sort of rough stone bowl down by the perv's head and then, well, fuck me if he doesn't set him on fire. I couldn't believe it. *Whoosh*. He went up like a thing."

"A candle," said Addy.

"Yeah, a human candle."

"Torch," said the Inspector.

"Yeah, that too. And then, just when you thought that was the end of it, the girl appears. She kneels down by the perv and gently puts his head between her knees. She didn't seem bothered by the flames."

"Dressed all in black like that," said Addy. "And with the flames flicking about she looked fucking terrifying and then ..." He shuddered and stuck his beanie back on.

"And then what?" asked the Inspector. The two young men looked at each other and then Dave said,

"She pressed her thumbs into his eyes and screamed . . ."

***

. . .and screamed. The fire leapt up, flames tumbling skywards, throwing flicks of orange light over Vee as if it were an artist flicking paint from the tip of a brush. Tears flowed from her eyes, a silver river, tarnished with the black of her mascara, full of pain and despair.

I watch her as I stand at the foot of the almost dead journalist. He twitches the last of his life away. Makka walks over to Vee and gently raises her up off her knees. There is no resistance. He turns her to face him and then envelops her in the folds of his cowboy coat. Hugging her. I can hear her sobbing.

"What did those fuckers do to you?" he says quietly.

I am simultaneously sad and happy. Sad for their pain and rage and the damage it has done to them, but happy because Makka has someone to care for and Vee has someone to care about her. We seem to step out of real time and into a moment of our own. All is quiet and peaceful.

And then we are back.

The flames die down as quickly as they had leapt up. The journalist is dead, and his soul is captured in the Soul Stone. I leave a message at his feet and pick up the bowl. It is warm to the touch and I can feel it humming.

Makka looks at me over the top of Vee's head. "Got him?"
I hold up the bowl and nod.

"OK, we better get going yeah?" Vee pushes him away gently and without turning to look at the eyeless corpse she walks off down an overgrown path that leads into the graveyard and the night.

"I guess we go this way," says Makka following Vee. "Come on."

I stow the Soul Stone in my bag and follow. As I jog to catch up, I notice two guys sitting like statues on a small tomb. I can just make out their horror-struck faces.

"Hi," I say, and they raise their hands in acknowledgement.

I smile.

***

Eve and the Inspector walked over to the body, which was covered by a white plastic sheet. Forensics were there doing their thing and Eve wondered what it took to be a forensic expert; a strong stomach at least. The two young witnesses had been shipped off to the police station to make statements so the atmosphere was a lot less jumpy.

"Any idea who he is?" asked Eve.

"Yes, according to his driving licence he is none other than Kit Hopkins."

"The tabloid hack?" Eve was surprised.

"The very same. Not a pleasant character by public account, misogynist, racist, and general hate generator. Considered a beacon of truth by the disgruntled far-right and, rather unfortunately, by those whose only source of information is the toilet tabloids. Personally, I've always considered him a total wanker, but hadn't put him down as a paedophile."

"So, he'll be missed?"

A breeze had managed to stir itself and pushed a few protesting dead leaves over and around the plastic-wrapped journalist.

"Well, I expect there will be some glowing obituaries in one or two parts of the press and the shittier parts of the internet, and we'll almost certainly get caned for failing to stop the killings." The Inspector sighed. "You know, when it gets out that it's kids carrying out these killings, the press will go mad. And when they realise one of them is an Asian, well . . ."

They stood in silence for a moment and watched a forensic investigator bag a large bloodied stone.

"So, another soul taken?" said the Inspector.

"Yes," said Eve. "But this killing was done for a different, or at least additional reason, don't you think?"

"Yes, I do." The Inspector looked down at the body. The breeze now played with one of the cover's edges, flicking it about absentmindedly. "It seems that Hopkins here is an abuser, and while I know I can't condone his murder, I can't help but feel sorry for the poor girl."

Eve nodded. "And so you should. This sort of abuse can destroy people. It leads to a plethora of life-long mental-health issues. Vee will not grow up to be the woman that she should have been."

"Sure," said the Inspector, who stood and continued to stare at the corpse. She seemed to be reflecting on Victoria's lost future. "Why did you call her Vee?"

"Out of habit I suppose," said Eve in what she hoped was a nonchalant manner. "I have a friend whose daughter is a Victoria, but everyone calls her Vee." Eve threw a sideways glance at the Inspector who had her eyebrows raised again. Damn it, how had she let that happen.

"Sometimes, Dr Rhodes, I get the feeling you have me at a disadvantage."

Eve shrugged. She and the Inspector caught each other's gaze for a moment.

"Now," said Eve, "Victoria's behaviour has shown us just how disturbed she has become. She has taken to the Boy's fantastical and murderous world without a second glance. It would appear that the values by which she judges the world have changed, almost certainly as a result of the internalisation of her trauma. The evidence we now have of her abuse helps us to understand why she is behaving the way she is, but still, to push out someone's eyes with your thumbs is beyond anything I've ever encountered."

"So, what we have here is both a revenge killing and a soul-collecting exercise. Two birds with one stone sort of thing."

Eve moved to the foot of the corpse and stood where the Boy had stood some hours before. At her feet, just discernible, was written the word *Purgatio*. "So, what are you going to do about it? The press response I mean," said Eve. The Inspector came and stood next to her.

"A pre-emptive strike. I think we need a leak to suggest that our dead friend here is a paedophile. It won't stop the verbal punches, but it'll help us to roll with them."

The smell of burnt hair, flesh and clothing wafted about and Eve coughed as the acrid fumes of overheated fat hit the back of her throat. At the head of the corpse was written with more clarity the words *Child Fucker*. Eve had no doubt that Kit Hopkins was an abuser. The Boy seemed to have been accurate with his killings so far.

"So, he's the second killing identified by the Boy as a paedophile. Any connection to Griffin do you think?" asked Eve.

"I don't know. It appears that Griffin did regularly abuse boys in the detention centre. Other staff members seem to be clean, but we get the impression they knew what was going on. Griffin was, by all accounts, an aggressive individual. We haven't finished investigating him yet, but resources are a bit thin on the ground and the Chief Inspector wants us to concentrate on catching the Boy. Interestingly though, Griffin had strong right-wing views and didn't seem to care who knew."

The Inspector waved a sensible-shoe-covered foot at the corpse of Kit Hopkins. "I'll get some digging done into the life habits of our dead man here and see what turns up."

She then crouched down by the corpse. "Given that there is a whole host of repugnant activities going on out there somewhere" – she nodded towards the glimpse of dawn – "it seems too coincidental that everyone the Boy has killed so far has far-right politics and/or sexual abuse tendencies in common. Let's see what the face of such horrors looks like, shall we?" She pulled back the plastic covering to expose the head of the journalist.

Eve looked at what had been Kit Hopkins. His face was so burnt that the beating he'd taken at the hands of Makka wasn't obviously visible. His eyeless sockets were black and hollow, revolting and at the same time fascinating – the broken entrance to a now derelict human structure. Eve was caught by her own stare and her overriding curiosity.

The world shifted.

She entered the dead space as easily as stepping through a door and was confronted by vast emptiness. The feeling of infinite nothing was overwhelming. She knew, or at least thought she knew, that this space was where the soul had been, the soul well as the Boy had called it. She had no sense of her own body, all she was aware of was her thoughts and the nothingness around her.

Nothing.

And then panic.

"Hey, Eve," she heard the Inspector say. "Are you OK?"

The world shifted back.

The Inspector had her by the arm, was helping her to stay standing.

"Sorry," said Eve as she regained control of her body. "Must be the shock of seeing the burnt face." She ran a hand over her eyes and through her hair. That was surreal. She really must be tired. She had let the Boy's imagery and words worm themselves into her subconscious. "I'm OK now." But Eve wondered if she really was. Reality had seemed, just for a moment, to have changed. She tried to shrug it off, but deep, deep down, she had believed it, believed what she had experienced. The words of the Boy came to her: *You could have been Arta.*

The Inspector covered the corpse again. "Apologies, Eve. I sometimes forget that most people aren't used to seeing such horrors. Let's get out of here."

They walked back to the church's lychgate in silence.

"So," said the Inspector as they reached the police cars, "your Boy seems to have lost his psychotic focus. He's hunting more than just far-right losers."

"Maybe. Or maybe his target group isn't far-right extremists."

"Paedophiles? But then that doesn't explain the deaths of the Nazi boys or the ex-bursar."

"No, I know, but I can't help but think there must be a connection."

"Maybe he is just fucking nuts and there is no connec–" The Inspector bought herself up short. Eve waited. She could see the Inspector was thinking, and by the look on her face she wasn't enjoying her train of thought.

"Hmm. Victoria's father seems to be taking centre stage here. How likely would you say it is that he knew or that he was involved in Victoria's abuse?"

"Statistically speaking" – Eve pursed her lips – "very likely."

The Inspector sniffed loudly and opened the rear door of a police car. Eve dropped into the seat offered. The Inspector leant in.

"Things may get a little difficult with the Chief Inspector. You bandy the word paedophile about and you'd better be certain of your facts, especially when your boss is friends with someone you might want to investigate." She stood back and straightened her coat. "A shit storm of cluster fucks does not begin to describe this," she said.

"No," said Eve. "It doesn't."

The Inspector gave a small parting smile and pushed the door shut.

And the day had only just started.

Chapter Twenty-Two

I catch up with Makka and we follow Vee who is marching with an unfocused purpose.

"Hold up girl. Where you goin'?" asks Makka. Vee keeps marching on.

"Away," is all she says.

"Well, OK, but can away be this way?" Makka gestures to a small road leading off to our left. Vee says nothing but turns left.

"Good," says Makka. "Bill's new squat isn't far, yeah?"

The road is well-lit by a number of shop fronts. One claims to be *Tasty Chicken*, another offers genuine *Turkish Kebabs* while yet another announces itself as *The Church of Scientology*. I ask Makka what this is.

"The world might think you're a mad little sod, but you've got nothing on that bunch of loose-brained fuck-monkeys."

I look in the scientologists' window, but its contents and Makka's comments leave me none-the-wiser.

We make a few turns and then take a narrow overgrown path that brings us to an iron gate set in a high brick wall. The gate is quite ornate, decorated with little spears and flowers – an interesting combination. I expect it has historic value. The gate is backed by some dirty looking hardboard that has been crudely fixed to the structure so we cannot see through. Makka pushes the gate open.

"Come on," he says, and steps through. Vee and I follow. We are in a small courtyard. It has an uneven brick floor, worn by use and weather and time, and its high walls give an enclosed and protective feeling. The courtyard is old and sleepy. The moon, which is waning now, makes a decent effort to light up the yard and at the same time illuminates the wooden-framed front of a whitewashed medieval building. A man is sitting on the ground next to a crooked door, his legs out in front of him and his head bowed. The silver light gives him an Elysian glow as if he is a statue carved from pure marble.

"Bill?" says Makka moving quickly over to the figure. He crouches down beside him and rocks him gently by the shoulder. "Bill."

Bill says nothing.

Vee and I join Makka and I crouch down too. Bill's eyes are open but they are past seeing anything. His hands, which sit in his lap, are bloodied and broken. Makka gently pulls Bill's coat aside and we see a large blood stain on his T-shirt.

"Fuck," says Makka and stands up looking around urgently. "We gotta go now. Come on." He grabs me by the collar and pulls me upright.

"What about Bill?"

"There's nothing we can do for him. The fuckers have killed him and they'll do the same to us if we don't get the hell out of here now." There is urgency in his voice. As we start off across the courtyard the iron gate scrapes open and three men emerge from its shadow. Makka doesn't break his stride and launches himself at the first man, grabbing him by the throat. At the same time, he kicks the second man in the groin. The kicked man deflates in a groaning exhalation.

"Enough," shouts the third man, "or I'll blow your tiny piss brains out of your thick skull." He has a gun. It's not like the Bursar's old army revolver. This one is sleeker, smaller and looks coldly ambivalent about its function.

Makka looks at the gun and squeezes the man's throat tighter.

"So, you're not dead, then," says the man. "See, I told you pair of brainless bollocks he wasn't dead. Pakis don't know when to die." He laughs.

The man turns towards me slightly and I can see it is Makka's father, although I think I had better refer to him as The Fuck.

"You killed Bill," growls Makka.

"No, I killed a useless hippy," says The Fuck. "But not before he brought us here. Now, let go of Jake's throat."

Makka releases his grip and the man coughs a few times and rubs his neck. He then punches Makka in the face. I think Makka saw it coming and tensed his muscles because the man seems to have hurt his hand in the process. Makka makes no sound.

The man on the ground gets to his knees. "I'm gonna kick your bollocks out of your fucking throat," he says to Makka, although he is having difficulty speaking.

Vee steps in front of him. She is streaming anger from every pore. I can see it drenching the old stone floor.

"What are you going to do about it, you stupid bitch?" says the man as he tries to stand. His voice is a little less strained. "Yeah? What?"

Vee kicks him in the groin just as he gets to his feet. He deflates again.

"Fucker," she says and spits on him.

"You, stop that or –" says The Fuck.

"Or what?" interrupts Vee. "You aren't going to shoot me because you have to return me to my father."

"True," says The Fuck. "But I can shoot this freaky little shit." He points the gun at me. "Should I?" He looks at Vee. "No? OK, then. Do as you're told."

It is too dark for me to catch his stare and I don't think he'd let me in anyway. There is nothing I can do at the moment, so I simply stand still and wait to see what happens.

"Get up," says The Fuck to the deflated man.. "We haven't got time for your arsing about." The Fuck waves the gun at us. It is like being in a movie. I'm sure it will all work out OK in the end. Movies usually do.

We are herded together and forced out of the courtyard leaving Bill's body. I take a last look at him. I am sorry that he has died. I liked Bill. I suppose Bill was taken in revenge, a fulfilment of the Old Testament's assertion that an eye for an eye is the way things should be. If the good side takes an eye does the bad side get to take an eye too? I suppose it does. It seems to me to be a morally neutral statement. It should have been more explicit. Perhaps then Bill wouldn't have died.

We are pushed back along the narrow overgrown path to the road and into the back of a Transit van. Disappointingly it is not new and black, but old, smelly and rusty blue. The deflated man is called Dog. I think this is because he looks like a dog. Dog binds Makka's and Vee's hands behind their backs with duct tape. He doesn't bother with me. I suppose I am no threat. Dog gets in the back with us while The Fuck takes the passenger seat and Jake drives.

"Are you called Dog because you look like a dog?" I say.

"Twat," says Dog and slaps me hard.

"No," says Makka. "It's because he fucks like a dog." He laughs at this.

"Shut the fuck up, Gandhi," says Dog, but Makka just keeps laughing. Dog punches him in the face, tears off a bit of duct tape with his teeth and forces it over Makka's mouth.

There are no windows in the back of the Transit van or any partition between us and the front seats. Light slashes in through the windscreen from streetlamps and car headlights, showing off our tiny tin world in slow stroboscopic vision.

Jake's driving is all acceleration and heavy breaking so we slide about the metal floor as there is no friction to hold us in place. It is not very comfortable. I count twenty-seven rivets in the floor before Jake slams the Transit van to a halt.

"You drive like shit, Jake," says Dog, who seems unhappy about the washing machine ride.

"Yeah? Well tough tits," says Jake, smiling.

"Get the boy and the Paki out," says The Fuck. Jake jumps down from the driving seat and opens the rear doors, and as Dog is about to step down Makka kicks him hard in the back with both feet. Dog leaves the van headfirst and cracks his shaven skull on the tarmac road. I think Makka is laughing behind the gag, but Dog isn't. He gets up and I can see a graze on this forehead. His eyes are bulging with anger and pain.

"You little shitty cunt," he says, and pulls Makka from the van, dropping him hard on the road. Jake and Dog start kicking him. Makka tries to curl himself up into a ball, but with his hands tied behind his back it is difficult. A well-aimed kick to Makka's head silences his struggle.

"Vee," I say. She is looking at the scene in anger. "Vee. Where do you live?"

"What?"

"They are going to take you back to your father. What's the address? We need it to find you later."

She tells me and then looks at Makka. "But I don't think you'll escape this."

"But if we do, we'll come and find you," I say, but cannot finish my sentence as I'm pulled out of the van by my parka hood. I land in the gutter next to Makka and catch my elbow painfully on the kerb. I look up to see Vee looking back at me. Her eyes are crying, but there are no tears. I think she believes this is the end of us, and perhaps she is right. The Fuck slams the rear doors closed.

"Right," says The Fuck. "You two, take this pair of jerk-offs down to the cellar. I'm gonna take jailbait here back to her daddy." He points at them. "Do not kill the fuckers. We'll do that when I get back."

"Yeah, yeah, yeah," says Dog, rubbing his grazed head, but it doesn't sound like he means it.

The Fuck moves his pointing finger between them. "You will wait – right?"

"Sure," says Jake. "No problem." He slaps Dog on the back. "Let's get 'em shifted."

The Fuck gets into the Transit and with a cough of smoke the vehicle takes off.

Vee is gone.

I recognise the street. It is the one we killed Mitch in, and I am lying in the gutter outside the White Hart. Before I get a chance to have a proper look around I am pulled to my feet and pushed and kicked through the pub's open front door. Inside there are two more doors; one has a large frosted glass panel making up its top half and I can hear voices sneaking out from behind it, the other is a chipped white wooden door. This is the one Dog opens. It leads down to a cellar.

The cellar is split into two. A dim light shows off the old brick arches that hang over each section. To the left, the cellar contains old beer crates, metal kegs, what looks like tubes heading up into the ceiling and other pub detritus. The right-hand archway is filled in with breeze blocks and has an old heavy-looking wooden door at its centre, although annoyingly, not at its dead centre. Dog opens this door and pushes me in. A moment later Jake and Dog reverse in dragging Makka.

There is a hook in the ceiling from which hangs a block and tackle. Much like the Bursar's cellar, this one has tendrils of horror tangled in the wooden mechanism. There is nothing else. Dog sees me looking at the ceiling.

"You scared?" He grins.

"No."

"Well, you should be."

I have heard this three times over the last few months, and perhaps I should be scared, but I don't know how to be.

"Yes, perhaps I should be," I say.

Makka hasn't moved. He is still unconscious.

"Can you get him some water or maybe some tea? I think he needs it."

Dog laughs. "Oh yes, sure. I'll give him some water." He stands over Makka, undoes his trousers and then urinates on Makka's head. Jake starts laughing. It is loud and violent and vengeful, and I have the sudden urge to tear his soul from his body, but once again the Angel does not stir.

"Hey, Paki, are you feeling better now?"

Makka doesn't move and Dog is getting cross. "Stupid Paki really is out cold." I think he wanted Makka to react so he could laugh at him.

"Come on, let's get a drink," says Jake. Dog does up his trousers and kicks Makka for good measure.

"Yeah, good idea."

They leave and bolt the door behind them.

I drag Makka out of the puddle of Dog's piss, leaving a watery trail streaked with blood, and pull off the duct tape binding his hands and feet. There is nothing to clean him up with, so I use the sleeve of my Parka. Makka groans as I do this, slowly bringing his hands to his face. His eyes stay shut.

"Why is my face wet?" he says after a moment.

"Dog peed on you."

Makka opens his eyes and tries to scowl, but his face is unable to accommodate the request. I help him sit up and between us we move him to the cellar wall.

"Pissed on by a Dog," he says and laughs and clutches his ribs. He looks at me. "We may be fucked. I can't see any way out of this shit storm."

"Maybe," I say, "but this might give us a chance." I hold up my sacrificing knife. "They didn't check my pockets." I rotate the knife and both Makka and I are caught by its violent beauty.

Makka laughs and clutches his ribs again. "You devious little shit." He looks at me, suddenly serious. "Even so, I'm not in a good way. Don't know if I can do much."

"Well, we have to try. We have to help Vee and we have to rescue my mother."

"Sure." Makka closes his eyes, "Sure. We'll give it a good go. Yeah?"

The sound of the bolt being pulled back interrupts us. Makka takes the knife from me and hides it in his coat pocket. The door opens just wide enough for a person to step through. They do and it's actually two people, Stacy and Holly.

"You look like shit," says Stacy as she eyes up Makka's broken state.

"What happened to your face?" says Makka, ignoring her comment.

Stacy moves her hair away from her face. "This black eye is from you, and the rest of my beaten face and body is courtesy of Garland. He was mad about you coming into his home. He reckoned it was my fault."

"Well, tough shit. You shouldn't have shacked up with that cunt."

"Look, I didn't come here to pass the sodding time of day with you. I've come to help you." Stacy is frightened. I can see the fear across her swollen face, hear it in her voice. Holly is holding her hand and I can see she has a bruise on her neck.

"Hello, Holly," I say.

"Hello," she says. "It's not very nice in here. It smells."

"Did you hurt your neck?"

"Daddy was angry. He doesn't like Rabbit."

Stacy pulls Holly close to her. Her eyes are bright with tears.

"What the fuck do you mean by help us?" says Makka. He is looking at Holly's neck.

"I'm taking her away," says Stacy. "He's going to hurt her. I know he is. He doesn't care for her. He's mixed up in something nasty, something to do with . . ." She mumbles and looks down.

"What?" says Makka.

"Children," she says quietly as if saying it quietly will make it less bad. "Something to do with kids."

"He's a child fucker?" says Makka, his features suddenly alert.x§

"No, I don't think so, not himself, but others . . . He's involved with others who are, I'm sure of it." She strokes Holly's hair. "I can't let him take Holly. I really think he would."

"What do you want me to do about it? Yeah?"

"Kill him," she says with anger. "You have to kill him. If you don't Holly and me are lost." Stacy looks at me for a moment, but I appear to be of little use in her desperate plan, so she refocuses on Makka.

"Listen, I hate you and I know you hate me, but right now we are the best chance each has of getting out of this shit. He will kill you, you know that, so what have you got to lose? Kill him. It's our only chance."

Makka is quiet. I can see he is thinking. Stacy is looking desperate at his silence.

"Please." She closes her eyes, shuts them tight as if this will help stem her rising terror at the possibility that Makka might say no. "Please."

I listen to the silence – it makes a ticking sound.

"You're right, I don't give a monkey's shit for you, but for her" – Makka nods at Holly – "I will help." He shifts uncomfortably against the rough brick wall. "I was gonna kill The Fuck anyway."

Stacy's relief is palpable, but she doesn't bother thanking Makka. "What's the plan then?"

Holly lets go of her mother's hand and goes over to Makka. Rabbit's head is poking out of her coat pocket, its big ears do a little floppy dance as she crouches down beside him.

"Does your face hurt?" she says.

"A little."

Holly kisses her hand and places it on Makka's cheek.

"There." She smiles. "Is that better?"

Makka looks taken aback, looks younger and vulnerable and innocent.

"Much better," he says, nodding.

"Good." Holly stands up and goes back to holding her mother's hand. Makka pulls himself to his feet. He seems to have found some new strength and I watch as the old Makka returns. His neck muscles rise. He is getting ready for action.

"OK. Go get the two twats upstairs. Tell them The Fuck wants them to start kicking the shit out of the Paki." He walks over to the door holding himself upright with care. "Get our bags off the wankers and then go to your car and wait. You do have a fucking car, don't you? Yeah?"

"Yeah. It's a white Fiesta parked a couple cars up the road."

"Good. Start it up and be ready to go."

Stacy nods. "Come on, Holly. We have to go now." We leave the room together and I watch Stacy and Holly climb the cellar stairs. The steps are too big for Holly, so she has to climb on to each one with the help of her mother. Rabbit seems to be enjoying the ride.

Makka shuts and bolts the prison door.

"In here," he says and moves through into the dimly lit other cellar room, the one with the kegs and crates. I follow him in and against the dirty white back wall I can see some large tins with 'paint stripper' written on them. There are also some old paint pots and brushes and a roller that is now rigid with unwanted dried paint. It looks like magnolia to me.

Makka picks up one of the tins. "You got a light?"

"A light?"

"Yeah, a light. You know, a match or a lighter."

"No."

"Fuck." Makka is unhappy, so I tell him Dog smokes and that he has a lighter. A blue one.

"If I didn't know you were an odd little fuck, I might think you do this kind of thing to wind me up, yeah?" He growls this out, but I can see he is grinning. I am not sure what he means, but I grin too.

Makka picks up an empty bottle. Its label reads 'Punk Ale'. He smashes the end off on the edge of a keg leaving the Punk Ale with a set of glass teeth, teeth that look ready to bite. He gives the bottle to me.

"You stab Dog in the back of the leg, yeah?" He shows me where he means using his own leg as an example. "You gotta stab him as hard as you can, really hard and twist it once it's in. I'll take out Jake with your knife. I don't want to kill 'em yet, right? Not yet."

The cellar door opens and Makka pulls me into the darker part of the room. I can hear Dog and Jake descending the stone steps.

"That Stacy is a right mouthy bitch." Dog doesn't seem happy. "She better not be fuckin' with us."

"I don't reckon she is. Did you see the state of her?"

"Yeah, Garland gave her a right going over 'cause she let the Paki into his house. Don't blame 'im. Didn't ruin her looks much." Dog laughs.

"You know she used to be a bit of a looker a few years back?"

Jake and Dog reach the prison door.

"What, 'er? No," says Dog pulling back the bolt.

"Yeah, nice tits an' all."

We attack. I do as Makka instructed and stab Dog as hard as I can in the back of his right leg. The Punk Ale sinks its glass teeth deep into his flesh through his cheap jeans. Makka didn't say which way to twist the biting bottle so I decide to twist it clockwise. Dog bellows and partially collapses, but still manages to catch me a blow to the side of my head with his flailing right hand. I am knocked off my feet and fall into the beer crates, scattering them about the cellar floor. Pain explodes behind my right eye. I can hear Dog yelping and Jake bellowing. I struggle out of the crate carnage and can now add the smell of stale beer to that of Dog's piss. My vision is a bit blurred, but I can see Makka kicking Jake into silence. Jake is holding his neck, which is pouring blood, and at the same time trying to fend off Makka. He is failing. The Punk Ale is still lodged in Dog's right leg, but he's pulling it out now and I think he might use it against Makka. He yelps in pain as the glass teeth reluctantly let go of their prey, but the pain must be great because Dog slumps heavily against the unbolted door. It opens inwards and Dog disappears through it, hitting the hard ground with a thump. Makka steps over Jake and follows Dog through the door. I can hear what sounds like meat being tenderised before Makka reappears.

"Get the paint stripper," he says. "Both cans."

I run to the back of the cellar and pick them up. They are heavy. I think they are both two thirds full. As I return, I find Makka dragging Jake into the prison cell where Dog already lies. Jake seems to regain some fight and tries to punch Makka. Makka's response is quick and brutal and Jake becomes lifeless.

Makka lays the two beaten Nazis together. He searches Dog's pocket and finds the blue lighter. Dog makes no effort to stop him.

We stand over them. Blood is pooling about their bodies.

"Fuck you," spits Dog. Makka says nothing but unscrews the cap of one of the tins.

"Fuck you," says Dog again. Blood snorts from his nose. "You're truly fucked when Garland gets hold of you."

"Yeah?" says Makka. "Really? What, more fucked than I was a few moments ago?" He starts to pour the paint stripper over the bloodied faces of the pair. "I don't think so."

Dog coughs and tries to cover himself with his hands. Jake makes a gargling noise but isn't really conscious.

Makka flicks the lighter.

No ceremony. No ritual. Just fire.

Their heads light up and they look like human matches. Dog makes an effort to brush off the flames, but he's too weak and just ends up setting his hands on fire. He starts a breathless scream.

"Bet you wish I would piss on you now, yeah?" Makka kicks Dog. "Well, fuck you." Instead he pours more paint stripper over the pair.

They burn.

Thick black smoke plumes up in a twisting dancing vortex bringing with it the smell of burning flesh and hair and clothes. The smell of death and of cleansing. I don't have the Soul Stone so cannot take their souls. It seems a waste.

"We better get outta here," says Makka, sniffing the air. "These bastards stink. Come on."

We leave the prison and Makka bolts the door. He then pours the rest of the first tin's contents over the door and sets it alight. We climb the stairs, leaving the burning pit behind us.

We come out into a small lobby. The door to the cellar is to the left of the inner door to the bar. I can hear the voices of drinkers seeping out from around its frame. Makka takes the second tin and empties it over the door, walls, and floor of the entrance. We step outside and he lights it up. Flames creep along the floor, up the walls and lick the ceiling in hunger. I can feel the heat immediately, and as the flames take hold, they start a mesmeric dance, moving with such liquidity that I begin to think of them as crashing waves of a cleansing sea. I have an urge to step into their midst and let them cleanse me.

"Over there," Makka says, pulling me by the arm and nodding up the dark road. He is holding his side as we half run, half walk away. I think his ribs are hurting. I expect the adrenaline of our escape may be draining away now. He lets me go as we approach Stacy's white Fiesta.

Behind us flames climb into the dark sky, glass smashes, urgent voices shout out in the night.

Behind us the White Hart burns.

***

Stacy drops us off down a side street some way away from the burning pub.

"Where are you going?" asks Makka as we get out of the car.

"To my sister's," says Stacy. She looks into the back at her daughter. "You better kill him. You know what he'll do if you don't."

"I will." He also looks at Holly. "And when it's done we'll be even, so you'd better make sure you look after her. We'll be back."

"Fuck you," says Stacy. "I don't need you or anyone else telling me how to look after my daughter." She puts the car in gear. "Just kill him," she says and drives off forcing Makka to take an urgent step backwards. The open door slams itself shut as they race up the road.

Makka watches until they disappear around a far corner.

"I need a wash," he says, sniffing himself. He slings his courier bag over his shoulder and winces. "And you smell like shit too," he says. Actually, I smell mostly of beer.

"Tomorrow we can rescue Vee," I say. I feel happy again.

Chapter Twenty-Three

We have spent the night in a launderette. Makka said we needed to wash our clothes. He does not like to be dirty. I don't think I mind very much, although I have not given it much thought. The launderette had a sink too, so we washed ourselves. A large black lady came in while we were washing and tutted at our nakedness, but on seeing our bruises and cuts helped us with our washing and even gave us some food. Her name was Tilda and she had warm friendly eyes. It seems to me the less people have, the more generous they are.

The sun is on its way. Light is streaming in from the east and the birds are singing. They sit in trees and on window ledges and on the façades of upright Victorian buildings. They ignore their surroundings and give themselves over to the joy they feel at being alive. Buses are roaming the streets and workers, early starters or late finishers, it's hard to say, are gliding through the first touch of dawn like transparent spirits. Members of the Dark Chorus are, as always, flitting about, searching, and for a brief moment the living and the lost appear to inhabit the same shadowy world.

Makka seems to be back to his old self. His face is puffy, and his side still hurts him, but he is talking with confidence again.

"So, we head to Vee's, kill her cuntish old man, grab his soul and then go look for The Fuck," says Makka. He is walking at some pace and I am jogging again to keep up. "And this time we kill him. No messing. Yeah?"

"Yeah," I say.

"Wait. CRAP. Where does Vee live?" Makka stops and looks at me as I overtake him a little. "Do you know where her old man's house is?"

"No."

"Shit." He runs his hands through his hair and down his ponytail. The steel muscles in his neck flex. "That's a bit of a bollock. I don't even know her surname. Do you?"

"No. I have her address though," I say.

"What? So why did you just say you didn't know where her house is?"

"Well, I don't know where it is." I can see he is expecting more. "I only have the address."

"That's the same fuckin' thing." He puts his hands in his clean cowboy-coat pockets and glares at me.

It's not, but I say nothing.

He laughs. "All right, I suppose it isn't quite the same. What's the address then?"

I tell him.

"Richmond you reckon? We're going to have to take a bus. It's a bloody hike out to that posh part of town."

"Can we sit upstairs, please?"

"Sure."

***

We alight just outside one of the entrances to Kew Gardens. I would like to go and have a look, but I know that now is not the time. Anyway, it is not open. We walk down Kew Road and turn off into a crescent with large houses spread out around a U-shaped private garden. It is quiet. Some houses have lights on, others are cloaked in the last moments of sleep. Vee's house is the fifth one on the left-hand side. It has a yellow front door atop some stone steps and is flanked by smooth white round columns, which hold up an ornate porch. A beautiful house that exudes pain and sadness and anger.

There is a white Jaguar parked outside. Makka feels the bonnet. It is warm.

"Didn't Vee say her old man had a BMW?" asks Makka, speaking quietly. Voices in the early morning travel far.

I nod.

"OK, so someone else is here. We need to be careful." He

looks down the small side-alley that acts as a divide between the house and the neighbouring building. He indicates with his head, and I follow him as he sets off between the houses. A wooden gate threatens to block our access, but it is unlocked. Makka rolls his eyes as he quietly opens it. We steal inside.

The garden is tidy, borders are straight, grass short, everything is in order. Dull. It is looked after, but without any affection.

Makka heads for the back door. It is a large white affair with the top half made of glass. A cat flap is cut into the wooden bottom section.

"Key," Makka whispers pointing through the glass to the lock on the other side. I can see a large key poking out of the keyhole. Makka looks through the lock from our side. "I think the key is straight on. I reckon I can push it out." He pulls out his knife. "Can you get your hands in the cat flap and catch it?"

I kneel down in front of the brown cat flap. It would have been better white. Its little transparent door doesn't want to open.

"It won't open," I say.

Makka looks at it and gives it a prod. "Fucking hell," he says too loudly for his own liking and then whispers. "How do cat flaps open then?"

I shrug. "Perhaps we need a cat."

"What? Where are we going to get a fucking cat from?" I can see he's thinking about kicking it in, but that would be too noisy. "We'll have to try something else," he says, moving off. He starts looking at the windows and the conservatory that juts awkwardly out on to the patio. It tries, rather unconvincingly, to suggest it has always been there, but it is a pretender like its owner.

I look into the garden and see a pair of eyes looking back at me from under a rhododendron bush. Cats eyes. I catch its stare and say hello. It is a friendly black cat with a white mark on its nose and it comes over to me to be stroked. I scratch it behind its ears and under its chin and it rolls over on its back so I can stroke its soft underbelly. It closes its eyes and purrs.

Makka reappears.

"Look," I say. "I found a cat."

He smiles. "Well, that doesn't surprise me. Can he get in through the flap?"

"She," I correct him. I encourage the cat to go through its little private door. It doesn't want to, it prefers to be stroked, but as it rubs itself against my hand which I have held out by the door the cat flap makes a clicking noise. I push on the flap and it opens.

I look at Makka who shrugs.

"Thanks," I say to the cat. It sits down and starts to lick a paw.

"Ready?" he says. I nod. I have both hands through the flap, stretched out to catch the key when it falls. Makka sets about his task. With a few angry words and some careful prodding with his knife the key falls and I catch it.

We are in.

The kitchen is white, floor tiles, table, chairs, cupboards, cooker and walls. The only colour comes from a bowl of fruit on the table. It contains three red apples, five satsumas, and four bananas. The kitchen is also very clean. Makka notices this too.

"Maybe he has live-in help," he whispers. "Eyes," he says pointing to his own eyes with two fingers on his right hand. He then points his fingers about the place. I have seen this sort of thing in a film, so I know what he means. I need to keep a lookout. I nod.

A soul flits by.

I can hear the faint sound of voices coming from somewhere above us. Two men, I think. Makka moves out of the kitchen in a slow-motion walk. I follow his exaggerated care. No noise. We enter a wide hallway, its floor is made from strips of polished wood, light coloured and warm. Makka looks up the stairs and then indicates that we should go into a room to our right. It is the living room.

It contains two enormous white sofas, a glass coffee table, and above a fireplace a large mirror housed within an ornate frame. It looks like it should contain a picture of maybe a boat in a rough sea or a portrait of an ancient relative, but for now it just paints my face back at me. My eyes are bright today. There are other bits of furniture dotted around the room that I think are just for the look of the place. They seem untouched.

Makka pulls me to the floor behind one of the sofas indicating urgently to be quiet. The voices are descending the stairs. They stop at the front door.

"So, we're clear. You'll have to get rid of Victoria," says a man with a sharp, clipped voice.

"Yes. Damn her. If she'd only play ball," says a voice that sounds like a news announcer.

"Well, it's too bloody late now. When we catch that murdering pair it'll all get out and Victoria is the only witness we have left."

"Yes, yes. I know." The announcer sounds annoyed and resigned. "And if Hopkins hadn't been such a randy little shit we could have nipped this in the bud. Never put your trust in a tabloid journalist, it's like sticking your tackle in a crocodile's mouth and not expecting it to bite the sodding thing off."

"Quite. Well, at least the irritating bastard is dead. Can't say I'll miss him." The clipped voice opens the front door.

"Right, see to it and I'll move things around my end. By the way, did Garland say how he caught your daughter?"

"No, not really. Something about a hippy giving him a tip off."

I can feel Makka tensing. The thought of poor Bill I expect. We also now know which one is Vee's father.

"His little HQ went up in flames last night, and two more of his bottom-feeding sidekicks burnt."

"Did they now. He can't have many left." Vee's father seems to be thinking. "The religious vigilantes?"

"No ritualistic killings this time, but the general feeling is that they are to blame. They killed the other two and our tame psychiatrist thinks they'll keep at the gang until they are all dead. Apparently it's not uncommon for these psycho types to pursue their fucked up scenarios to a deranged end."

"So Garland may well have had them and let them slip through his fingers. I shall have to have words."

"You do that. This could all be over if he'd handed them to us." I can hear the clipped voice outside now. "Right, I'm off. I hope not to see you for a while."

"Likewise," says Vee's father.

The door clicks shut, and footsteps ascend the stairs.

We get up from behind the sofa. "Time to get to work," says Makka. "Here's the plan. Go out the back and come around to the front door and ring the bell. Vee's old man will answer it and think you're on your own. Get him to go through to the kitchen. I'll wait here and then when you're in the kitchen I'll go upstairs and find Vee. We'll come back for you and kill the twat, yeah?"

"OK." I smile.

Makka nods. "Good." He looks out of the front-room window. "The white Jag's gone, and there's no one about. Go."

I go.

There is a flaw in our plan; the door doesn't have a bell. I wonder about going back to tell Makka this, but I think he would probably just call me a twat and tell me to use the door knocker. I use the door knocker and wait. I like the yellow door. It is the same colour as the mini we stole when we escaped from the detention centre – a beautiful burnt panama yellow.

The door opens and Vee's father stands before me in a smart pink jumper and blue trousers. He is wearing leather slippers.

"I have come to take your soul and feed it to the angel from the kingdom of light," I say.

He looks down at me through a pair of tortoiseshell rimmed glasses. "Have you indeed?" he says.

"Yes. Also, can I have an apple? I'm quite hungry."

He looks around. "And the other one? Where is he?"

"Not here. May I come in now?"

Vee's father stands aside and I enter his house once more. I make for the kitchen.

"Looks like I don't have to tell you where the kitchen is." He walks close behind me. I can feel his stare and can also feel Makka heading up the stairs.

I take an apple from the bowl and bite into it. I am actually hungry.

"So, you're the prophetic mad child, or perhaps I should say psychotic mad child. Where on earth did you dig up this whole religious vigilante idea from?"

I take another bite of the apple.

"It is difficult for people to understand that what I do is a consequence of my role as Arta, as someone who has to pursue the path chosen for him in order to save lost souls and to restore a celestial being to heaven. However, you will be one of those that will understand." I take another bite and chew for a moment.

"Really? You really think that?" Vee's father laughs.

"Yes, you will understand at the point at which oblivion takes you."

Vee's father shakes his head. "You really do have a problem, don't you?" He looks at me and blows his cheeks out. "So, what to do with you, what to do with you?" He adjusts his glasses. "I should hand you over to the police, but I think I might call Garland. He seems to have a real beef with you, and in particular with the other one – Mica, isn't it?"

"Makka. Yes."

"I think it best he takes you and disposes of you in some imaginary way."

"Where is Vee?"

"Vee?" He laughs. "Victoria, you mean. She's been calling herself Vee ever since her mother died. Stupid, childish name."

"Is she here?"

"None of your business, I'm afraid. Now, time to call Garland. First things first, I'll need to secure you. Don't want you running off."

Vee's father grabs me by both arms. I start to count.

"One, two, one, two, one, two . . ."

"What are you doing?"

"I'm trying to count in time."

"Why? What's wrong with you?"

"Nothing, I just wanted to help Makka get his timing right."

"Makka? For what?"

"This," says Makka stabbing Vee's father in the back of each thigh in time to my counting. He does it twice – a four/four rhythm.

Vee's father lets out howls of pain. His face creases up and his eyes shut as he reaches out to the backs of his legs.

Makka stands clear as the injured man stumbles falling against the clean white table. The fruit bowl slides from its surface and smashes into numerous tiny pieces on the hard floor. Fruit bounces about, scattering itself as it pleases. A banana lands at my feet. I pick it up.

The injured man bellows again as he finds the floor. He lies on his back clutching at his legs.

"Fucking hell. My legs. My fucking legs." He is breathless with pain.

"Yeah," says Makka, "they are your fucking legs. Hurt, do they?"

"Of course they fucking hurt, you bastard. You stabbed me. Jesus, they hurt."

"Where's Vee?" says Makka. "She's not upstairs."

"She's not here, you fucking moron." He screws his face up in pain. "Jesus," he says again.

"Where is she then?"

The soul that I saw earlier flits by and pauses by the stairs. I can hear its voice, disturbed and urgent. Like most souls, its ramblings make little sense, but there is something about this one. I concentrate on it.

"Garland has her," says Vee's father. "He took her away for safe-keeping. OK?" He moves himself trying to ease the pain. "Now fuck off," he shouts.

"He is lying," I say.

"No shit," says Makka.

"I'm not. Search the sodding house if you like. She's not here." He drops his head on to the floor and closes his eyes. Makka looks at me expectantly. I look into his eyes and smile.

"Vee's mother knows where she is," I say. Vee's father's head jerks back up.

"What the hell are you talking about? She's dead." He laughs through gritted teeth. "I know they said you were nuts, but I didn't think you were simple as well." He pushes himself up on his elbows. "I suppose you can see ghosts and spooky shit like that." He laughs again and grimaces. "Christ."

"In a manner of speaking, I can," I say. "Vee's mother's soul is here. She's by the door under the stairs."

"Oh good," says Vee's father. "Well, help yourself, you mad shit. Go and take a look." He doesn't sound convincing.

I leave the kitchen and pull open the glossy white door that stands unobtrusively under the stairs. Inside is a vacuum cleaner – a little red Henry with a smiling face, a broom, some boxes and some hooks with coats and bags and umbrellas hanging from them.

"See," shouts Vee's father. "Nothing. Your spook is a fraud, just like you."

The soul hovers by the Henry and then disappears through the floor. I smile. I have found Vee.

"Makka, Vee is down here, but we need to pull the floor up."

Makka appears and looks in the cupboard.

"OK," he says, pulling out the Henry and the boxes and throwing them into the hall. "How do we get the floor up?"

I shrug.

"Fucking great." He turns to the sound of the door handle being rattled and races into the kitchen. I follow him.

Vee's father has pulled himself across the floor and is trying to open the back door, but his legs aren't working. Makka pulls his head back by his thinning hair and punches him hard in the face. He yelps and his glasses fly off to join the escapee fruit.

"Here's the deal, paedo. You tell us how to get into the cellar and I won't stick forks in your eyeballs, yeah? I'll get through that floor one way or another so you might just as well make it easy for the both of us."

"There is no fucking cellar," says Vee's father. I think he is sounding desperate. "The boy is a fucking loon. You must know this. Give it up. Come on."

Makka pushes him to the floor and starts pulling at the kitchen drawers until he finds what he is looking for. He waves two forks at Vee's father.

"Unfortunately for you, I'm also a fucking loon, yeah? And now I'm goin' to stick these forks in your eyes." He smiles, but it is not a kind smile. Vee's father tries to crawl away, but he doesn't get far.

I realise I am still holding the banana. I start to peel it. I am not sure if I really like bananas, but while I wait, I think I will give them another go.

"OK, OK," says Vee's father waving his hands about in an effort to ward off Makka's attentions. "For fuck's sake get those forks out of my face." Makka stops. "Half the floor is a sprung trapdoor." His head sways and he seems to be having trouble focusing. "Press down hard and it'll pop open." His head flops backwards and he collapses on the floor. He has lost the colour in his face which now matches the white tiles of the floor.

"Watch him," says Makka, and he goes off to open the trapdoor. The banana tastes a bit floury, so I put it down on the table. Vee's father is now lying on his back looking up at the ceiling. I stand next to him looking down. He moves his unfocused gaze from the ceiling to me and I catch it. I wander through the turbulent coloured clouds of his consciousness, find the soul well and descend.

I watch his soul for a while, looking for some colour redemption in its curling and twisting contents. There is none. It is black. Crisp's Law is upheld.

I leave.

Makka reappears in the kitchen just as I am thinking about having a go at a satsuma. He has Vee with him, and she has let him put an arm around her. Protected, but her head is bowed, and she looks lost.

I go over to her and crouch down so that I can look up into her face. She doesn't look at me.

"Vee," I say, but there is no response, so I reach out and touch her cheek. The physical connection works and she turns her gaze towards me, and I carefully move into her head. I am not sure what I am looking for, but I am certain I can do something to help. Her mind is full of colours, the purples and dull reds I have seen before, but they are in chaos; unorganised, confused. I come across a deep purple orb of consciousness turning in on itself again and again and again. I think this is the essence of Vee. It is not looking out, not managing the consciousness around it, but simply shutting itself off – hiding. I intervene, gently stopping the inward turning, relaxing the turbulence. After a moment the orb becomes stationary and then sends out tendrils into the distressed consciousness. A semblance of organisation returns. I gently back out.

"Vee?" I say again. She looks at me. She is back, but so is the pain from which she ran. She lets tears drop from her lashes, but makes no sound. Makka holds her tight. I am not sure this is right. Why must she endure such pain for everyone else's benefit? The Angel stirs. I don't think it is comfortable with my thoughts. We stay in the moment until the cat comes through the cat flap and miaows loudly. Vee pushes her tears away with the palms of her hands.

"I need a shower and a change of clothes," she says. She looks at her father, who seems to be unconscious. "Is he dead?"

"Not yet," says Makka.

"Good. Don't kill him until I come back down." She leaves the protection of Makka and heads out of the kitchen.

"Shall we have a cup of tea?" I say.

***

"Eve." It was the Inspector on the phone. "News from the front line. My rattling the cage about Victoria's father has got the chief threatening to shove a red-hot Chevy up my arse."

Eve was looking out of her flat's large rear window watching the thunder clouds roll about the sky. She took a sip from the fresh espresso she had just made.

"Eve? Are you there?"

"Yes. Sorry. So, it's as you thought?"

"Afraid it is. I'm not to investigate the connections between the victims. The Chief says that at best it's circumstantial and at worst it's downright harassment based on a delusional conspiracy theory."

"So he's not convinced by the evidence from our acid-dropping hippie friends then?"

"Nope. But I think he is wrong. Two more of the Thuggery burnt last night. No ritualistic elements associated with the deaths, but the general feeling is that it was the work of the boys. Eye-witnesses say they saw two young men leaving the building just before it went up in flames."

"Do you think they caught our trio after they killed Hopkins?"

"Yes, I'd say so. The Nazi goons were killed at the pub opposite the site of the first killing – the shopfront one. They burnt the place to the ground. It was a miracle no one else died."

"What about Victoria?"

"My guess is the goons took her back to her father – but I can't go anywhere near him at the moment. Of course, he should have contacted us, but if we're right about his involvement in the abuse ring then that's unlikely."

"What? Even though Victoria is directly involved in most of these crimes?"

"Yes. Look, Eve, I need concrete evidence that Victoria is there before I can go steaming in. As much as I want to, I have no intention of getting busted back to sergeant."

"OK, so what if I go? I could make the trip under the guise of wanting some background information on Victoria and her past mental health issues. To be honest, the state she's in there ought to have been a tome on her, but actually there's nothing.

"Sure. If you're really up for it. I'll need solid proof though – my career will be on the line here." She sighed. "But if you find some proof, I'll risk it. I mean shit, we have what we think is a paedophile ring being wiped out by religious vigilante killer-children."

Eve was still watching the clouds. They appeared to rear up and then charge into each other with brutish aggression, like some alien animal on the Siberian steppes.

"If Vee's father is at the heart of what turns out to be a

paedophile ring then, well, don't you think it likely that the Chief Inspector is involved?"

There was silence at the end of the phone – a deep silence. Eve waited. The cloud animals fought it out and, as is usually the way in such fights, the biggest animal won.

Thunder rang out in triumph.

"Yes," said the Inspector. "Yes," she said again, "quite probably."

"I'll go to Victoria's home at some point today and see what I can find. Address?"

"I'll text it over to you. Just be careful, Eve. There have been a lot of deaths associated with this case. If things go all the way to the top, then everything is just going to get worse."

"Sure. By the way, what was with the Chevy reference?"

"Oh, it was on my mind. I'm thinking of buying one – a red one."

***

We push back the white sofas in the living room leaving an expanse of beautiful polished wooden floor and then drag Vee's father into the newly created space. We've bound his legs together and his arms to the side of his body with cling film. He seems to have recovered a bit and swore at us when we moved him.

"Look, I'll trade you," he says. "You lot just fuck off and leave me here, and I'll give you some information that will make you a fortune. Seriously, a fortune."

"Oh, yeah?" says Makka dropping on to one of the sofas.

"Yes," says Vee's father craning his neck around to look up at Makka.

"So what is this info then?"

"It's a bunch of videos of some very important people doing stuff they shouldn't. I mean, you can extort the shit out of them. Really."

"You videoed your fucked-up sessions?" Makka looks disgusted.

"Of course I did. I'm not stupid. This kind of business

needs some protection. I knew I might need some leverage at some point, so I taped the lot."

"And what? The sick bastards didn't notice?"

"No. Too trusting. I guess they thought everyone was in it together. Safety in numbers." Vee's father puts his head back on the ground. "I'm feeling really shit now. Not sure my legs work." He closes his eyes. "So what do you say?"

I take a sip of my tea. I can see Makka is thinking about it, but I don't think he is after the money.

"I'll think about it," he says. "Now, shut the fuck up."

I leave the room.

I am going to catch Vee's mother's soul. It's sad and anxious and I want to help it – give it some peace. I find a large jar of coffee in the kitchen, Columbian extra strong, and tip out its contents on to the table. I have some night-lights in my bag and so get one out, but before I drop it into the jar, I notice a slim wine-red candle sitting on the windowsill. It looks like a delicate bloodied finger. Next to it sits a box of matches. I put the night-light away and retrieve the candle and its matches and then cut off the top of the waxy finger. I light a match and melt some wax. It drips in thick dollops like coagulating blood on to the bottom of the jar and before it sets, I plant the fingertip into its stickiness. This is a much better arrangement for Vee's mother's soul than my simple night-lights.

I take the jar out into the large hall and at the base of the stairs I draw my symbols.

I sit on the bottom step and wait.

After some time, Vee comes down the stairs and at her feet is her mother's soul. I lean forward and light the trap. Vee looks at it as she passes, but says nothing. She is dressed in clean, mostly black, clothes: thick black tights, a black skirt much like her old one, a deep red shirt, and a black jumper that seems to me to be more of a collection of holes than a jumper. She has her hair pulled back and her eyes are once again framed with black mascara while her lips are painted deep purple. I like the look, but I don't think it would suit me. I am not sure if boys are supposed to wear make-up, but I don't see why not.

Vee's mother's soul leaves Vee, drawn to my flickering trap. I lean forward and clear a path in the chalk letting the soul drift in. The fire tongue seems to sense its presence and extends itself in the soul's direction. There is a moment of stillness and then the trap pounces.

The lid goes on the jar. It is done.

I walk back into the living room carrying the jar. Vee is standing at the feet of her father.

"I'm OK," she says to Makka. "Really, I'm fine."

Vee's father opens his eyes and looks up at his daughter.

"Victoria, you've got to stop this nonsense. Come on, let me go now and we'll sort this mess out."

Vee says nothing.

"Victoria? Vee? You know I love you. All this is because I love you. You know that, don't you? Deep down you know that. Vee?" His voice is faint. I think he's having trouble staying conscious. Vee looks at me, and I know what she's asking. I shake my head.

"He has nothing left," I say.

"What do you mean, nothing?" says Vee's father. "What's that supposed to mean? I love you, Victoria. I can make this all better. Really I can. Just let me go."

"He was going to kill you," says Makka. "We overheard him talking to some other paedo. Apparently you're the last witness."

"Don't listen to them, Victoria. Please, I wouldn't harm you. Please."

I think Vee's father knows this is the end. Fear has been building up in him for a while, leaking out of his skin, falling between the tiny cracks in the floor.

Vee doesn't look at him. She looks at Makka. "Can you shut him up please."

"Sure."

"NO. Vee, wait."

Makka leans out of his sofa seat and punches Vee's father in the face. The man's head rocks back and hits the wood floor hard with a loud deep ring. Blood trickles from his nose and his head drops to one side, but he keeps talking.

"Enough. Stop it. I order you to stop it now. Victoria, do as you're told. Stop this now."

"Get the cling film," says Makka to me. I do as I am asked.

Makka wraps the transparent film around his head a number of times, covering his face and mouth and nose. He cannot speak now.

"There," says Makka as we watch Vee's father wriggle about trying to get a breath. His inadequate kicking movements soon stop as he runs out of oxygen. Just as he starts to pass out, Makka leans forward again and pierces the covering with one of his long thumb nails. Vee's father sucks at the air, desperate to get a good breath. The small hole makes a whistling noise, a bit like a kettle.

"Paedo here," says Makka, nodding at the whistling man, "tells me that he has videos of all the sick shit they got up to. He wants to trade it for his life. Your call, girl."

Vee reaches into a small pocket in her skirt and pulls out a key ring with three little plastic sticks on them. One is red, another green, and the third and largest stick is grey.

"I heard him from upstairs," she says. "He always assumed me and mum were too stupid or too frightened to notice things." She bends over and dangles the plastic sticks in her father's cling-filmed face. "Well, he was wrong. I've always known where he hides these memory sticks." She stands upright and tosses them to Makka.

"Let's get on with it." She looks at me again.

I hold up the jar. "This is your mother's soul."

Vee stares at it for a moment. "Good. She can watch," she says.

I put the jar down with deliberate care on a little white three-legged table. She'll have a good vantage point from there. I take some chalk from my pocket and draw a square around Vee's father. I then encompass it in a circle. I take out the Soul Stone from my bag. It is warm to the touch, and as I peer into the polished blackness of its bowl, I can just make out the fleeting and flitting shadow of the journalist's soul. It is desperate to get out. I place the Soul Stone above Vee's father's head. I take some lighter fluid out of my bag, but Vee stops me.

"Use this," she says, going over to a corner cabinet and taking out a bottle. She gives it to me. The label reads *Macallan 1964*. "He loves this stuff more than he ever loved me, he might as well burn with it."

Makka takes the bottle from me.

"I'll pour," he says.

"Can I have your knife?" asks Vee.

I give her the blade. She stands over her father, a leg each side of his body and then sits down on his chest. She pulls the cling film apart and cuts open the pink jumper to expose his chest. Then very deliberately places the tip of the blade between the fifth and sixth rib on the right.

"I'm ready," she says. Her father tries to rock her off but is now too weak and too bound up to dislodge her.

Makka hits him hard on the head with the whisky bottle, which seems to stun him. He then uncorks the slender bottle and pours the light-gold, burnt-wood smelling liquid into the small breathing hole. Vee's father chokes, coughs, tries to swallow the alcohol, but Makka is pouring it in too fast. The liquid spills over his face, head and throat drenching him.

"Now," says Vee.

I light him up and watch as the blue flame takes hold, spreading out, burning. Makka and I stand back and watch.

The cling film starts to melt around Vee's father's mouth. He is free to speak.

"Victoria, please, I beg you. Stop." He chokes. "Stop, please, stop."

"That's what I said to you and your disgusting friends. I begged you to stop, but you didn't. You fucking well didn't." Vee tightens her grip on the knife handle. "So neither will I." She leans on the knife with all her body weight and the blade buries itself in her father's chest up to the hilt, piercing his loveless heart. Flames lick her fingers but she ignores them.

He bucks violently, just the once, and then lies still. Vee slowly stands up and then comes over to us. There are no tears. She lets Makka put an arm around her. We say nothing but watch and wait. I can hear the Soul Stone humming – it is also waiting. And then the soul appears, drawn out of the body by the flames that dance over the dead man's burning face. The Soul Stone wastes no time. Its own flames dart out, barb hooked and accurate, skewering the soul in a split second. The soul tries to flee but is no match for the pulling-power of the stone. It disappears into the ancient artefact's dark prison.

It is done.

Chapter Twenty-Four

Makka says it is time to go. We have fed our captured souls to the Angel. We did that in the dining room. It had dark wooden panelling and felt like a suitable place to carry out the ceremony.

Vee's pain is still great, but I think it is a little less. We have had a good breakfast and I have spent some time stroking the cat. I asked Makka if we could take the cat with us, but he said, "No way. You and Vee are enough. Anyway, cats do whatever the fuck cats like to do. You can't make 'em do stuff they don't want to. She'll just piss off."

I don't think I agree, although I have never looked after a cat. I suppose our freedom might be coming to an end soon, though, so perhaps it is best she doesn't come along. But I do like her. She has soft fur and beautiful green eyes.

I return to the living room to leave our message for the police. I am just finishing off writing '*Purgatio*' when there is a loud knock on the front door.

"Fuck," whispers Makka from the hall. "It's the psycho doc."

The Angel stirs.

I can feel it pulling the threads of our futures together, pulling it to a point as if offering us a chance to find some personal closure. A reward maybe? I need to act now if I am going to take this chance, so I add a message just for Dr Rhodes at the feet of the cleansed.

There is a second and equally loud knock.

"Quick," says Makka. "She's goin' around the back."

I leave the living room and am ready to go. Vee descends the stairs carrying her black rucksack.

"You good to go, girl?" asks Makka. She nods, but then

rushes into the living room and emerges with her mother's soul jar. She jams it into a net pocket of the rucksack.

Makka nods, opens the door, and we run. And the cat runs with us.

***

Eve considered knocking for a third time, but then she noticed a passageway leading to what she supposed to be the back garden. She descended the front steps and took what she knew was a furtive look around before heading to the rear of the house. The garden was neat and tidy, manicured to within an inch of its life. It had no soul.

A back door beckoned to her, so she approached and peered through its glass upper panel into what she assumed would be a neat, tidy manicured kitchen. But what she saw was an explosion of fruit and cutlery and coffee and blood, all sprinkled with a coating of fine bone china granules. She felt her heart start to race. Fear or excitement?

She tried the door. It was unlocked, so she opened it and carefully stepped in. "Hello? Anyone there?"

Nothing.

But not empty.

She picked her way through the grotesque floor art and into the hall where her nostrils were assaulted by a now familiar smell – burnt flesh and hair. The streaks of blood, like tramlines, ran up the hallway and then off into a room. She took the virtual tram, but before she arrived at its destination, she noticed that the front door was ajar.

They'd been here when she knocked.

She closed her eyes. She could almost feel what had happened here – the rituals. They left a trace in the air, but not in the air of the real – in the air of the realm of the Dark Chorus. Eve felt no anxiety at this, and that surprised her.

She opened her eyes and looked out into the road and over to the communal garden. She was sure eyes were looking back at her. She smiled.

"Who the fuck are you?" said a man, leaping up the steps

towards her. She hadn't seen him coming and it took her by surprise.

She blinked at him. "None of your business," she said, stepping back and trying to shut the door.

The man kicked at it and the solid wooden edge hit Eve in the face. She rocked backwards and fell on to the stairs. The man was inside. He slammed the door behind him.

"Right. Where's that twat Parks?"

Eve was in a lot of pain, but fear kept it at bay. She held one hand over her damaged face, but she could still see her attacker. She said nothing.

The man looked around and took in the bloody tramlines, the smell and the chalk ritual markings he was standing in. He went into the living room.

Eve got to her feet. She could run, but a morbid curiosity took her into the living room too.

A man, Vee's father, she assumed, was lying bound in cling film, his chest exposed, a deep looking wound above his heart, and a burnt face – blistered and black and covered in glue-like beads. Melted cling film? There was a bottle of whisky on the mantelpiece.

The man took the bottle down, smelt it and then took a long draw on it. He turned to her. "Who the fuck are you?"

"I might ask you the same."

He took another drink and simply stared at her. Eve had seen this kind of stare before. He was unstable, probably violent, and certainly struggled with some kind of psychosis. She guessed he was one of the Thuggery, and given the number now killed off, he might well be the only one left. The head thug probably? She opted to answer his question.

"My name is Dr Rhodes," she said, and noticed the man raise his head in acknowledgement. Did he know her? "And I'm a psychiatrist working for the police. I came around to interview Mr Parks about his daughter, Victoria."

"What do you know about Victoria?" he said.

"Nothing. That's why I came round."

The man stared at her again. He had his hand in his coat pocket, and she could see he was gripping something tightly. A knife?

"I've called the police and reported the murder," she said. "They're on their way."

"Is that supposed to frighten me?" He certainly didn't look concerned. Perhaps he'd read her bluff.

"I'm just making sure you understand the situation."

"Oh, I fucking well understand the situation." He tapped the chalk words 'Child Fucker' with his foot. "Yeah, I understand all right." He put the bottle back on the mantelpiece. "And I know how this is going to end."

"Do you know who did this?"

"Oh yes. The mad little psycho and the Paki."

"Do you know why they are killing people?"

The man looked at the other chalk words at the foot of the dead Mr Parks. "Stop asking fucking questions. Now, what does that say?" He pointed at the Latin words.

"'*Purgatio*' means cleansed. The other words say . . ." Eve thought for a moment and opted to lie. "Fed to the Guardian Angel, king of the heavenly realm of light."

"That right?"

"If you worked for Mr Parks then you'll be a target, you know? They'll come for you."

The man laughed out loud but without humour. "I'm banking on it. Those two fucks are going to die."

"Why not go into police custody? If you kill them, you'll end up in jail yourself."

He laughed again. "No I won't. I've protection. High-up protection." He looked at the "Child Fucker" words again. "And my protection tells me you've guessed why the mad fuck is killing certain people. Yeah?" He grins at her.

Oh, shit.

"And you know what? You're right." He pulled a knife from his pocket. "Looks like you're about to become another victim of the religious nutter."

She felt cold. There was no bargaining with him; he would kill her.

She pointed at the whisky bottle. "Whisky bottle," she said.

He turned and looked at it. "What about it?"

She ran.

The distraction gave her just enough time to open the front door, but as she stepped through it she felt a sharp pain race across her shoulder. He'd managed to slice through her coat and cut the flesh across the bone.

She ran.

And careered into two policemen coming up the path to the door.

"Dr Rhodes?" said one of the men. "Are you OK?"

The other policeman noticed her shoulder and ran to the front door. It slammed in his face.

"Round the back," said Eve, breathless with pain and adrenaline. "The gate's open."

The policeman took off. He came back moments later clutching his face. "The bastard floored me and took off over the back fence."

"How did you know I was here?" said Eve. "I didn't get a chance to make a call."

"Don't know. Ask the Inspector."

Just then a police car pulled up and the Inspector stepped out of the passenger side. She looked at Eve and at her cut shoulder.

"You look like shit," she said, without any apparent sympathy. "I told you to be careful."

"Yes, well, things took a turn that I hadn't been expecting. How did you know I was here?"

"We had a call from your psycho boys. Makka told us we'd better get over here quick. He said, and I quote, 'The Fuck has just turned up and I wouldn't give a pig's dick for the psycho doc's chance of getting out alive.' 'The Fuck', by the way, turns out to be Garland. He's the boss and, I think, the final member of our little Nazi gang." The Inspector looked up at the house. "What will we find in there?"

"We were right, Inspector. Vee's father was an abuser and he is well and truly dead. Sacrificed. Garland tried to kill me because he said we'd guessed right. The paedophile ring goes high up. He said he had protection."

"Did he say who?"

"No."

"Right, well it's too late for a cover up now. Before I was warned off by the Chief Inspector, I put a couple of colleagues on to looking for connections. Turns out that Parks here knew Griffin. He regularly visited children's high security homes thanks to his work with the Ministry of Justice, and Griffin always showed him around Thorndyke House."

Eve was sitting on the grass verge and winced as she removed her coat.

"Do you want an ambulance?" asked the Inspector.

"Is it deep?"

"Scratch," said the Inspector taking a cursory look at the wound.

Eve doubted it, but she knew the Inspector would have told her if it were bad.

"Leave it. So, what about the Trapt?"

"Well, initially it looked like there was no connection" – she pushed her hair back although none had come adrift – "but Trapt liked to keep records. Not just the names and what have you, but also notes about how each of the kids had come to be there. Most were delivered to him by a Mitch Bourn."

Eve nodded. "The first killing."

"Exactly. I'd guess that most of the kids were identified by Griffin, picked up by the Nazi gang, abused, and then when they were finished with given to Trapt for disposal. One well-organised sick paedo ring. I can only guess that the abusers are wealthy and well connected. We have two possible leads right now. Victoria and Garland."

"What about the Chief Inspector?"

"No evidence yet, but he's not going to shut me down on this now. I've passed this by a number of inspector colleagues who I trust, and they're on board. I'm working with the Children's Welfare Unit – it's their jurisdiction and there's more than enough evidence to suggest the ring exists." She nodded towards the house. "I'm guessing we'll find more evidence here."

Damn it. The police would see the chalk note the Boy left for her . . . but so what? If they read it and then caught the children, it'd all be over. Good.

No, not good. Eve realised she didn't want them captured. A realisation that the Boy's world existed, that he really did carry the last shard of an Angel, that lost souls wandered the earth waiting for salvation. She had seen it. And she couldn't deny it anymore. Just as she couldn't deny the existence of the mirror-world she'd been able to see when she was young. It *had* existed, and it still did. Just because she couldn't see it any more did not negate its realness.

The front door opened, and a policeman came out.

"I'm just going to take a look," said the Inspector.

Eve got to her feet. "I'll come with you."

Once inside, they were shown to the living room. Vee's father's body was as she had last seen it. She noticed that one of its feet had a leather slipper on it. The other, she supposed, had been lost in the affray.

"'Child fucker'," the Inspector read out. "'*Purgatio*'." She turned her attention to the other chalk words. "Can't make these out."

Eve looked at them. They were certainly unreadable now – thank God for that. They must have been scuffed out during her escape. "That might have been me when I escaped. Sorry."

"Did you get a chance to read them?" said the Inspector.

"They said, 'Fed to the Guardian Angel, king of the heavenly realm of light'."

"Nice," said the Inspector. "Religious wankery at its best. Right, you push off home now and get your shoulder looked at. We'll catch up tomorrow for a statement."

Chapter Twenty-Five

Eve had gone to the local hospital but, nasty though the cut was, it didn't need stitches – her coat had protected her from the worst.

She was back in her flat now, and it had gone eleven, but she wasn't ready for bed. She sat at her kitchen table, lights off, staring at the jar that she had placed at its dead centre. She had no trouble seeing it now. The soul glowed in the dark and danced gently on the tip of the flame from the night-light. She thought about the words the boy had left for her at the scene of his latest cleansing: "Temperance crypt midnight tomorrow. Bring my mother's soul."

She felt a little bad that she'd lied to the Inspector about what they said. The Inspector was one of the good people, but the Boy wasn't ready to be caught yet. The Boy needed his mother. She thought about her own mother, locked away in a secure unit, unable to respond to the medicine or to the therapy or to her . . .

She would visit her mother tomorrow, she decided. She would look, really look, to see if there was anything she could do.

***

"Tomorrow night you say?" asks Makka when I tell him about the message I had left for Dr Rhodes. We're sitting on a bus-station bench watching the tide of the afternoon wash up people and then wash them away as they go about their business. Vee has said nothing since she killed her father. The cat is sitting on my lap. Her ears twitch as I gently stroke the top of her head.

"Yes."
"At the Temperance Hospital crypt?"
"Yes."
"Why?"
"It is time to rescue my mother." The cat kneads my legs.
"Yeah? And what about my mother?" The tendons on his neck rise and he runs his hand through his hair. "Every breath The Fuck takes dishonours her. What about her rescue?"
It had been all Vee and I could do to stop Makka breaking cover when he saw The Fuck arrive at Vee's house. I can feel his desperation. The earlier failure has upset him.
He gets up, suddenly agitated. His anger erupts. "FUCK." His frustration is overpowering him. "FUCK," he says again, and some people move away from us. He is attracting attention from a group of young men at another stop.
"We're going to get fucking caught soon. I can't keep us safe much longer, yeah?" He takes a step towards me and Vee and the cat. "And I have to kill The Fuck before we get caught. You understand? I might never get the chance again. FUCK."
The cat puts her head down and miaows. The group of young men think twice about getting involved and wander up to a stop farther away.
The ferocity of his anger fades as quickly as it came. I can see his eyes are glistening with tears.
"I have to kill him," he says and then turns away from us. His shoulders drop and his head hangs down.
Vee gets up and goes and stands next to him. She says nothing, but her presence seems to help him and after a moment he stands upright again. I am glad Vee is here. He turns back to me and the cat and takes a deep breath.
"OK, we get your mother's soul back and you do whatever it is you have in mind and then we kill The Fuck. Yeah?"
"Yeah," says Vee.

***

The night is on us again, and Makka is keen to get us off the street.

"Cops everywhere," he says. "I thought the Tory fuckwits had cut the Met."

I have no idea what he means, but he's been talking non-stop since we left the bus depot. He seems conflicted: happy and sad, angry and calm, aggressive and friendly. I think it may be something to do with Vee. I know I'm not very good at understanding how people talk to each other without words, but I would say they've been doing a lot of non-verbal communication. I think this is good, so I am once again happy.

We head down a street lined with large Victorian terraced houses with portico columns holding up balconies over large solid doors. Sash windows and large white bricks front all the houses. They look expensive. The third one along is empty. Its windows are boarded up from the inside and a small sign on the door says *Protected by Bynard Security*. The house is strange. It makes me stop and insists I take notice.

I do.

And then I remember.

"Makka, we can spend the night here," I say.

He and Vee have walked a little way further down the street. They turn. "What?" He looks at it. "It's trussed up tighter than a psycho in a straitjacket. We aren't goin" get in there."

I say nothing but stroke the cat's head, which is poking out of my parka. Makka sighs and walks back to me. He raises his eyebrows and tries the door. To his surprise, it opens.

"Well, fuck me," he says.

The street is busy, but no one seems to be paying us any attention, so we go in and shut the door. The house is making a low purring sound. I look at the cat and she looks back at me and then starts purring too. The hallway is large – dark but for some streetlight bleeding in from around the boarded windows – and clean. It is not empty.

I head up the stairs.

"Hey, wait up," says Makka. "Gotta be careful, yeah? Could be others here."

"There are," I say, and keep going. Vee follows me up the stairs.

"Well, shit, we need to be careful then. How the fuck do

you know there are others here?"

Vee, the cat and I reach the landing and I head for the next set of stairs. I hear Makka come bounding up behind us.

"Wait up," he says and overtakes me. "I'll go first."

"OK," I say.

"Right." His status is now reinstated. "So where am I going?"

"Next floor, front room."

Even in the dim light I can see Makka giving me a quizzical look.

"I've been here before," I say and feel this is a little inaccurate so add, "Actually, my memory has been here before."

I don't think Makka is any the wiser.

He heads up the stairs and we follow. The door to the front room is open, and sitting on the floor with their backs to the far wall looking at us are two young people. They are dressed identically, have identical shaved heads, identical faces, and identical smiles.

Makka walks in and looks around. "It's empty, you twat."

I look at Vee. She sees nothing, but I can see she feels a presence.

I sit down opposite the pair and let the cat out of my parka. She sits next to me and watches the twins too. Makka is about to say something when Vee touches his arm.

"I don't think the room is empty, Makka," she says. "Leave him for a bit."

Makka stares at her for a moment and then nods. "OK, sure. Let's check out the rest of the house, yeah?" They leave me and the cat.

The twins say things to me but not with words. I simply know what they want as if I've always known. And what I know is that the end of our crusade is not close at hand, but neither is it unattainable. They have come to tell me what I need to know to finally cleanse the soul, but I think this will take time. For the moment, though, I will focus on saving my mother and helping Makka to kill his father.

The twins tell me that they were born decades apart, and

into different families, but are genetically identical. They were born for a purpose; they are the Restorers – the ones tasked with fitting the shattered soul of the Angel back together. They are not dead, they have souls, but having stepped into the world of the Dark Chorus thousands of years ago, they can now only exist in that world. The salvation of the lost souls is their salvation too and, despite their beautiful smiles and their youthful looks, I can feel the weight of their tiredness.

They get up and leave through the wall. I hope I see them again soon, but it's hard to say.

The cat stretches and wanders off. She is curious to see the rest of the house. I follow her out of the front room and spend a little time investigating the house myself. I notice there are a number of the Dark Chorus drifting about here. And they give me an idea, so I think I will collect a few of them. They can help me with my plans for my mother's soul.

I find Makka and Vee in what is clearly the kitchen.

"I need some jars and a cup of tea," I say.

"Of course you do," says Makka, rolling his eyes at me.

I think there will be some jars in the cellar. After all, this house used to belong to Charles Janenssen.

***

Eve's mother had been much the same when she had visited the following afternoon. Snippets of conversation could have been taken for any sane person talking in general, but then she would blindside the unprepared with tangents and obscure trains of thought. Sometimes these would be frightening to Eve's mother, and she would curl up and cry out in horror. Other times she would react violently and have to be restrained and other times the thoughts were simply impossible to follow, and this would frustrate Eve's mother. Eve had managed to catch her mother's stare but was immediately disorientated by the chaos of colours that confronted her. She would need more time and practice to see if she could make any inroads into helping manage the chaos.

Eve was quite aware that she herself might be suffering

from some form of psychosis. After all, believing you can see lost souls and thinking that you have the ability to move into someone's mind and manipulate it in some way is lunacy, no doubt about it. But she could no longer doubt what she thought she saw, what she thought and felt she could do. Unlike the Boy, though, she knew better than to vocalise such thoughts.

She had decided to take her car to the Temperance Hospital and was now sitting in the driver's seat having parked up in a side road. She had a large handbag with her, and inside it was the Boy's mother's soul.

She took a deep breath and exhaled loudly. If she had to regret this, she hoped she'd be alive to do so.

She opened the car door, clutching her bag, and set off towards the hospital.

The night had turned cold, frost cold, and was producing a cleansing chill that seemed to pull the grime and badness out of the air and wrestle it to the ground to be absorbed into the earth.

Eve approached the door she had slipped through a few weeks ago. It was slightly ajar, but she still had to pull hard to open it enough to squeeze past its defence. She'd come prepared with a small torch, and she switched it on now.

The wooden counter loomed into view. It cast an imposing and muscular shadow on the peeling wallpaper. Eve hadn't considered the possibility that entering a deserted building in the middle of the night might be frightening, but fear was trying its hardest to make itself felt.

She moved the torch beam to the hole in the back wall that gave access to the hospital itself. A movement through it caught her eye, but when she focused on the spot, all she saw was the stillness of the dark.

Fear was playing with her.

She climbed through the hole carefully, shining her light around the Victorian hall. Its former splendour was still evident; it seemed to be trying to pretend it didn't mind its dishevelled look. Now, where was the crypt? She had thought about this earlier, guessing that its entrance must be somewhere down the tunnel the Boy had made his earlier escape through.

She headed for the alcove where Makka had killed one of the Thuggery. The torn entrance was still there, so she stepped through this second portal and cautiously made her way down the giant, dirty white-tiled wormhole.

Almost exactly at its midway point, Eve found the newly created doorway to the crypt. Bricks had been removed from the tunnel wall and placed in two tidy stacks each side of the entrance, like guards awaiting her arrival.

She smiled.

"Don't make a fucking sound," whispered a voice into her ear as a hand covered her mouth.

She dropped the torch. Something cold and hard pushed against her cheek. Metal. A gun barrel?

"Pick up the torch. Slowly. And give it to me. No noise." It was Garland.

Eve nodded. Garland took his hand away from her mouth and she felt the gun barrel pressed to the back of her head.

Shaking, she picked up the torch and passed it behind her.

"Thought you'd fobbed me off with your stupid translation of those chalk words, didn't you? I knew you were fucking lying. I scuffed out the words, but I remembered. *Cras nocte*. Doesn't take a sodding rocket scientist to look things up. *Tomorrow night*." He let the torch beam play over the crypt's entrance. "Didn't expect to end up here when I followed you, though."

He pushed her forward. "In. Any sudden movements, I'll shoot you. And no, I don't give a flying fuck that it's in the back, or that it's murder. I've done worse."

The entrance was quite small and narrow, so Eve had to turn sideways and crouch a little to squeeze through. She stood in the crypt and waited for Garland to follow. Light splashed about as he made his way in. He stood next to her and shone the torch around, halting its travel when it picked out the Boy who sat on a large tomb that was positioned in the middle of the crypt.

The Boy was facing them. His legs hung down and he had his hands flat on the tomb's stone lid. The hood of his coat was pulled up, but Eve could see his face. He smiled at her. A cat sat next to him.

"Hello, Dr Rhodes," he said. "Thank you for coming." He seemed unconcerned by the presence of Garland.

"Where are the other fucktards?" asked Garland. He waved the torch around but didn't seem keen to let the Boy out of its focus.

"About. I see you brought my mother."

"Yes," said Eve.

"Shut the fuck up," said Garland. "Tell me where the others are, or I'll just have to shoot you through that fucked-up head of yours."

The Boy ignored him. "Relax, Dr Rhodes. Relax and things will become clear. Trust me."

Easier said than done, but Eve tried. She knew he'd said it for a reason.

She closed her eyes, ignored the pressure of the gun barrel on her back, ignored the presence of Garland, and summoned the feeling she had last night when, without effort, she had seen the dancing soul of the Boy's mother.

Then she opened her eyes.

The crypt was alight. Dozens of jars were on the tombs, the floor, and in the alcoves. The iridescent light from captured souls filled the space, flickering in synchronicity with the flames from the dozens of night-lights that held them. It was breathtaking. Utterly beautiful.

She could see Makka just to her right and Vee to her left. They were so close she could touch them, but in the dark world of Garland they were hidden.

"Where are they?" said Garland. He was becoming anxious. The detachedness of the Boy was unnerving him. "Where ARE THEY?" But he was only rewarded with another smile.

"Fuck this." He raised his pistol and aimed it at the Boy, but as he pulled the trigger Makka hit him on the side of the head with a lump of medieval carved stone. Eve thought it looked like a serpent's head.

Garland staggered sideways from the blow and dropped the torch as he bumped into Vee, but managed to get a shot off in the process. Vee pushed him hard in the back sending him towards the centre of the crypt. He lost his footing and fell heavily, losing his grip on the gun.

The torch went out.

The crypt was now utterly dark and beautifully light.

***

I can see the amazement on the face of Dr Rhodes. The Dark Chorus is beautiful, and here, in this ancient crypt, they shine with a particular radiance. Makka and Vee had the same look when I helped them to see what was hidden from them.

The Fuck shouts at me and raises his pistol, but I know Makka will stop him. The sound of the pistol firing is muffled by the confined surroundings, but I can feel the pressure in the air change. It pops my ears, but not before I feel a sting on my cheek and my parka's hood flicks off my head to hang down my back. The Fuck staggers under the blow from Makka's stone serpent and from the violent push from Vee, and falls to the ground. I watch his gun skitter off across the dirty stone floor as the torch goes out. The gun is not too far from The Fuck, but he can't see it.

Makka looks at me and grins. "Sorry, yeah?" he says. "I wasn't expecting him to get to the shooting bit so quick." He raises his hand to the healed cut on his face, the one I gave him in the detention centre. "Well, I guess we're even, yeah?"

He steps forward to stand behind The Fuck and kicks him hard in the ribs, just as he's getting to his feet. He drops back to the ground.

"Fuck you, you Paki bastard," he says, kicking out with his feet. But Makka can see by the light of the Dark Chorus and easily sidesteps the swinging foot. He moves around The Fuck and picks up the pistol.

The Fuck hears the clink of metal and freezes. I can see Makka turning the pistol in his hand.

I look at Dr Rhodes.

"Are you all right, Dr Rhodes?" I ask.

"Yes," she says. She's looking around at the scene, at

Makka and Vee and me and the cat. "Yes," she says again. "Are you going to kill Garland?"

I get down from the tomb and stand in front of her.

"No," I say.

"What?" Makka stops playing with the gun and looks up sharply. "We bloody well are." He points the gun at The Fuck's head. "I'll do it now and fuck his soul. Yeah?"

"I am going to do something worse," I say.

"You don't scare me, you little shit," says The Fuck.

I'm not trying to scare him.

"Look," says Makka, "take his fucking soul, yeah? But let me kill the bastard. I gotta kill him after what he did to my mother."

"Oh, yeah and what the fuck did I do to your mother?" says The Fuck. He is trying to crawl as quietly as he can in the direction of the exit. Makka kicks him to a halt.

"You know what you did, you shit. You fucking well raped . . ." Makka kicks him, "her and . . ." he kicks him again, "it killed her."

The Fuck groans and then laughs. "You stupid bastard. That's not how it was." He pulls himself into a sitting position with his back to the central tomb. His hand gropes for a weapon of some kind. "She was fucking beautiful. I didn't rape her. Oh, we shagged all right, and she wanted it as much as me."

"LIAR." Makka hits him with the pistol butt. I cannot help but think we're in a film again.

"Wait," says Dr Rhodes. "Are you saying you're Makka's father?"

The Fuck pulls himself up again and puts a hand to his head. "Fuck, you're smart. No wonder they made you a doc. Yes, I'm the Paki's father, but trust me, I hate the piece of dribbling piss more than you can imagine."

"And you killed Makka's mother?"

"No. The stupid cow got pregnant. I told her to get rid of it, but she wouldn't. Makka killed her. He killed her by getting born. She wanted the bastard but the shame, oh the fucking shame of it all."

I can see Makka. He is standing still, so still that he looks like one of the crypt's carvings. This conversation isn't good for him.

"He killed her, not me. And he knows it."

I think Makka believes this, perhaps he always has, but I don't think this is right.

"Did you love her?" says Dr Rhodes.

"Fuck, no. She was a Paki. I just wanted to know what it was like to fuck one."

I expected Makka to react, but he doesn't. He didn't seem to register the hateful comment. The Fuck senses Makka's detachment, senses a victory. He starts to feel his way towards the exit again.

"Makka," says Vee, going over to him. "Makka." She touches his hand. He responds to the physical contact and looks into Vee's eyes. They stay like that for a moment and it appears Makka sees what he needs to see and in one quick bound he has The Fuck by the hair, pulling his head back and placing the pistol to his temple. He turns to me. "Tell me if he is telling the truth. Tell me if he raped my mother."

I crouch down in front of The Fuck. I can see him, but he cannot see me. I need him to look at me properly.

"Vee, do you have your lighter? He needs to see my eyes."

Vee crouches down beside me and flicks her Zippo into life. The Fuck and me look at each other over the smoky orange flame. He is defiant and cataracts of darkness put up a strong defence. But today is not a day I will be denied, and I force my way in.

And I find the truth. And it is not what I expected. There had been love, a very strong deep love, but it had turned into an equally strong and deep hate. I cannot see narratives, only emotional results, so I cannot say what created the love or drove the hate. But evil is now in charge and there is no colour left in his soul. It is pure tar black and Crisp's Law is upheld.

I withdraw.

I stay looking into his eyes, and I think of Makka.

"He lies," I say, truthfully. But the lie he tells masks a different story to the one Makka believes. I don't think he raped Makka's mother, but I am not going to say so.

The Fuck's eyes widen. "You little shit," he says as Vee flicks the lid on the Zippo and his world drops into darkness again.

"It is time," I say, but at that moment The Fuck pushes himself to his feet. His head connects with Makka's chin and Makka flies backwards, dropping the gun. It lands next to The Fuck who hears its metallic clatter as it comes to rest on the stone floor. He grabs it in one hand and with the other he grabs my throat and drives me to ground putting a knee on my chest.

"No one fucking move. NO ONE. Or I shoot the psycho." The Fuck puts the gun to my forehead. He can't see me, but if he pulls the trigger now, he will definitely kill me. I can see Vee and Dr Rhodes standing still, but I can't see Makka.

"I'm going to get up now. No one make a move." He stands dragging me up with him. "If I hear any sound I'm going to shoot. Got it?"

"Got it," says Makka from behind us. The Fuck turns and fires into the darkness. The bullet hits one of my jars, which shatters releasing a soul. It starts up a babbling chatter and drifts off. The Fuck pushes me forward, but he is disorientated by the dark and we're staggering towards Vee and not the exit. Vee is holding the cat. She smiles at me and then throws the cat at The Fuck's face.

The cat lands, claws out. The Fuck yells and lets go of me, grabbing at the cat with his hands. I think he might kill the cat, so I grab one of his arms and hang on. Vee attacks too, grabbing the other arm as The Fuck pulls the trigger. Another ear-popping moment, but the bullet misses anything organic and instead takes out the stone eye of a knight standing imposingly in one of the corners. Dr Rhodes grabs the gun hand and keeps it away from me and Vee. The cat leaps for safety and the struggle stops. Makka hits The Fuck on the head with a stone hand and he collapses.

The crypt goes quiet, its stillness cut only by our heavy breathing. And then Makka laughs. He holds up the stone hand.

"The hand of God."

But I don't think so. I think it is more likely the hand of a saint.

"Twat," says Makka when I tell him this.

The cat jumps up on to the central tomb looking pleased with herself. I scratch her behind an ear.

"Nice throw," says Makka to Vee.

She shrugs. "I know."

"So, what are you going to do now?" asks Dr Rhodes, dusting down her skirt and retrieving her handbag and my mother's soul.

"Kill him," says Makka. "Do you have a problem with that?"

"Well, yes," says Dr Rhodes. "That's murder. You can't just kill people you don't like. He's your father."

"Not as far as either of us is concerned," says Makka nodding at the unconscious figure. "And it's not that I don't like him – I fucking hate him."

I need to show Dr Rhodes the state of The Fuck's soul. She has the ability to come with me and see for herself.

The Fuck takes the opportunity to moan and make some small movements. Consciousness is returning.

"Makka," I say,. "Can you sit him up?"

Makka does this without much care, ramming him into a sitting position against the central tomb. We all stand in front of him except the cat who is now laid out on the tomb lid hoping someone will stroke her. I crouch down.

"Come," I say to Dr Rhodes and hold out my hand. She takes it and crouches down beside me. Vee knows what I want and fires up her Zippo. I take the Soul Stone and some lighter fluid from my bag and place the stone next to The Fuck. I pour some of the flammable liquid into the smooth indent of the bowl. Vee touches the pool of liquid with the smoky flame and it purrs into life.

The cat starts to purr too.

"Catch his gaze, Dr Rhodes," I say, but can feel her reluctance. "I will be there. You will be safe. Trust me."

I catch the blurred stare of The Fuck and wait. I know she will come. Her enlightenment is almost complete. A moment later Dr Rhodes joins me. I connect with her presence. It is the equivalent of taking her hand. I navigate the clouds of colour and the thunder of thought and lightning of anger and pain and find the soul well.

THE MIND IS SO BEAUTIFUL. THE COLOURS SO VIVID, THE MOVEMENT SO POWERFUL. IT FEELS LIMITLESS.

IT IS, I say. THERE IS NO BOUNDARY TO THE MIND, TO CONCIOUSNESS.

DO THE COLOURS HAVE MEANING?

I THINK SO, AS DO THE PATTERNS THEY MAKE. BUT I HAVE A LOT TO LEARN SO CANNOT REALLY TELL YOU VERY MUCH.

WHERE ARE WE GOING NOW?

TO FIND HIS SOUL.

We descend.

The Fuck's soul hangs by its ethereal threads. It is tar black. It offers no colour, no movement, no empathy. It offers nothing but hate, a deep evil so powerful that it has destroyed the celestial gift that connects us. I do not know what happens to such diseased souls when they pass on, but this one will never find out. It will be cast into oblivion.

I can feel Dr Rhodes' horror, her fear, and her understanding. I sometimes wonder at my own lack of fear and my difficulty in understanding what people feel or are thinking. Dr Rhodes is not like me in that sense. She is deeply empathetic and that would stop her being a true Arta. I do not easily take on the pain of others. It has only been my recent relationship with Makka and Vee that has opened up that vista to me. I think this is why I can do what needs doing to restore the Angel and why my mother could not.

It drove her to insanity.

BETWEEN US WE CAN BREAK THE BONDS THAT HOLD THIS EVIL, I say.

CAN WE?

YES.

I focus on opening up a conduit to my own soul and to that of the Angel. I concentrate and the link develops and from it flies a barbed tendril, which pierces The Fuck's soul surface, hooking it like a speared fish.

I pull.

The Angel lends me some strength, but I need more.

HELP ME, DR RHODES. WE MUST PULL IT FROM ITS BINDINGS.

I can feel Dr Rhodes join me. She takes a virtual grip on the tendril and pulls. And it is enough. The ethereal bonds tear and the dark soul is now anchorless, free to be pulled from the body. It thrashes about trying to escape, but it is no match for our combined strength. We pull it from the soul well, through the colours of the mind and out into the crypt.

LET GO, DR RHODES, I say.

She does, and so do I.

The Soul Stone pounces.

It is done.

I watch as Dr Rhodes blinks and recognises that she is back in the real world. She now understands that the Dark Chorus exists, is a reality.

"Done?" asks Makka looking at me. I nod.

"OK, let's kill The Fuck and get out of here."

"There is no need," I say. "Look at him."

Makka bends down and slaps The Fuck's face. There is no response. The look on his face is fixed and it is one of utter terror. "What the fuck have you done to him?"

"Taken his soul. Unlike the others, we didn't need to kill him to do it. With Dr Rhodes help we could pull it free. He is conscious but is adrift in oblivion."

"You should kill him," says Dr Rhodes.

"You've changed your tune," says Makka.

"No. It's just that I've seen oblivion and it is terrifying." I can see Dr Rhodes shudder. "It would be kinder to kill him."

I can see this has the opposite effect on Makka. He stands up, stretches and then strokes the cat. "Glad we decided to bring you along," he says.

"That is wrong. You said –" but he interrupts me.

"Twat." He smiles. "Let's go."

I look at him and think I understand. He is joking.

I pick up the cat. "Yes, let's go," I say.

We collect our things and climb through our crude hole back into the tunnel. I take a last look around the crypt. We have left the jars with the souls in. They are happy and quiet and will hopefully remain undisturbed until I complete my task. They offer a light source that shows the beauty of the human condition, but The Fuck cannot see that, or anything, ever again. He sits where we left him. This will now be his body's tomb.

We rebuild the wall, carefully putting each brick back in its original place.

I turn to Dr Rhodes. "Do you have a car?"

Chapter Twenty-Six

I awake to sunlight streaming through the curtainless window of the room. We are back at the asylum where my journey started. I am so comfortable that I don't think I'll be able to get up and wonder if I could lie here in this soporific moment forever. But I need a cup of tea, so I pull myself up and out from under my blanket. Around me lie Makka and Vee and Dr Rhodes and the cat. They are all asleep.

I am happy. Perhaps the happiest I have ever been.

I leave my sleeping friends and head down a familiar corridor to the kitchen. Miraculously, the gas is still connected and the teabags I had left from my last stay are still here. I boil the kettle and make a cup of tea. I close my eyes and let the fragrant steam flow over my face. It offers a gentle caress, its warm touch leaving droplets of tea on my eyelashes and giving a tea-enhanced sheen to my skin. It is important that I stay looking young, especially today.

The early sunlight that washes through the building is fresh, and although I have only slept a few hours, I too feel fresh. Last night we fed The Fuck's soul to the Angel and I have fulfilled the promise I made to Makka. His father is no more. I hope this will help him, but I think there is more to his anger than the evil of his father.

"Do you mind if I join you?" says Dr Rhodes. I had been so immersed in my thoughts that I hadn't heard her approach the kitchen.

"No," I say. "Would you like a cup of tea?"

"Please."

I make her a cup but cannot offer any milk.

"That's fine," she says. As I watch, she holds her face over the cup and lets the steam gently buffet against her skin.

I smile.

"Dr Rhodes, a while ago I said that the resolution to my mother's problem depends on you."

"I remember." She still has her eyes closed.

"Do you know what I want?"

"Yes, I think so."

"Are you willing to do this for me?"

Dr Rhodes says nothing, but breathes in the steam.

I wait.

"Will I die like Mrs Johnson?" she asks.

"No."

She nods. "Will I still be me, do you think?"

"I think so. I am still me, although I have never been alone. The Angel has always been there." I pause for a moment and give it some more thought. "I think you will still be you." I shrug. "But you might know or feel things that you don't know or feel now."

Dr Rhodes opens her eyes and nods again. "This will tie us together for life, won't it? I'll always be part of the Dark Chorus from now on?"

"Yes," I say. "But the Dark Chorus was already there for you to see. Even if you say no, you'll continue to see it. I don't think you'll be able to stop seeing it now."

"I won't kill anyone for you, for the Angel. You understand that don't you?"

"Yes, I'm not asking you to do anything but carry my mother's soul, to give her a semblance of life and help her pass on when your own time comes."

I am looking at Dr Rhodes, but I drop my eyes. My desire to have my mother back is so strong that I can feel tears welling up – such an alien feeling. I'm not sure I'll be able to stop them if they decide to spill out. I am certain the rescue of my mother can only be done voluntarily – any other way, and it will fail.

Dr Rhodes touches my shoulder and I look up. I can see she is thinking of her own lost mother and perhaps thinking what it would be like to have her back. Her empathy washes over me and I wish again that I could have such a gift.

"I will do it," she says.

Tears leak from me.

Makka and Vee appear. They both look refreshed too. Makka looks at me and I smile despite the tears. He raises his eyebrows, takes my tea from me and gulps down a mouthful.

"Fuck, that tastes like piss. Any milk?"

***

I have drawn out the symbols, lit the night-lights, and placed my mother's soul jar so that Dr Rhodes can see it. She is lying on her side facing me, her head resting on her arm. I am sitting on one of the triangle's points while Makka and Vee sit at each of the other two. The cat is sitting next to me. She doesn't have to be here, but I think she is curious. Cats are like that. I have also placed the Soul Stone, which represents the Angel, above Dr Rhodes's head.

We are all here. We are ready.

I lean forward and unscrew the lid of the jar and blow out the anchoring flame. My mother's soul slowly rises. As it clears the jar's lip, I catch it with my stare – not with a piercing barbed hook but with gentle soft tendrils. I hold it still and wait.

Dr Rhodes takes a breath, exhales and then catches the soul in her own gaze. She takes it away from me, gently cradling it with her own ethereal tendrils. I drop my stare and simply watch. In a slow and controlled motion, Dr Rhodes pulls my mother's soul towards her, and then between blinks the soul is gone. Dr Rhodes eyelids fall shut.

All I can do now is wait.

I get to my feet. "Time to make the call, Makka," I say.

"Yeah? Are we sure?" He looks to Vee, who nods.

"OK," she says.

I pick up the Soul Stone and leave The Screaming Room. I have one last thing to do before we surrender ourselves to the police.

We agreed last night that we would do this. It will protect Dr Rhodes, and Makka said we would get caught soon anyway. Better to know when and where. He also said he had a plan to get us our freedom but that it may take a while. "Those fucking paedos will make it happen, yeah? 'Cause if they don't, they're fucked."

I don't mind waiting, but I wonder what will happen to the cat.

I find the handle-less metal door that leads to the garden and follow the winding path that takes me out to my singing beech tree. The ghosts of those that have trodden the bark-strewn route before me now line the path, silently raising their hands to me in salute, a joyous recognition of success.

I hope they are right.

I reach the tree and stand before it for a moment. It has no new leaves to accompany its singing, but a light breeze plucks at its branches and a few old, dry leaves who have clung to their high perch create a tympanic sound of welcome, a sound that I acknowledge with a bow of my head.

The tree's trunk is large. I think it would take two and a half men holding hands to encircle it. It is strong, and I can feel life coursing through it, sending energy up to the branches, preparing the new leaves for spring. Although I know trees grow out of the earth, it is hard to imagine this particular tree having ever done so. It looks like it was deliberately driven into the ground by a giant, fully formed, charged with the task of guarding those around it. And it is the guarding nature of the tree that I am now interested in.

At its base, where two large roots briefly surface like the arched backs of whales, I clear some decaying leaves and dig at the soft soil. I create a hole deep enough to accommodate the Soul Stone. I need it to be safe because I will need it again, but I suspect that may not be for a while. I wrap the Soul Stone in a cloth that I took from the kitchen and place it carefully in the hole. It is warm and humming quietly. I push soil around and over the artefact, burying it, and cover the disturbed ground with the decaying leaves I moved earlier. I stand back and look down at my work. The hiding place is invisible.

I thank the tree and tell it I will be back.

I retrace my steps but stop at an old bench. It is one I have sat on before and I now sit on it again. I let my mind wander and it pulls up a memory, one I am so familiar with that I could write down every aspect, every detail, every smell and feeling it generates without having to play it out in my mind's eye.

A brick-vaulted room lies exposed, lit by smoky yellow lanterns that throw long-legged dancing shadows about the place. To my left, an opening offers me a glimpse of a steam train, small and compact, sitting on a track that disappears into the blackness of a tunnel. This world is sooty. In front of me, on the ground, tied up with coarse rope, is a man. He is gagged with a dirty cloth. His face is pock-marked and his eyes wide with fear and hate. His clothes are not modern, and I now know they are late Victorian. He is lying in a chalk square, which is enclosed in a circle. The two shapes touch at the square's corners. Lit candles are in place at these junctures. It is the ritual, and the prisoner is about to be cleansed. I watch as a well-dressed man with a beautiful long cashmere coat sets down a jar with a small flickering candle in it. He stands over the trussed-up man and takes several deep breaths before he busies himself with collecting the man's soul. I watch the soul emerge, dark and ruined. It hangs in the air for a moment and is then grabbed by the fire-jar.

Collected.

The well-dressed man picks up the jar, turns and looks straight at me. I like this bit the best. I think he can see me. He has deep green eyes and a full rich-black moustache. He smiles. He is my great-great-grandfather, Charles Janenssen.

And then the link to my mother's soul rings out, as clear as a plucked guitar string, a long summoning sound that only my soul can hear.

She is here.

I run and run and run.

***

Eve was with her mother again, carefully trying to undo the knotted and tumultuous coloured clouds of consciousness that were afflicting the poor woman. She'd had some success. Her mother had become less agitated, calmer. She had moments where she acknowledged her daughter with love and tenderness.

Eve gently pulled away from her mother's mind and sat back. Her mother sighed and then closed her eyes. They were sitting together looking out into the grounds of the mental health unit, part of an old Victorian asylum that was now modernised and clean and safe. Rabbits festooned the lawn, a sea of twitching ears and fur and bright eyes.

Eve was content.

That morning a small package had arrived for her. Inside was a large-capacity memory stick and a note that simply read – *it's time to get us out.*

She closed her eyes and relaxed and as she did so she could feel the link to the Boy's soul. It was strong and bright and pulsated with energy. He was alive and well.

The Inspector had always referred to him as 'her' boy, and now he really was her boy. He was simultaneously her patient and her son, as she was his psychiatrist and mother.

The Boy's mother smiled.

Printed in Great Britain
by Amazon